THE APPOMATTOX SAGA

6

GILBERT MORRIS

✯

The Shadow of His Wings

Tyndale House Publishers, Inc.
Wheaton, Illinois

Library of Congress Cataloging-in-Publication Data

Morris, Gilbert.
    The shadow of his wings / Gilbert Morris.
        p.   cm. — (The Appomattox saga ; 6)
    ISBN 0-8423-5987-7
    1. United States—History—Civil War, 1861-1865—Fiction.
 I. Title.   II. Series: Morris, Gilbert. Appomattox saga ; 6.
PS3563.O8742S48   1994
813′.54—dc20   94-28708

Printed in the United States of America

99 98 97 96 95
9   8   7   6   5   4   3

To James and Murlene Golden—
Our Golden Missionaries.
You have given Johnnie and me so much
over the past years!
All of us need to see the gospel
walking around, and to us,
you two have demonstrated Jesus Christ
and the power of his gospel
to transform lives.

CONTENTS

Part Four: Josh

GENEALOGY OF
THE APPOMATTOX SAGA
THE ROCKLINS

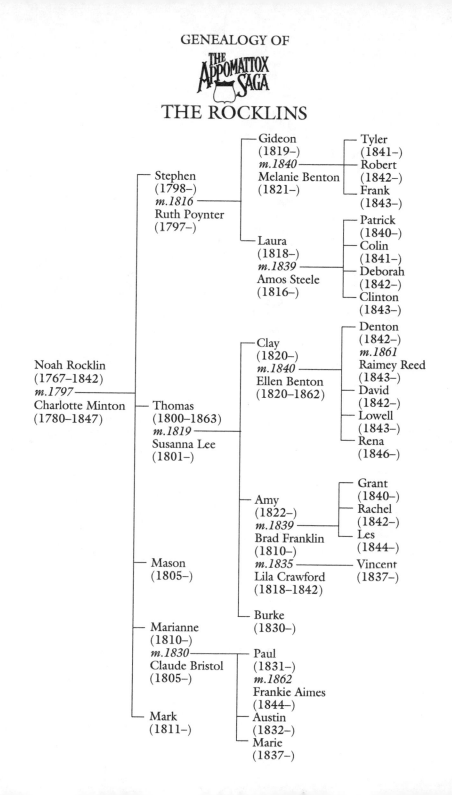

THE YANCYS

Buford Yancy
(1807–)
m.1829 ———————
Mattie Satterfield
(1813–1851)

— Royal
  (1832–)
— Melora
  (1834–)
— Zack
  (1836–)
— Cora
  (1837–)
— Lonnie
  (1843–)
— Bobby
  (1844–)
— Rose
  (1845–)
— Josh
  (1847–)
— Martha
  (1849–)
— Toby
  (1851–)

PART ONE
Rooney

CHAPTER ONE
Flight from Vicksburg

✦

For most people terrible dreams come in the dead stillness of the night. They lie awake longing for the morning when they can escape into the world of reality.

For Rooney Smith, however, night was a welcome refuge where she escaped from the nightmarish days. She spent her waking hours fighting off men who moved through the slums of Vicksburg, for at the age of seventeen, she was a very attractive young woman. All day long she cleaned hotel rooms on Beacon Avenue, the worst street in the worst section of a river town noted for violence and vice. By the time she reached home she was sick of the vile remarks and the grasping hands of men.

But no matter how bad the days, when she closed the door to the two-room shack she shared with her mother, Clara, and her brother, Buck, the nightmare ended and she could rest. Her mother worked in a bar called the Gay Lady and usually came home at dawn—when she didn't stay out for several days. So each night Rooney closed and barred the door, making a safe haven for her and Buck. The two of them read together, played games by the hour, and—most important—were safe in the dilapidated shanty.

Late one Thursday, Rooney arrived home and shut and barred the door. Weariness flowed through her so that she leaned back against it, closed her eyes, and let the fatigue drain out of her. As usual it was not the physical labor that debilitated her, but the feeling of uncleanness.

Opening her eyes, she shook her shoulders, then made a fire and heated water. Buck would not be home for half an hour, so she took a bath in a number ten galvanized wash-tub, sluicing herself with the warm water, and when she stepped out, dried off, and slipped into a clean dress, she felt most of the bitter, distasteful memories of the day slipping away.

Dark was falling fast, and she looked out the small window for Buck. He worked for a butcher, and she'd warned him to be home before dark. She began to put a simple meal together, and when the knock came at the door, she went at once, a smile on her face. Lifting the bar, she opened the door with a smile, saying, "It's about time you—"

But it was not Buck, and a chill ran through the girl as she saw the big man with pale blue eyes. Quickly she tried to shut the door, but he put out a big hand and seized it. "Now, this is something I like!" he sneered. "Come to see Clara—but reckon you'll do better." He stood there holding the door as Rooney tried to force it shut, and with no effort he pushed it back.

Rooney backed away, saying as calmly as she could, "My mother's not here. You'll have to go now." When she saw that he made no move to leave but grinned more broadly, she lifted her chin. "You get out of here!" she said.

"Now, don't be like that, sweetheart." He was a tall, heavily built man with yellow hair and a wide mouth. "I'm Dement Sloan. Know your ma *real* well." The catfish mouth drew upward into a leer, and his pale blue eyes shone with a glitter Rooney had seen in many men. "Now you and me, we can have ourselves a good time!"

Sloan let his eyes run up and down the girl's trim figure, took in the oval face, the short-cropped, curly auburn hair, and the large dark blue eyes now wide with fright. The fear in the girl pleased him, for he'd rather see women's fear than try to earn their admiration or love. Stepping inside, he kicked the door shut with his foot and stood there staring at her. "I brought us a bottle," he said, taking a brown bottle from his inner pocket. "We're gonna have us a real good little party, little girl!"

Rooney backed away, her eyes darting around, but there was no way of escape except through the door that Sloan blocked. "You—you better leave or I'll scream!"

Sloan set the bottle down on a battered table and advanced toward her. He was drunk and had come to find Clara Smith, having enjoyed her favors in the rooms over the Gay Lady. He was a handsome brute and a womanizer, though his taste ran to the coarser types found on Beacon Street. The sight of the young girl brought a surge of lust, and he grinned as he moved toward her.

Rooney twisted, moving behind a chair to escape the man, but he seized it and threw it aside. "You need a man, sweetheart, and I'm the man you need!"

Fear shot through Rooney, and she made one desperate attempt to fling by Sloan, but he caught her by the arm. "Come on, honey, don't be so shy!"

Suddenly the man released her arm and crumpled to the floor. Rooney was startled to see Buck suddenly standing in the room.

"It's me, Sis," Buck said. Rooney blinked, and her eyes focused on the face of her brother. "You OK?"

"Buck! What—" Rooney stopped speaking as she looked at the form of Sloan on the floor. He was lying on his back, and his eyes were wide open. A wound gaped like an open mouth on his scalp, just over his left ear, and blood dripped steadily onto the wooden floor. Wildly Rooney looked up to stare at the small form of her brother.

He met her gaze, then suddenly tossed down the heavy iron poker he'd been holding. It clattered on the floor, startling Rooney, and he said in a frightened voice, "I—I think I killed him, Sis!"

Rooney stared at Buck, then dropped to her knees beside

the still form. Fearfully, she put her hand on the broad chest, then looked up to whisper, "No—he's alive!"

The explosion of violence had robbed Buck of all but fear. "I come in and he was hurtin' you, Rooney." He was an undersized lad with brown hair and large brown eyes, his cheeks now pale as paper. "I had to stop him!"

Seeing the boy's panic, Rooney got to her feet and drew him close. "I know, Buck! I know you did!"

He began to tremble, his thin form shaking in her embrace. "Will—will they hang me for it?" he whispered. Pulling his head back, he stared at her, his eyes wide with fear. "Will they, Sis?"

"No! No, they won't!"

"If he dies, they will!"

Rooney said quickly, "He's not going to die." But looking down, she saw that the man was well dressed, obviously not a drunk or a bum. He'd come to Beacon Street, as many men did, for drink and women.

The police will believe him—not Buck and me! The thought flashed through Rooney, and instantly she knew they had to move him. "We've got to get him out of here, Buck."

Buck was almost paralyzed with fear, but he was a quick-witted boy. He had to be to survive among the dregs of Vicksburg! "Yeah, that's right," he said with a nod. He glanced down and shook his head. "He's so *big*, Rooney."

"I know, but we've got to do it!"

Turning quickly, she moved to the door, opened it, and stared outside. "It's pretty dark outside. We have to get him into the alley."

"When he comes to, he'll tell on us, Sis."

"Maybe not—maybe he won't remember. He's drunk, and he's been hurt."

Hope touched Buck's eyes, and he nodded. A thought came to him, and he exclaimed, "I know. We can use Tip's cart!"

At once Rooney nodded, relief in her face. "Go get it, Buck!"

The boy left the shack in a flash, and Rooney stood there, staring down at the still, pale face of Sloan. Her knees were weak, and she was nauseated with fear, but she forced herself to remain calm. Soon she heard the sound of iron wheels rolling and opened the door.

"I got it. Lucky Tip left it here." He was pulling a low four-wheeled wagonlike affair used by a neighboring brick-layer to haul his bricks. It was only a little over a foot off the ground and had sides no more than four inches high.

"Come on, let's get him on it," Rooney whispered. The two of them advanced on the unconscious man, and she said, "Grab this arm, and I'll take the other one." She hated to touch him, but fear of what might come to them from the law was greater than her revulsion. They took a strong grip on the man's arms and tugged with all their strength. He weighed at least two hundred pounds, and by the time they had gotten the still form to the door, both of them were gasping.

"We'll never get him into the cart, Buck!"

"Lemme put the wagon up to the door so we don't have to drag him any farther than we have to."

It was the only way they could have managed it, and as they tried to lift his massive body into the cart, his head struck the edge of the wagon with an ugly sound that made Rooney cry out, "Be careful!"

But Buck ignored her. "Come on, Sis!" he gasped. "We've got to get him outta here!"

As soon as Sloan's body was loaded, Rooney grabbed the tongue of the wagon, and the two of them dragged it down over the cobblestones. The loud rattle it made sounded like thunder to both of them, and Rooney expected someone to appear at any second. However, they reached the small opening that led between two of the shacks in the dilapidated row without a sign of anyone on the street. Quickly they wheeled the vehicle into the alley. "We'll have to roll him off," Buck whispered. "Got to take Tip's wagon back."

"All right." Rooney cradled the lolling head of the helpless man as they pulled him off, then carefully placed it down. She felt a wetness on her palm and knew it was fresh blood.

"Come on, Sis—we got to get outta here!"

Rooney swallowed hard, then rose and followed Buck. As they stepped out of the alley, a voice cried out, "Hey! What you doin' there?"

Glancing down the street, Rooney saw the form of a man emerging from the darkness. Panic ran through her, and she wheeled, crying, "Run, Buck!" But Buck was already fleeing, and she ran with all the speed she could muster.

"Stop! Stop right there!"

The voice broke the stillness, and doors began to open, but the man was heavy, and the youthful pair ran like rabbits, dodging through alleys that Buck knew as he knew his own hand. They crossed two streets, then burst onto a street occupied by warehouses and other large buildings.

"I . . . can't run any farther, Buck!"

"Me neither!"

They stopped and looked around the dark street. The windows of the warehouses caught the gleam of a few flickering streetlights. To Rooney they appeared to be opaque eyes staring at them. "Can you hear anything, Buck?" she gasped.

Buck listened hard, then shook his head. "No. I—I guess we got away."

The two stood there, holding their breath, listening hard. The silence of the street washed over them. Faintly they heard the sound of a wagon rattling over cobblestone, but it was blocks away. Fear and the hard run had drained them both, and now they felt a tremendous sense of fatigue.

"What'll we do, Sis?"

Rooney stared at Buck's pale face, noting that his lips were unsteady. She was stiff with fear herself but managed to say calmly, "We've got to get away from here."

His eyes grew wide with shock. "You mean . . . leave Vicksburg?"

"We can't stay here. That man will have the law on us."

"But where'll we go?"

Rooney had no idea of how to run away. She had no money on her, and they had only the clothes they stood in. But she had to do *something!* "Let's go see if anybody's at the house," she said finally.

"What for?"

"I have a little money, and we can get our clothes." She saw him hesitate, then said, "We'll look real careful, and if anybody's there, we won't go. But if the coast is clear, we can run in, grab our stuff and the money. Then we'll see."

It was not a good plan, and she dreaded going back to the house, but they had to have *something.* "After we go there, we'll have to go and tell Ma what happened."

"All right, Sis."

Her brother's agreement came quickly, and she knew he was afraid. Putting her arm around him, she squeezed him. "It'll be all right, Buck. We'll get away."

Rooney was a resourceful girl, but this assurance was for her brother. She felt hollow inside and dreaded to go back to the house. She also was terrified of what her mother would do, but she could think of nothing else. "Come on, Buck," she urged. "We'll make it!"

★   ★   ★

Alf Swanson, the bouncer at the Gay Lady, stepped out into the alley to catch a fresh breath of air. The smoke-laden interior of the saloon aggravated a hacking cough that had troubled him for days, and he coughed, hawked, and spat on the ground, glad for the relief. It was well after midnight, and he couldn't leave until the place closed down.

"Mr. Swanson!"

The burly bouncer started, for the voice caught him unprepared, seeming to rise out of the ground. He'd thought the alley deserted, and he growled suspiciously, "Who is it? Who's out there?"

"It's me—Rooney."

Swanson had thrown himself into a defensive position at the sound of the voice, but as the form of a young girl appeared out of the shadows to his left, he relaxed, dropping his fists.

"It's you, is it?" he said, surprise in his gravelly voice. "What in the world are ye doing here this time of night?"

"Buck and me are in trouble, Mr. Swanson."

Swanson stared at the girl, then looked over her shoulder and saw the boy. He was a hard man, but had admired the way Rooney had fought to keep herself above the level of her mother. "Trouble? What kind of trouble?"

Rooney hesitated, but she had learned to like the big man. He had always been roughly kind to her and Buck. He had never tried to touch her and had given her some protection from time to time. Swanson was not a man who liked the law, Rooney knew, and she had no other way to turn. "A man named Dement Sloan came to our house a little while ago. . . ."

Swanson stood there listening, saying nothing, but when the girl finished, he shook his head. "Too bad you got caught" was his only remark.

"We have to get away from Vicksburg," Rooney said quickly. "Can you get our mother to come out here so we can talk to her?"

"I'll do that. Wait here—and keep out of sight."

Swanson stepped inside the saloon and walked directly to Clara Smith. She was sitting at a table with a man who looked bored. "Clara, got to talk to you," Swanson said.

"Can't you see I'm busy?" A harsh note was in the woman's voice, but it was no harsher than her appearance. She had been an attractive woman once, but had grown gross and hard. Her hair was dyed a brassy yellow, and any natural color her cheeks might have had was buried under a layer of paint. Her lips were a wide gash of scarlet, and her eyes were sunk back into her head, giving her an unhealthy appearance. She wore a low-cut green dress, but she had lost weight and looked thin and bony.

The man drained his drink, got to his feet, saying, "I got to leave anyway. See you next time, Clara."

As the man walked away, Clara cursed Swanson, but he snapped, "Shut up and come with me."

"Come where?"

But Swanson took her arm and piloted her out of the bar. When they were in the hall that led to the alley, he stopped and related what Rooney had told him. "And they got to get out of town, Clara—you, too."

"Me? I ain't done nothing!"

"The man was put down in your place. His name is Dement Sloan, a swell from uptown. He'll have friends, the big people up there," Swanson snapped. "You on such good terms with the law you can convince them you had nothing to do with it?"

Anger grew in Clara Smith until she trembled—and she began to curse and rave, her hands outstretched like the talons of a monstrous bird, her nails red as blood. "I'll *kill* those crazy kids!" she cried, her eyes bright with rage.

"Shut your mouth!" Swanson took the woman's arm, and his iron grip closed on it like a trap. "The fellow was attacking your daughter! Don't that mean nothing to you?" But he didn't wait for her answer. "Listen, you're drunk, but not so drunk you can't understand. The judge told you the last time you was up if you came before him again, it'd be the pen for you. You want to go there, Clara?"

Fear touched the woman's sunken eyes, and she shook her head and shivered. "No! I'd—I'd die in that place!"

"All right, then you got to get away."

"And go where?" Despair came into her thin face, and she began to cry. The tears ran down her cheeks, leaving tracks in the caked makeup. "I ain't got no money!"

Swanson released his grip. Reaching into his pocket, he pulled out a roll of bills. Peeling off several of them, he thrust them into her hand. "That'll be enough to tide you over until you can get another place."

"But *where*, Alf?" She saw the look that crossed his face and asked, "What is it? You think of something?"

"Maybe I have." Swanson was not a quick thinker. He took an idea and chewed on it before speaking it. Clara had learned this and waited nervously until finally the big man said slowly, "Richmond . . . that's where you better go."

"Richmond? Why'd I want to go there?"

"Because it's the capital of this here Southern Confederacy, that's why." When Swanson saw the blank look on her face, he snapped with irritation, "There's a war, ain't you noticed? Richmond's got thousands and thousands of men in the army there to protect her—a ton more than around here. And men is your business, ain't they, Clara?"

Swiftly the thin face of Clara Smith changed, for she understood this kind of reason. "Lots of soldiers there in Richmond?"

"Be purt' near a million, I guess." The tough, battered lips of Swanson twisted in a humorless grin. "Get every one of them boys to give you a dollar, and you'll have a million dollars, Clara."

"Well, I dunno—"

Impatiently Swanson swore. "Clara, you ain't young, and you're sick. Time was mebby when you could call your shots. But now," he shrugged and said evenly, "you need to be where the men ain't so particular."

For one moment anger brightened the woman's eyes— and then they dulled. "You're right, Alf, but Richmond's a long way."

"I got a friend works in the boiler room on the *Natchez Belle,*" he said. "She'll be pulling out at dawn. I'll get him to stow you somewhere—no fare. She'll dock near Memphis, and you can get a train from there to Richmond—as long as the trains are still running."

"But I ain't got no clothes—nothing!"

"All right, I'll go to your place. If it's clear, I'll get your stuff." Alf stared at her. "Now, you know—?" He broke off suddenly, thinking hard, then said, "Listen, Clara, I got a friend in Richmond—at least, he was there last I heard. Got a place, sort of a hotel and bar. About like this one, I reckon. His name's Studs Mulvaney. Won't be hard to find him and his joint. Look him up and tell him I said to give you and the kids a break."

"All right, Alf—and thanks."

"I'm doing it for the kids, Clara." Turning, he led her to the alley, then called out, "Hey, Rooney!"

When the girl and boy appeared, he said, "You and your ma's leaving for Richmond. Let me get my coat and gun, then we'll coast down and see if we can get your stuff, Clara."

Swanson left them alone, and Buck said, "Ma, I'm sorry, but I had to hit him."

Clara stared at the thin face of the boy. For one instant she almost flared out at him, but she was too tired. She shook her head, saying only, "One place is as good as another, I guess."

Several hours later, the ghostly form of the *Natchez Belle* slipped away from the docks. The smooth brown water of the Mississippi dropped in a shining waterfall from her paddles, catching the first rays of the rising sun. The engines throbbed, the drivers sending the huge paddle wheel into its rhythmic pattern, churning the water to a white froth.

Deep inside in a storeroom filled with flour, potatoes, and cans of food, Clara sat on a stool, her head down. Rooney saw that she was sick and came to stand beside her. Timidly she put her hand on her mother's shoulder. "It'll be all right, Ma."

Clara looked up, despair in her eyes. "No, it won't." She shook off her daughter's hand and turned her back to stare at the bulkhead.

Buck was staring out a porthole, entranced. "Look, Rooney!" he whispered. When she joined him, she saw the shoreline slipping by very rapidly. "We must be going real fast," he said, his eyes large. "Wish we could stay on this ol' boat for a long time!"

Rooney, filled with dread at the specterlike thought of the future, nodded and put her arm around him.

"So do I, Buck!" she whispered sadly. "So do I!"

CHAPTER TWO
Lowell Meets a Pair of Generals

✦

Clay Rocklin stood idly under one of the towering oaks that lined the driveway leading up to Gracefield. He could hear the sound of laughter from the big white house and had been thinking of how unlikely it was that the Rocklin family would ever gather in exactly the same way. *The war is wearing us all down,* he thought sadly. *There'll be empty places here by the time it's over.* He was happy for the lull that permitted the Rocklins to gather at Gracefield for a brief time before the spring campaigns drew the Army of Northern Virginia away.

He half turned to go inside and join the others when a rider suddenly appeared on the road leading from Richmond. At first he thought it might be a courier with a message from regimental headquarters recalling them to duty, and then he saw that it was a civilian. He waited until the rider turned into the circular driveway, then exclaimed in surprise as he recognized his uncle Mark Rocklin. Moving forward as his uncle drew up, he called out to him, "Mark!"

Mark Rocklin pulled the bay stallion to a halt, glanced around, and came out of the saddle. "Clay, how are you?" He wore an expensive black suit that suited his tall figure, and despite his fifty-two years, he was still lean and strong. Clay could not speak the thought that leaped into his mind as the two shook hands: *The best looking of the family—and he's wasted his life!* Mark had been the wild one of Noah Rocklin's sons, leaving home at an early age and never returning except for brief visits. Clay knew he'd been a riverboat gambler—and worse—but had always felt a strong affection for Mark.

"You came just in time, Uncle Mark," Clay said. "We managed to sneak a family reunion before the army gets goin' full steam again."

Mark studied the uniform Clay wore and remarked, "You're a captain now. I didn't know that. Are your boys all in the army?"

"Dent and Lowell are in my company. David's taking care of the home front." Something about Mark's appearance disturbed Clay. Lines were etched around his lips, and a somberness in his dark eyes revealed some sort of tragedy. But Clay knew that he could not ask what had aged his uncle. *He'll tell me if he wants me to know, and wild horses couldn't drag it out unless he's ready.* "Come on in. Everybody will be glad to see you."

"The prodigal returns home?" Mark smiled slightly. He turned to Clay, saying, "I couldn't get here for your father's funeral. . . ."

Clay recognized that this was Mark Rocklin's apology for many things and said, "I understand, Mark. We can't always do what we'd like, can we?" Then, wanting to break the moment, he said, "Come on! Let's join the crowd."

When the two entered, Clay called out loudly, "Set another plate! We've got another Rocklin to feed!"

Clay's mother, Susanna, was the first to get to Mark. She greeted him with a fierce hug, and the rest of the family waited for their turn. Clay watched as Mark smiled as he greeted each of them, thinking, *Something's wrong with Mark. There was always some sort of shadow over him, but it's worse now.*

After the greeting of Mark, the men were gathered in the drawing room while the women were in the kitchen. Food was the answer to many problems for women, and they gave themselves to it. The house was filled with the smells of fresh bread and pastries, and Dent said, "Raimey says there's been enough food cooked to feed a whole company." Glancing at his father, he said soberly, "I wish we could save some of it. We'll need it when we go out to fight the Yankees."

"Oh, Dent, we'll make them run next time—just like we did at Fredericksburg!" Lowell Rocklin spoke up from where he stood beside the fireplace. He was shorter and more muscular than his father and his brothers and perhaps for this reason held himself very straight. He had brown hair and hazel eyes that reflected his indignation. Seeing doubt on David's face, he lifted his voice, "Isn't that right, Father?"

Clay shook his head. "Depends on a lot of things, Lowell. The Army of the Potomac's got one hundred thousand men. We can't match that."

Lowell gave the classic Southern answer in a confident voice. "Any Confederate can whip five Yankees!"

Dent Rocklin grew sober, and he touched the scar that marred his face. "You don't still believe that, Lowell? At Manassas those Yankees fought like wildcats when they were cornered. Every battle since then, too."

The talk went on for some time, Lowell standing erectly, stating that the Yankees would turn around and run for Washington as soon as the action started. The others were less certain, and it was Mark Rocklin who said, "Hope you're right about it, Lowell." He gave Clay a strange look, saying abruptly, "Can you use another soldier in your company, Nephew?"

Clay blinked in surprise, caught off guard. "Why, I think we can find a place for you, Uncle Mark. The Major needs an aide, and you'll look the part."

"Meaning I'm too old to carry a Springfield along with the young fellows? Probably right." Mark nodded. He saw the doubt in their faces and gave a brief explanation. "I guess you've all felt that I didn't care about the South. I've given you cause enough to think that. I've been a pretty worthless fellow—but when a man gets older, he wants to be a part of something more permanent. For me, it's this family. I—I'd like to join it . . . belatedly."

"You've never been out of it, but now you'll be right in the middle of the Rocklin mob!" Clay knew that his uncle would never say much about his past, but that this was his appeal to be accepted. "It'll be good to have you, Uncle Mark."

David had said little, but now he spoke up. "And I'd like to join, too, sir." He spoke to Clay, and there was an unhappiness in his eyes. "I can't stay home and grow potatoes while the rest of you fight!"

"David, we've been over this," Clay said slowly. "Somebody *has* to stay here and see that the food gets grown. The army can't fight unless it can eat."

"Anybody can run this place!"

"No, they can't, David." Dent spoke up. *"I* couldn't. You were working and learning how to run Gracefield from the time you were twelve years old. And what was *I* doing?" He lifted his hands in a gesture of helplessness. "I was out raising the devil!"

Mark kept quiet but was troubled over David. *He's always been the quiet one; Dent the colorful twin, Mark thought. Now he feels left out. I wish Clay would change his mind. The boy needs a chance.* But he knew that he'd forfeited his right to direct the family by his own irresponsible behavior, so he said nothing.

Finally David fell silent, and it was Lowell who looked now at Dent, his commanding officer, and grinned. "You think the Bluebellies will run, don't you, Dent?"

Dent returned the grin. "I'm no expert. We'd better get Stonewall Jackson in here to settle the question. . . ."

Clay slipped away as the talk turned to the coming battles and went to the kitchen. His mother was stirring a large pot filled with something that smelled good. He put his arm around her, asking quietly, "You all right?"

"Yes. Are you?"

Clay gave her an odd look, for she knew him better than he knew himself. "No, but that'll pass, I suppose. Things like this are always hard." At that moment Melora came through the door accompanied by Rena. She was in the midst of a story, and Clay was glad to see the smile on his daughter's face.

"I started home," Melora said, "but I had an idea, so I turned around and came here. I wanted to talk to Rena."

"What are you two plotting?" he asked. "You look like you're up to some outrage."

"Rena's coming to our house," Melora answered. A smile turned the corners of her full lips upward. "I'm going to teach her how to raise pigs."

"Can I, Daddy?"

Clay looked at Rena, nodded at once. *Be good for her to be with Melora,* he thought. "Why, sure. Every cultured Southern belle should learn the gentle art of raising pigs." He gave her a hug, adding, "Be sure you take a bath before you come back."

"Oh, Daddy!"

Clay and Melora watched the girl flounce away, and Melora said, "You shouldn't tease her so much, Clay."

He grinned suddenly. "I always teased you when you were a little girl. You turned out fairly well."

Melora tried not to smile, then gave it up. "I was a lot tougher than Rena."

"You were, for a fact," Clay said thoughtfully. He glanced at Melora and then noted that the other women had gone to deliver the food to the men. "Melora, watch out for her, will you? With me having to go away and her mother gone, she needs someone to talk to, to trust."

"I know. That's why I asked her to come and spend some time with me."

"Besides, she'll have to get used to you being her new momma!" Clay teased, winking at his beloved.

"Rena's fine," Melora stated evenly. "It's *you* I believe who needs some mothering!"

19

Clay chuckled. "You have a way of rapping out with the truth. You always did that, even when you were ten years old."

"I did it when I was six," Melora returned, her eyes twinkling with the memories of the days when he'd first come into her life. She'd been only a child, but she'd fallen in love with Clay Rocklin from the beginning. She knew one day soon she'd be his wife—but that day was not now.

"Let's go join the others, Clay," she said. "When do you and the other men have to be back?"

"Dent will have to leave tomorrow. Lowell and I have a little job to do in Richmond, so we'll have a little more time."

"Bring Rena tomorrow. We can all look at the pigs."

He smiled at her, and they went into the drawing room to join the others. Clay felt a sense of relief that Melora had stepped into the responsibility of caring for Rena. He had discovered that Rena was very dependent on him, and now that Ellen was gone and he would be away on duty for yet another summer, she needed someone. *Nobody better for that than Melora,* he thought.

★ ★ ★

Gen. Jeb Stuart pulled his horse up shortly and put his direct gaze on the two men who had halted their own mounts to let him pass. He was headed out of Richmond, but the general always had an eye for a good horse. "Well, now, that's a right pretty mare you've got there, Private," he observed.

"Thank you, General," Lowell said, returning the salute, then added boldly, "that's a pretty fair animal you're riding."

Clay had recognized the officer riding beside Stuart at once as Gen. James Longstreet. Longstreet pulled a black cigar from between his teeth and laughed softly. "The boy sounds mighty confident, General. And that *is* a nice mare he's riding."

James Ewell Brown Stuart bridled. "She can't beat Skylark!" Jeb Stuart was a colorful figure, and he was also the leader of the Confederate cavalry. He was proud of his ability—and his horse. "Private, you're not thinking your horse can beat mine, I hope?"

"Yes, sir, I'm afraid I am."

Longstreet laughed in delight. He himself was a plain man, and the flamboyant Stuart sometimes aggravated him. He gave Clay a look, seeing the resemblance at once between the two men. "Your son, Captain?"

"Yes, sir. I have two sons in the Richmond Grays."

Longstreet was impressed. "Have you now?" he murmured. "That's admirable." He considered Clay, then the mare Lowell was riding. "Are you of the same opinion as your son—about the mare?"

Clay grinned. "She's never been beat, sir!"

Stuart saw the sly look of amusement on Longstreet's face. "Well, sir," he announced firmly, "that record is about to be broken!"

"You're not going to race an enlisted man, are you, General?" Clay asked with alarm.

Stuart's face was hidden behind the bushy black beard, but his eyes twinkled with humor. "I do it all the time, Captain," he said gleefully. "That's how I enlist my cavalry." He looked at the terrain, then lifted his gauntleted hand, pointing to a single tall pine in the middle of a pasture. "To that tree and back, Private—what's your name?"

"Lowell Rocklin, sir, and this is my father, Capt. Clay Rocklin."

"Gen. Longstreet, you give the signal," Stuart commanded. He brought his big stallion around so that he faced the tree, and Lowell did the same. As soon as they were in position, Longstreet shouted, "Go!"

As the two horses exploded into action, Clay said nervously, "Sir, my son is in a no-win situation. If he loses, his record with that mare is broken, but if he wins—well, nobody ever made any money beating a general!"

Longstreet looked at Clay, puffed on his cigar and nodded. "That's pretty wise, Capt. Rocklin, but don't worry. Your boy won't beat Gen. Stuart."

Clay watched uneasily but saw with some relief as the two horsemen made their return that Longstreet was right. Stuart beat Lowell by three lengths. Lowell pulled up, crestfallen, but Gen. Stuart said heartily, "You have a fine animal, young fellow, and you're a fine rider." His blue eyes gleamed. "Jine the cavalry! Nothing like it!" He gave Longstreet a caustic grin, adding, "Any yokel can dress up and march around with a musket, but I need young fellows like you! We're the eyes of the army. Why, Gen. Lee wouldn't make a move without me and my boys!"

Lowell was fascinated by the colorful Stuart and glanced at Clay. "Sir? Do you think I might?"

"Have to ask Col. Benton for a transfer, I guess."

Stuart suddenly lifted his plumed hat, waved it, and shouted, "Do it, Private!" He spurred the stallion and drove off shouting with a wild whoop.

Clay stared after Stuart, then put his gaze on Longstreet. "Sir, he's quite a man, isn't he?"

Longstreet nodded. "For what he does, there's nobody better."

"Do you think Gen. Stuart really wants me in the cavalry, sir?" Lowell asked.

Longstreet smiled. "Every young fellow in Virginia wants to join Jeb Stuart, and if he extended the offer to you, he means it." He nodded to Clay. "Come along, tell me about those boys of yours, Capt. Rocklin."

Clay was flattered by the general's interest, and he gave a brief sketch of his boys. "This one is the best horseman of us all—best in the county." Clay smiled at Lowell, adding, "In my opinion, General, the best *anywhere!*"

Longstreet noticed Lowell flush at his father's praise. "Don't be embarrassed, Private. We're going to need the best from everyone to hold off the Yankees."

"May I ask your opinion of the enemy force, General?" Clay inquired cautiously.

Longstreet shrugged. "I expect you know he's coming with as big an army as has ever marched on this continent. He's got everything he needs—guns, ammunition, artillery—even balloons."

"Even *what*, sir?" Lowell asked with surprise.

"Balloons, Private." Longstreet nodded. There was a sober quality in the man, a steadiness that controlled all that he did and said. He was, Clay knew, the most reliable of all the Confederate generals, and Lee put much confidence in him. "Fellow named Thaddeus Lowe has come up with a new idea. Makes big balloons out of silk, fills them with hot air. They have baskets underneath, and the Federals send up an officer to get the position of the opposing troops."

"I haven't heard of that, sir," Clay said with interest. "Does it work?"

"They tell me it does, though I haven't seen it myself." Longstreet took the cigar out of his mouth, studied it, and added, "I hope it doesn't, Captain, because they have them and we don't!"

"Just a big balloon filled with hot air?" Lowell asked with surprise. "Why, that shouldn't be much trouble, General."

Longstreet turned his head to study the young man. "We had one last spring for a few days, and we sure could use every advantage we can muster. Private, if you want to serve the Confederacy, you make one of those things for me. I'll promote you on the spot to sergeant."

"Really, sir?"

Longstreet nodded. "You'd be a lot more use to the Cause doing that than riding around with Gen. Stuart—" Longstreet suddenly realized what he had said and added hastily, "Of course, we couldn't do without Gen. Stuart and his boys, but when the Yankees hit us, how are we going to know where they are? They'll know where *we* are! They'll have spotters up in those blasted things telling them where every man we have is located."

Lowell stared at Gen. Longstreet, his eyes narrowing. "Sir, I can do it!"

Longstreet had not been serious, but at the intent look on Lowell's face, he grew sober. "Do it then!" he snapped. Looking at Clay, he nodded, saying, "If your boy can come up with an observation balloon, it might make a big difference when we go into action." He nodded shortly, then rode off toward Stuart, who was waiting impatiently up the road.

"Never thought we'd be talking with two generals, Father!"

"Nor did I." Clay gave Lowell a quick look. "Did you hold your mare back?"

"Sure did! I've got more sense than to beat a general at anything!"

Clay laughed loudly. "Come on, Son, we've got work to do."

As they rode into Richmond, Lowell said suddenly, "I could make that balloon, sir."

Clay was startled, for his mind was on other things. "Why, I guess you could, Lowell. You were always good at inventing things." He considered this intent young son of his carefully. "You going to try it?"

"I'd like to, sir."

"Well, I'll ask Col. Benton to give you some time for this project. Shouldn't be too hard since Old Pete asked you to work on it."

"I'm going to have a try at it." Lowell's hazel eyes glowed. "Say, wouldn't that be something?"

"Wouldn't *what* be something?"

Lowell pointed up to where a red-tailed hawk was sailing high in the air. "To be up there with that fellow!"

Clay glanced upward, studied the steady flight of the bird, then nodded and smiled. "Yes, that really *would* be something, Son!"

CHAPTER THREE
Chimborazo

Studs Mulvaney, owner of the Royal Hotel, was not a man prone to granting favors. But he'd taken Clara Smith on as one of his "hostesses"—dance hall girls—only because Alf Swanson had asked. Studs had given the woman a room on the second floor—a room that would be used to entertain men. She looked so ill and tired after her hard journey from Vicksburg, Studs had surprised himself by saying, "Take a few days to rest up, kid." Afterward on his way to his office, he'd had second thoughts. Looking over to Bugs Leggett, his one-legged swamper who was cleaning up, he remarked, "She won't make it, Bugs, but I got to do it. Owe Alf a big one."

"Wot about the girl and the kid?" Bugs demanded. "Pretty girl like that, she'll be trouble if she don't come across."

"Yeah, I guess that's right. Go get her, will you, Bugs?" After the swamper thumped out on his wooden leg, Mulvaney leaned back and stared at the picture of the coyly smiling nude on his wall, though not really seeing it. He was a huge man, well over six feet, with the battered features of an ex-prizefighter. He was nearing fifty now and growing fat, but was still rough enough to serve as his own bouncer. And the Royal Hotel needed a tough bouncer, for although

25

it might qualify as a hotel insofar as it had rooms that could be rented, it was more of a saloon and a dance hall than anything else. And the rooms upstairs, where men followed the women, were paid for in bribes to the police each month.

When a slight knocking on the door drew his attention, he got up and walked to the door. Opening it, with a nod of his head he motioned in the two who stood there, then closed the door behind them. Staring down at the pair, he stated bluntly, "This ain't no place for kids."

Rooney said quickly, "Mr. Mulvaney, Buck and me can work. You got to have cleaning, and we're real good at that." She was frightened, but held her head high. "Just give us a corner someplace to sleep in, and we'll work for our room and board."

Mulvaney had made up his mind to get rid of the pair, but he liked the girl's spunk. Taking the stub of a foul-smelling cigar out of his mouth, he stared down at them uncertainly. The boy, Buck, piped up, "And I can take messages and run all your errands—and I can do anything else you need done."

"Can you now?" Jamming the cigar between his battered lips, the big man thought hard. *I can use the boy, but the girl could be trouble if any of my customers get an eyeful of her.* Still, he liked the girl's steady look and asked abruptly, "You're a good girl, ain'tcha?"

Rooney's cheeks reddened, and she nodded. "Yes, sir."

"Well, I'll do what I can for you." He thought hard, his eyes almost hidden in their sockets. A thousand blows had formed scar tissue that pulled his thick eyelids down so that he was slit eyed, but Rooney had learned to know the looks of men. Studs Mulvaney, she was sure, though hardly a civic leader, wasn't one of the bad ones.

Mulvaney reached a decision. "C'mon, I'll show you what I got. Might work out, might not."

Rooney and Buck followed the big man out of his office. It was only the middle of the afternoon, and the saloon was almost empty as he led them through it to the stairs near the back. They creaked under his weight, but he ignored the sound, turning at the top to his left. The hall was lined with doors, and there was a strange, thick odor that both young people noticed. At the end of the hall Mulvaney opened a door, and Rooney looked cautiously inside. It was some sort of storage room with mops, buckets, chamber pots, and other equipment piled carelessly around.

"See that ladder?"

Rooney and Buck saw a ladder composed of two boards nailed to the wall with two-foot-long pieces nailed across to form a rough sort of ladder.

"Yes, sir."

"Well, up at the top there's a room—sort of. Go up and look it over, then come back down here."

At once Buck scrambled up the ladder, and Rooney followed, trying to keep her skirt around her legs, but glancing down, she saw that Mulvaney was staring down at the floor.

At the top of the ladder, she stepped off and found herself in a garret room—more or less. It was composed of a floor, four walls, and a peaked roof. Someone had boarded up the attic of the Royal Hotel, slapped a door in one side and a single window in the outer wall that looked down on Sixth Street. The walls were covered with yellowing newspaper, and the furniture consisted of two cots, one table, a chair, and a battered washstand.

Buck stepped over and pulled the window open. "Hey, we can see everything from here, Sis!"

Rooney stared around at the room, and a great relief came to her. *It's like a little tree house,* she thought. *We'll be safe here!* Aloud she said, "We'll make us a real home here, Buck."

As she descended the rungs of the ladder, her mind was already working on how to fix up the room. Stepping to the floor, she said, "Oh, Mr. Mulvaney, it's just what Buck and me need!"

"Pretty rough for a young woman, ain't it?"

"Oh no!" Rooney's eyes were glowing, and she spoke with excitement. "Buck and me can fix it up fine! Can we work for you?"

"I reckon so." Mulvaney saw the two exchange happy glances and shrugged. "Guess we can round up some bedding and stuff. Buck, go find Bugs and tell him to see what he can dig up." As soon as Buck disappeared, Mulvaney looked down at Rooney.

"See that door?" He shoved some boards aside and with a grunt opened a door that had been concealed behind them. "It goes out to some stairs, see? Used to be a fire escape, I reckon. Somebody made this closet and closed it off." Puffing blue smoke like a miniature engine, he considered Rooney, then said, "Wouldn't be too safe for a young girl to be in the hotel. You better use these stairs."

Rooney was relieved and said, "That'll be nice, Mr. Mulvaney."

"Can you cook?"

"Oh yes! I can bake biscuits and cook just about anything, if it's not too fancy. I worked for a café once, just washing dishes at first, but then I got to help the cook all the time."

"Guess that's what you'll do, then. C'mon, I'll show you the kitchen."

When they had descended the stairs, Rooney followed the owner through the bar into a dining room that held half a dozen battered wooden tables flanked by an assortment of chairs, then through a swinging door. "Hey, Chin, this is your new helper. Her name's Rooney."

Rooney faced a small, thin Oriental with a smooth yellow face. "Looney?" he said in a sibilant voice. He bowed three times, saying, "Wely nice, Looney!"

"It's *Rooney!*" Mulvaney growled, but turned to the girl with a smile. "He can't talk American good, but he's a pretty fair cook. You give him a hand."

"I'm glad to know you, Chin." Rooney smiled. She had never known a Chinese, but she felt that she would be safe with this one. That was always the test with any male: *Will I be safe with him?* "Maybe you can teach me to make Chinese food."

"Ah, yesss!" Chin's head bobbed up and down, and he grinned, exposing yellow teeth. "You be glate hep to Chin, Looney!" The thin, undersized cook had never mastered the *R* of the English language, but he said, "You know how to fix pot loast?"

"He means pot *r*oast," Mulvaney said, grinning. "Come on, we'll see if Bugs and your brother got anything fer your room."

★　★　★

Rooney perched on a high stool, peeling potatoes with quick, efficient motions of a small knife. Across from her, Chin chopped meat into small strips with swift, accurate blows of a razor-sharp cleaver. This never failed to amaze Rooney, for the diminutive cook used his left hand to position the meat, his nimble fingers shoving portions of the rich, red beef into place. Chin never seemed to look at the meat and withdrew his bony fingers just in time to escape being cut off by the blows of the heavy cleaver. He jabbered constantly as he worked, and Rooney had grown fond of him.

"You're going to chop all your fingers off one day, Chin," she remarked when the cook slammed the gleaming cleaver down, missing his fingers by a fragment of an inch, slicing the tough beef cleanly.

"Ho! Chin nevah miss!" As if to show his helper the truth of his words, he sent a staccato echo as he struck the beef a rapid series of blows. Each blow, Rooney saw with amazement, sliced a thin section of raw beef from the bone, and when the sound stopped, Chin held up the slices, triumph in his black eyes. "No fingas!" he crowed, then laughed silently at the girl. "You tly now?"

"No!" Rooney smiled, shaking her head. "I'll stick to peeling potatoes. What kind of pies do you want me to make for supper, Chin?"

"Ah—thlee apple and two laisen." Gathering up the beef, Chin proceeded to pull down pots and pans, making a terrific clatter, while at the same time raising his shrill voice to ask, "You like it heah, Looney?"

"Yes. Buck and I both do."

"I glad," Chin pronounced. "You fine young womans! Make good pies." His wise eyes came to rest on her as he tossed the ingredients for the meal together. He was a lonely man, cut off from his homeland by thousands of miles, and there were only a handful of Orientals in Richmond. He had lost his wife and children to an epidemic of cholera that had broken out aboard the ship bringing them to America and had never married again. His only interests were reading a small collection of books printed in his native language and playing cards. He was an inveterate gambler, and he had been overjoyed when Rooney had accepted his offer to play cards. He was, Rooney quickly discovered, a terrible gambler. She never played with him for money, of course, but even over their simple games Chin got so excited that she learned to beat him easily. "Don't get excited when you have a good hand," she had cautioned him. "And sometimes just *act* excited when you have a bad hand." But Chin was incurable and lost his wages at the gambling tables as soon as he received them. "You're really working for nothing for Mr. Mulvaney, Chin," she censured him more than once. "He pays you for working, and you turn right around and give it back to him at the card tables."

"I beat him next time!" was his inevitable reply.

Rooney had learned to survive the dangers of the Royal—primarily by keeping herself out of sight as much as possible. She worked hard in the kitchen, only going out to serve in the dining room when necessary. And she *never* went to the bar or the second floor—*never!* It was not so dangerous for Buck, so he sometimes went up the inner stairs, but Rooney had learned caution in a hard school. Always she left the kitchen by the outer door that opened into the alley and climbed the rickety stairs that led to the small closet, then climbed the ladder to the small room she shared with Buck. She had said once to Buck, "Let's make a rope ladder, then we can come up here and pull it up after us. Nobody could ever get to us."

"Aw, that'd be too hard," Buck had answered. He had learned to fit into the world of Richmond's lower denizens, the men and women who roamed the raw streets and alleyways. He was a sharp lad and was earning money, making himself useful to Mulvaney and other saloon owners along the street. There was always need for someone to take a bottle or a message, and men were careless with their money.

Rooney was aware that Buck was being hardened by the life they were forced to live, and despair came to her when she could find no way to protect him. She worried over his future, wanting him to have more than he did. All the love she could not lavish on parents, she gave to him. Until recently he remained fairly innocent, but he was growing up, Rooney saw, and the boys he was beginning to spend time with were a bad influence.

She sat there peeling potatoes and listening to Chin tell about his youthful days in China. It was quiet in the kitchen, and she liked being in the kitchen with the little cook. Rooney had learned to enjoy the simple things, savoring them for the moment. Her life had been a tightrope, and only by some sort of miracle had she been able to keep her purity of body and mind in the midst of a raw and violent world.

The door swung open abruptly, and Rooney's mother came in. "I gotta have some money, Rooney," Clara demanded. "I know you got some, so let's have it."

Rooney reached into her pocket, took out the three dollars she had left from the small amount that Mulvaney paid her. She handed the sum to her mother, who snatched it and stared at the girl suspiciously. "This all you got?"

"Yes, that's all."

Clara stuck the bills into her bodice and started to speak

but was seized by a coughing fit. Her thin body was racked by the deep tearing coughs, and Rooney leaped up and ran to get a glass of water. Holding it toward her mother, she said urgently, "Mama—drink this!"

Clara seized the glass, and the water spilled over her chin as she tried to gulp it. Finally she sputtered and the coughing grew milder. Taking a shallow breath, she stared at Rooney with hollow eyes. "I got to go to the doctor," she muttered hoarsely. "I ain't feeling good."

"Maybe he'll give you some medicine for your cough," Rooney encouraged her. Timidly she placed her hand on her mother's shoulder, adding, "Maybe you should take a few days rest."

Clara gave Rooney a look of anger, mixed with despair. "There ain't no rest in this business." She turned to Chin. "You got any cough medicine, Cookee?"

"Ah, yesss." Chin bowed with a sharp, jerky motion, turned, and went into the door that led to his small room just off the kitchen. He came back at once with a brown bottle in his thin hand. "Vely good for you," he insisted, then added a warning, "but make you sleep long time!"

The sick woman stared at the bottle, pulled off the cap, and sniffed at it. Blinking her eyes, she gasped, then looked at Chin. "Smells bad enough to be good. Thanks, Cookee." She gave Rooney a weary glance, asking, "You feelin' all right?"

"Yes, Mama."

Suspicion came to Clara Smith's faded eyes. "Stay away from these men. None of them is any good."

"I will."

Clara lifted the bottle, drank two swallows, then lowered it. A contortion twisted her features, and she gasped, "What is this stuff, anyway?"

"Vely good for sick womans," Chin insisted, his head bobbing up and down. Concern came into his smallish eyes as he added, "Not much. Too much and womans die!"

His words caught at Clara, turning her face suddenly still.

She lifted the brown bottle, stared at it, then muttered, "There's worse things than dying, Cookee." She gave Rooney a look filled with bitterness, turned, and left the room.

"She vely sick," Chin said quietly, shaking his head. "Not a good place for sick womans!"

All afternoon as Rooney helped Chin with the cooking and later when she washed dishes, she thought about her mother. She had been ashamed of what her mother did for a long time, but there still remained a love for her. Finally she said good night to Chin, left the kitchen, and climbed the stairs and then the ladder up to her room. Carefully she lit the lamp, then took off her dress and undergarments and washed as well as she could, using a large enamel washbasin. All the water had to be hauled up to the room, but Buck had devised a method so that both of them could bathe. He'd found a twenty-gallon wooden barrel and—with Mulvaney's help—had hauled it up to the tiny room. The difficulty was in filling it with water, but he and Rooney had solved that by hauling up water from the alley using a rope and a two-gallon wooden bucket. Now as Rooney bathed herself with fresh water, she relaxed. When she was clean, she dried off, put on a thin dress she used for a nightgown, and went over to sit down at the makeshift desk—really a part of a door over two boxes. Picking up a book, she sat there and read until she grew sleepy, then put the book down. It was a story about an orphan named Jane Eyre, and somehow the book spoke to her. She read poorly, making the words out slowly, but even so, the plight of the young English girl touched her heart. *Funny that I can feel so sorry for a girl who's not even alive,* she mused as she sat hunched over the book. *With all my troubles, it's silly to read about somebody else's.*

Going to her cot, she lay down but didn't go to sleep at once. Finally fatigue caught up with her, and she drifted off. The noise of Buck climbing the ladder woke her instantly.

She sat up and waited until he stepped inside, then said with a touch of rebuke, "It's too late for you to be out, Buck."

Buck shrugged and tossed his cap on the floor. He began undressing but made his defense by saying, "Big poker game across the street at the Chez Paree, Sis. Some big wheels in it." He stripped off his shirt and as he washed, added, "I took them some whiskey and sandwiches, and then one of them sent me downtown with a message. Gave me five dollars."

Rooney didn't like it but knew that neither of them had little choice. "What was all that noise earlier tonight?"

"New bunch of soldiers come in—from Alabama I think." Buck pulled off his trousers, then his shoes and socks. Stretching out on the narrow cot, he closed his eyes.

"Do the men say the Yankees will come here?" Rooney's world was delicately balanced. Any small event could send it rocking, and as poor as her condition was, she clung to it desperately. She knew little about the war. For her the only issue was: Will the Yankees come? If they came, she might lose her place, and she could not face that.

"Dunno, Sis." Buck opened his eyes and said, "There's been lots of our men hurt in battle so far. One of the men in the poker game was a soldier—a doctor."

"What did he say?"

"Said it was real bad. He said he'd cut off arms and legs until they made a pile high as his head!"

"How awful!"

"Some of them wuz Yankees, though."

Rooney tried to shut the image of such a bloody scene from her mind. "Where do they take the wounded soldiers, Buck?"

"The officer said they haul them back to Richmond in wagons. Said lots of 'em are took to houses, and the people take care of them." He thought hard, then added, "He said there's a big hospital here, out on the edge of town. Can't say the name of it right . . . Shimboozo—somethin' like that." He was very sleepy and muttered, "He said they ain't no space or near enough doctors, and some of the wounded have to be put on the floor. Says some of 'em will just die with nobody to take care of em. . . ."

Rooney glanced over and saw that Buck was asleep. Rising, she went to him, leaned over, and kissed his cheek, then turned and blew the lamp out. For a long time she lay in bed thinking of the wounded men who were dying because there was nobody to take care of them.

"I could at least get them water and wash their clothes." She lay still, and a determination came to her. "I'm goin' to that place. If Mr. Mulvaney will let me!"

★　★　★

Phoebe Yates Pember, matron at Chimborazo Hospital, looked up from the raw stump where a leg ended and stared at the youthful girl who'd come into the infirmary. The ward was packed with cots, and some of the men with less-serious wounds were on blankets on the floor. The smell of blood, urine, and sweat filled the room, and there was a constant low muttering from men in pain.

"Well, what is it?" she demanded, staring at Rooney. Mrs. Pember had not slept well in a long time, and her nerves were ragged. It was not only the constant strain of men dying for the lack of simple care, but the opposition she had received from the doctors. They had let her know that male nurses were needed, not female! But she had a letter from President Jefferson Davis stating that he would be pleased if the medical department would give Mrs. Pember charge over a ward—and none of the doctors had the nerve to deny that letter!

But the staff had made Mrs. Pember as uncomfortable as possible, withholding supplies and giving her the most worthless of the male nurses and orderlies. And they had assaulted her verbally if not physically, making their talk around her as crude and rough as possible.

But Phoebe Yates Pember had forged ahead, throwing herself into the work of saving wounded Confederate soldiers. Ignoring the opposition of the staff, she had struck Chimborazo Hospital, Ward 12 like a small tornado. When her energy had produced the smallest death rate in her ward of any in the entire hospital, the doctors were forced to shut their mouths, though her success seemed to anger instead of please them.

Some help had come from the women of Richmond, but not nearly enough. Mrs. Pember looked at the girl with large blue eyes and snapped again, "Yes, what is it?" The stump she was working on was not well done, and she silently raged against the carelessness of the "surgeon" who had done such a poor job on the soldier.

"I've come to help with the soldiers, ma'am."

Mrs. Pember began to bandage the stump, then looking up, she spoke more gently. "Help with the soldiers? Are you a nurse?"

"Oh no! I—I just thought I might do something. I could feed them and get them things—maybe help with the washing."

"What's your name?"

"Rooney Smith, ma'am."

"Do your parents know you're here? You're very young, and this is rough work."

"My mama . . . won't care." Rooney stumbled over the words, then lifted her chin and stated, "I'm used to rough living. All I want to do is help."

A smile came to Mrs. Pember. "All right, Rooney. I'm glad you've come. How much would you like to work?"

"Oh, I can work all morning, Miz Pember! I cook in the afternoons, so I couldn't work then."

"That will be fine. Now, if you'll just stay with me, I'll show you how to change bandages." She hesitated, then said, "Some of the wounds are very bad. Do you think you can do it?"

"I don't know, ma'am," Rooney answered quietly. "I'll try."

Mrs. Pember liked the girl. She distrusted people who

made rash promises, and Rooney's reply pleased her. She turned to face the young soldier with the missing leg. "Think you'd like to have this pretty young woman for a nurse, Billy?"

The soldier was no more than eighteen. He was so thin that his eyes looked enormous in his face. But he smiled faintly and nodded. "Sure, Miz Pember. I'd like her just fine."

"Get Billy some fresh water, will you, Rooney? And try to get him to eat a little soup."

"Yes, ma'am," Rooney agreed. Quickly she got the water, then sat down and smiled at him. "This looks like good soup, Billy. I'm going to sit here and feed it to you, so just make up your mind to it!" He reminded her of her brother, Buck, and Rooney was glad to see him smile weakly.

"Yes, Miss Rooney, I'll sure do my best," he whispered. Billy Cantrell had been thinking of his own sweetheart, Ruth Wentworth—wondering how she would feel when a one-legged man came back to her. He'd been thinking about how Ruth loved to dance, and the thought had brought despair to him. Somehow it helped that this young girl was willing to sit with him. Maybe Ruthie would have him with one leg after all!

CHAPTER FOUR
Shadow Bluff

★

The Richmond Grays fought savage battles since their baptism of fire at Bull Run. Their ranks were thinned, and the shock of battle had dulled their spirits. The entire Confederate army was shrinking from combat losses, and Gen. Lee sought desperately to fill the empty ranks and garner supplies for the coming onslaught of the Army of the Potomac.

But even in that "slack" period between fall and spring, there were skirmishes all along the borders of Confederate territory. One of these involved a small Federal force that suddenly appeared along the northern border of Virginia. A daring young officer, Maj. Phil Ramsey, had obtained permission to raid the scattered troops now guarding that area. He had planned a surprise attack, but his force had been detected by scouts who had relayed the news to Richmond. The Richmond Grays were part of the force that had been sent to deal with the attack and had engaged in a sharp battle with Ramsey's men at dusk. They had fought themselves into a stupor, and all were thinking of what would happen at dawn. Lowell looked up bleary-eyed at a large hill or plateau that rose more than a hundred feet high ahead of them. "What hill is that, Sarge?"

Sgt. Waco Smith was sitting down, his back against a tree. A bloody rag was tied around his forehead, but he looked more alert than the members of his squad. "I dunno," he said, shrugging. "This is your country, ain't it? You're supposed to know it better than me." Waco was a Texan, and his heritage showed in the .44 he kept strapped to his side, just as he'd worn it when he was a Texas Ranger. He looked past Lowell to Clay, asking, "You know that hill, Captain?"

Clay Rocklin nodded, then came to sit down in front of the fire. "I think it's called Shadow Bluff," he said. He had impaled a piece of beef on his bayonet and held it over the fire. When it started to sizzle, he eyed it critically. "Looks good. I'm hungry as a wolf."

"Not enough meat for our company, Clay." Lt. Bushrod Aimes had come over and squatted down beside Clay. "Course, there's not as many of us eating now. The Yankees whittled us down some this afternoon."

Clay nodded. He and Aimes were old friends and shared many memories. "Guess that's right." He looked over at the sleeping men, adding, "Leo didn't make it, Bushrod."

"How many of us does that make?"

Clay shook his head, counting silently. "I don't know the count for sure, but I'd say about a dozen."

Bushrod stared at him, his eyes red rimmed and his face drawn with fatigue. "That's almost a quarter of the company. We can't take much more of this, Clay." He stared up at the looming face of Shadow Bluff and shook his head. "I hope we don't have to take that hill tomorrow."

"I think we'll have to try." Clay pulled the meat out of the fire, tore off a morsel, and tasted it. "About right." He cut the meat into portions and called out, "Lowell, you and Mark come to supper. Enough for you, too, Bushrod."

"I've eaten." Aimes got up and walked over to where the first platoon was camped, saying, "Watch yourself in the morning, Clay. Don't let any of your boys be heroes!"

Mark Rocklin had come over to sit beside Clay. He looked dark and saturnine in the gloom, his face highlighted by the flickering tongues of yellow flame. He had served as an aide to Col. Benton since enlisting but had wrangled permission from the colonel to accompany the attacking force. Taking a portion of the meat, he chewed it, watching as Clay dealt out slices to Lowell and Waco. He felt old and out of place among these young men, though at the age of fifty-two he was able to outmarch many of the younger men. He was a handsome man, his features patrician and his hair almost as black as that of his nephew Clay Rocklin. Glancing over at Lowell, he asked, "Still thinking about joining the cavalry, Lowell?"

"In a minute if I had the chance," Lowell said with a big grin. He had always admired his uncle Mark, and the two of them had grown very close since Mark had enlisted. "Don't see many dead cavalrymen, do you?"

Mark laughed suddenly and nudged Clay. "You didn't teach this young whelp much respect for tradition, did you?"

Clay smiled at Lowell, but his eyes suddenly became serious. "I'm going to teach him some respect for those Yankee sharpshooters." He waved his chunk of meat at Lowell, adding, "You keep your head down tomorrow, Lowell." He'd had to pull the young man down more than once in the battles and had seen too many go down for good.

Lowell grinned, jibing at his father, "You always stay down, don't you, Capt. Rocklin? Never see you moving around when the lead starts flying." He enjoyed the look on his father's face, for Clay was always moving about when the situation was worse.

Waco, seeing the expression on Clay's face, remarked slyly, "Seems like I been through all this before. Remember Bull Run? The three of us—and Lt. Rocklin, too—was staring at the Yankee guns jist like we are now."

Lowell nodded. "I never will forget the way you charged up that hill to get Dent, Father. Right in the teeth of the Bluebellies. You remember that, Waco?"

"Sure do!" the Texan said with a grin. "I was saying hello to St. Peter all the way up. Bob Yancy was with us, too, as I think on it."

Lowell grasped his knees, his face rapt as he thought of that battle, shook his head slowly, and gave his father a look of admiration. "I don't think Dent would have made it if you hadn't led us up that hill."

Clay was uneasy as always when anyone referred to that time. He himself saw nothing heroic about that wild charge—not for him, at least. It was his own son who was in danger, and a man could do no less.

Clay stated brusquely to Mark, "Keep this young firebrand under control, will you?"

"Do my best, but you know how these Rocklins are—stubborn as blue-nosed mules!"

All three of them laughed at Mark's definition, and Waco watched them with interest. "Must be nice to have kin beside you," he remarked.

"Not very smart," Clay answered at once. "We ought to be scattered out so that we'd have less chance of all of us getting hit."

Waco looked up at the hill in front of them. The Federal campfires winked out of the darkness like malevolent eyes, and the Texan shook his head. "I got a feeling about goin' up that blamed hill in the mornin', Captain." He shaved off a morsel of meat with his bowie knife, put it in his mouth, and chewed it slowly. "I shore don't want to go up there. Let the Bluebellies have it!"

Clay looked at the bulky mass of Shadow Bluff, and a chill ran through him. "I guess we don't have much choice, Sergeant. They're there, and we've got to drive them back."

At dawn the attack began, and Clay had time to say to Waco, "We're going to get hit hard. Watch out and try to save as many as you can!" Then he advanced at the head of the men into the raging battle. He lost sight of Lowell and thought, *I hope Mark takes care of him!*

But both Mark and Lowell were in the front of a line that hit the Union center. Mark held Lowell back for a while, but the younger man ran straight at the enemy. Mark cried out,

"Lowell—you fool, get down!" When he saw that Lowell was not going to stop, he ran after him.

The Federals opened up with a volley that tore huge gaps in the gray-clad ranks, with salvo after salvo of exploding case shot. Mark saw Lowell go down, and with a wild cry he ran to where the young soldier had fallen. But before he got there he was struck in the stomach by a force that lifted him off his feet and threw him backward. The sun seemed to explode, and as pain ripped through him, he thought, *My God! I'm being killed!* And then he fell into a blackness that blotted out pain and thought instantly.

★ ★ ★

Clay's face was black with powder, and he called out, "Don't press the attack, men. They're retreating, and that's what we came for."

As the battle finally ended, Waco turned to Clay and said, "Your boy Lowell and Mark got hit, Captain."

The two of them hurried to where some of the wounded had been placed under a towering elm. Clay stumbled toward them, bent down, and saw that Lowell's eyes were open. "Son! Are you hurt bad?"

Lowell licked his lips, but seemed fairly alert. "N-no, I don't guess so. Just got sliced across the shoulders. But Uncle Mark, he's in poor shape."

Clay took a deep breath and squeezed Lowell's hand. He turned to Mark and saw the crimson blood that stained the gray uniform—and his heart sank. *A belly wound. He'll never make it!*

But Clay regained control quickly, saying, "Go back to that farmhouse, Sergeant. Commandeer all the wagons they've got. We've got to get the wounded to the hospital!"

As Waco dashed off to obey the command, Clay looked at the wounded men who were groaning and writhing on the ground. His eyes were filled with grief, not only for his own kin, but for all of them, Northern and Southern men alike.

He bent over and whispered, "Son, I'm taking you and Mark into Richmond. You'll be all right."

Lowell nodded weakly. "We gave 'em the best we had, didn't we, sir?"

Clay nodded wearily. "Yes, Lowell, you did real fine! All of you boys did real fine!" Then he took a deep breath and rose to his feet. The battle was over, but as always, the suffering was only beginning.

The trip back to Richmond was hard on the wounded. Three of them died on the way and were buried beside the road. Finally they reached Chimborazo, and Clay got the wounded admitted. He waited outside until the surgery was over, then moved into the ward where Lowell and Mark were lying on cots.

The surgeon was still there, and Clay asked, "My son and my uncle—Doctor, how are they?"

The doctor was a short, heavy man with tired eyes. Glancing at Lowell, he nodded. "He's not bad. He'll make it." His eyes turned to the still form of Mark, and he shook his head. "I'm not hopeful about your uncle. Took a minié ball in the belly. I dug it out, but you know how bad a stomach wound can be."

"What are his chances, Doctor?" Clay asked, his eyes fixed on the two still forms.

"God knows." The doctor shrugged wearily, then turned and walked away.

CHAPTER FIVE
"Just a Few Scraps of Silk!"

★

Within a week Chimborazo had become the biggest thing in Rooney Smith's life. She did her work with Chin in the afternoon and spent her evenings in the tiny room over the Royal—but she lived for the mornings.

Rising early, she dressed quietly, descended from the garret room to the alley, then made her way through the deserted streets of predawn Richmond to the hospital. Chimborazo Hospital was a sprawling affair perched on a high hill near the western side of Richmond. It eventually numbered 150 wards, each under the care of an assistant surgeon. The wards were housed in one-story buildings, 30 feet wide and 100 feet long.

At first Rooney had been confused by the jumbled fashion in which the wards were scattered but quickly learned that they were all grouped into five divisions, or hospitals. Mrs. Pember was in charge of Ward 12 in Hospital 2, and it was in that ward that Rooney worked.

As she climbed the steep incline leading to the hospital, she thought of how quickly she'd learned to help with the soldiers. Mrs. Pember had only let her clean at first, but when it became obvious that Rooney was a natural nurse, able to clean patients and change bandages quickly without flinching at the dirt, the smells, and the awful wounds, the matron had at once used her in this capacity.

The sun was creeping over the city, bathing the white

45

hospital buildings in a golden red glow as Rooney entered the building where Mrs. Pember had her office. She passed through the center of the ward, speaking to men who were awake, remembering some of their names. Their eyes followed the slender young girl as she moved down the aisle, but there were no rude remarks.

She paused beside the bed of one of the patients who was sitting up staring at her. "Hello, Claude," she said, coming to stand beside him. He was a new patient, having come in only three days earlier, and he was, on the whole, a rather sorry specimen. He was lean as most of them were, but his hair lay over his shoulders in lank strands, and his fingernails were long, like claws.

"Claude, when are you going to let me cut your hair and your nails?"

The soldier stared at her and blinked with determination. "Never!" he spat out. "I done promised my ma I wouldn't cut my hair till the war's over. And I use my fingernails 'cause I couldn't get a fork when we wuz on the march."

Shaking her head with amusement, Rooney said, "Why, Claude, your mama would purely *thrash* you if she saw that dirty ol' greasy hair! And we've got plenty of forks here—you know that!"

But Claude shook his head stubbornly, and Rooney gave up. "If you'll let me clean you up, I'll write that letter you've been after me to do."

The eyes of the soldier brightened, and he sat up straighter. Then he seemed to consider this a weakness because he slumped down and shook his head. "I promised my ma," he muttered.

"Let me know if you change your mind."

Rooney left, and the man on the bed next to Claude, a pale young man of eighteen with one arm, jibed, "Claude, you ain't got good sense! That purty young thang wantin' to purty you up, and you laying there sulled up like a pizen pup! I allus knowed you Georgia crackers wuz dumb!"

Rooney didn't hear this remark, but later when she came

out of the supply room with fresh water and bandages, Claude said abruptly as she passed, "Wal—I reckon you can do it, then."

Rooney wanted to laugh, but she had learned that most of the young men were highly sensitive, so she said only, "That's fine, Claude," and set about cleaning him up. As she worked with a pair of scissors, cutting his hair carefully, Claude's friends began calling out advice. "Don't let them things slip and cut his ears off, Miss Rooney. He's ugly enough as he is!" "Save them fangernails, Nurse. They're the purtiest thing they is about ol' Claude!" "Better hose 'em down with turpentine, Miss Rooney!"

Rooney smiled at them, knowing that it was a lonely life they led. Most of them were from Georgia and had no visitors. There was nothing to do for those who were bedfast except lie there and stare at the ceiling, and even the more mobile of the wounded could only talk or play endless games of cards. Her heart went out to them, and when she wasn't actually tending to their physical needs, she usually sat and talked to the worst cases or wrote letters home for the men.

"There!" she announced finally, rose and stepped back to admire her work. "Don't you look nice! Wait—I saw a mirror in the office." She disappeared through the door and was back soon with a small, round shaving mirror. "Look at yourself," she commanded.

Claude cautiously held the mirror up, as though it were a musket that might explode in his face. Billy Willis jibed, "Thet mirror is doomed! It'll break into a million pieces with a mug like that lookin' into it!"

But Claude had fixed his eyes on the mirror. He held silent and still for so long that the room grew quiet. Finally he lowered it and stared at Rooney. "Did you do all *that*?"

"I guess so, Claude. Do you like it?"

There was a long pause, and the tall lean soldier stared at Rooney with astonishment and admiration. *What in the world is he thinking?* Rooney wondered.

Then Claude lifted his hand, stared at the neat nails. He

47

moved his fingers as if to be sure that they actually *were* his own. Finally he crooked his index finger at Rooney in a gesture of command.

When Rooney leaned forward, Claude's voice dropped to a low pitch. "Air you married?"

"No, I'm not, Claude."

Claude Jenkins rose higher in the bed. He pushed his hair with one hand into a semblance of a wave. A faint color fluttered over his hollow cheeks, and stretching out a long bony finger, he gently touched Rooney's arm and with a constrained voice whispered mysteriously, "You wait!"

Rooney giggled, and hoots went up from the patients. As Rooney moved down the ward, changing bandages, she was pleased at the way she'd handled the matter. Later, when she met with Mrs. Pember to get instructions, she found that the matron had heard of the incident.

"I suppose you'll be leaving us, Rooney," Mrs. Pember said, catching the girl off guard.

"Why . . . why, no, ma'am! I don't have any thought of such a thing!"

Mrs. Pember's face was placid as a rule, but now she smiled, which made her look much younger. "You won't be marrying Claude, then?"

"Oh, Mrs. Pember," Rooney exclaimed, her face rosy, with a smile on her lips. "That's just some of his foolishness!"

"The whole ward was talking about it. I'm glad I'm not going to lose my best nurse." The matron noticed the flush of pleasure that came to the girl's cheeks at the compliment and wondered again about Rooney's circumstances. She was a woman of quick discernment and knew most of her staff well, but Rooney came and left, saying nothing of her life on the outside. A sudden thought came to her, and she asked cautiously, "You're not married, are you, Rooney?"

"Oh no, ma'am."

"I thought not, but girls are marrying very young these days. Too young, I'm sure." She studied the smooth cheeks of the young woman and asked, "None of the men have . . . bothered you, have they?"

"Oh no, Mrs. Pember," Rooney replied instantly. "They're all so sick, and most of them are real scared. A few of them try to flirt with me, but they don't mean anything by it." A soft compassion appeared in Rooney's large dark eyes, and she added thoughtfully, "I have to nurse my little brother when he gets sick. He's only thirteen, and these are grown men, but somehow some of them remind me of him—kind of like they are little boys."

"You've done fine work with them, Rooney. Not only with the bandaging and other work, but they all like you." A weariness came to Mrs. Pember's black eyes, and she said softly, "They need a woman's gentleness, and they see that quality in you."

"Well—it'd take a pretty mean person to treat them bad," Rooney said. "They got hurt fightin' for the South, so the least we can do is to take good care of them."

"Please, just don't marry Claude!"

Rooney giggled, then asked, "I'll bet some of them try to take up with you, don't they, Miz Pember?"

"Why, I wouldn't allow such a thing!"

The matron's reply was sharp, but the next day Rooney was going through the ward with her when Mrs. Pember got a taste of male admiration.

After showing Rooney how to apply a particularly difficult type of bandage, the matron straightened up to find a tall, rough-looking soldier staring at her directly. Rooney noticed the man, too, and wondered if he would speak to Mrs. Pember.

The soldier was evidently on a visit, for he looked healthy and strong. And he had a pair of bold gray eyes that he fixed on Mrs. Pember, giving her his full attention. Mrs. Pember gave him stare for stare, but if she hoped to embarrass the tall soldier, she was not successful.

Without taking his eyes from the matron or saying a word, he began to walk slowly around and around her in a narrow circle. His sharp eyes took in every detail of Mrs. Pember's dress, face, and figure, his eye never fixing upon any particular feature, but traveling incessantly.

Rooney wanted to laugh, so comical was the soldier's rapt attention, but she didn't dare. *Let's see how she handles this kind of thing,* she thought. She watched as Mrs. Pember moved her position, but the soldier shifted his to suit the new arrangement—again the matron moved, but the tall soldier, his eyes fixed upon her, moved constantly. Rooney would not have been surprised if he had asked her to open her mouth so he could examine her teeth, but he never said a word.

Finally the men lying on the cots began to laugh, and Mrs. Pember's cheeks began to glow. She'd never been bested in such a contest, but her stern glare had not fazed the soldier, who was now twisting his neck like an owl.

"What's the matter with you?" the matron demanded. "Haven't you ever seen a woman before?"

"Jerusalem!" the soldier whispered in a slow Texas drawl, keeping his eyes fixed on Mrs. Pember. "I never did see such a nice one. Why, you're as pretty as a pair of red shoes with green strings!"

The compliment almost destroyed Mrs. Pember's dignity, and she wheeled and almost fled from the ward.

Rooney stared at her dumbfounded, for she had admired the woman's strong spirit. She had seen Mrs. Pember stand up to officers who tried to humiliate her and send them away feeling the barbs of her speech. But the Texan had done what they had failed to do, and Rooney said to the soldier, "You sure did get a good look at Miz Pember."

"Wal, now," he breathed, still staring at the door where the matron had fled for refuge. "I been to six battles, three county fairs, and two snake stompings, but I ain't never seen nothin' like her!"

Rooney expected Mrs. Pember to comment on the Texan, but she never referred to it. It pleased Rooney to know that this woman she admired so much could be—well, just a *woman* after all!

★ ★ ★

Lowell awoke with a terrible headache and a tongue that felt like a piece of raw rope that had been soaked in tar. His lips were so dry that when he tried to lick them, they felt rough even to his swollen tongue.

Dimly he was aware that there were a large number of men in the long room, and as he lay there trying to sort it all out, he remembered the battle.

I've been shot!

Fear ran along his nerves, and he checked his limbs, noting with a weak relief that he had the usual number. Then he tried to sit up, and vivid slashing pain caught him across the back. It was as if a whip made of fire had been brought across his shoulders, bringing an involuntary cry of pain from his throat.

"Now, you don't be moving so much." Cool hands were on his forehead, and Lowell peered up to see the face of a young woman.

"Where . . . is this place?" he gasped.

"Chimborazo Hospital. Now let me help you sit up, and you can have a drink."

Her strong hands lifted Lowell to a sitting position, then a glass of water was placed at his lips. Grasping at the glass, he downed it thirstily, then begged, "More—please!"

"You can have all you want," the young woman said. As she held another full glass to his lips, she said, "Be thankful you don't have a belly wound. They can't have water, just a wet cloth on their lips."

The water, tepid as it was, seemed to Lowell the best thing he'd ever tasted. "Thanks, Miss," he whispered. "That was sure good!"

"You feel like lettin' me bandage your wound?" The girl, Lowell saw, was very young—and pretty, too!

"Are you a nurse?"

"No, just a helper, but the doctor wants your bandage changed. He said to clean the wound out, too."

"I guess you better do it," Lowell said, nodding. He was wearing a shirt that she pulled from him very gently. Her hands were cool and very steady as she removed the old bandage. "Is it bad?"

"No, not bad," she assured him. "Bullet plowed a sort of ditch across your shoulders. I'll bet it hurt when you got shot."

"Not so much at first," Lowell said, remembering. "Kind of knocked me out—but it got to hurting later. I think the doctor gave me some medicine to make me sleep."

"Laudanum, I'd reckon. Say if I hurt you."

Light as her hands were, the raw flesh was painful. Lowell endured it, however, and once when she had to bend over to bring the bandage under his arm, he was startled when her firm body pressed against his side. Quickly he looked at her, noting the curly hair and the clear eyes, as well as the smoothness of her cheeks. After seeing little but rough, bearded men for days, the girl looked like an angel.

"What's your name?" Lowell asked as she helped him put on a clean shirt. "I'm Lowell Rocklin."

"My name is Rooney Smith," she said. Looking down at him, she said, "Your pa, he was here earlier. Guess you didn't know it, though."

"Father was here?" Lowell remembered a little then of how his father had brought him and Mark back to Richmond in a wagon. And then he demanded, "My uncle Mark—is he here, too?"

"Well . . . yes."

Noting her hesitancy, he was afraid to ask, but he had to know. "How is he?"

"He's alive," Rooney said slowly. "The doctors, they operated on him again after they brought him here. I heard one of them tell your pa he didn't have much hope for your uncle."

Lowell sank back on the bed, his eyes cloudy. "He can't die!" he muttered.

Rooney looked down on him with pity. She'd seen so

many die, yet she had not become hardened to it. Each death was a fresh grief to her, and she knew that the young man on the cot was suffering.

"He's real dear to you, your uncle?"

"Yes, he is." Lowell looked up at her, somehow anxious to talk and to explain how he felt. "He's always been good to me, and he's had a bad life."

"He married? Got children?"

"No. He never married." Lowell lay there silently, then said, "I guess that's why he always seemed so . . . well, sort of *left out*, you know? A man's not whole all by himself."

Lowell's statement came as a surprise to the girl. Her lips grew tight as she thought, then she nodded. "That's nice, Pvt. Rocklin," she whispered. "I guess none of us are much without somebody to love."

She turned suddenly and disappeared before Lowell could thank her. He had no idea of the time and could only lie there until the sun rose. All around him he could hear the slight cries of pain as men moved on their beds, and he wondered if one of them was Mark. He made up his mind to talk to the doctor the first chance.

Father—he'll know about Mark, he thought. *I'll bet he'll be back tomorrow.* Then he thought of the young woman, wondering who she was. *She sure knows how to treat a fellow gentle.* The thought stayed with him, and he found himself looking forward to seeing her in the clear light of day.

She looks pretty in this dark, he thought sleepily, *but she's probably real homely in daylight.*

★ ★ ★

Clay came down between the two lines of beds, turning to speak to the patients. He'd gotten to know many of them during the five days he'd been coming to visit Lowell and Mark, and he paused long enough to stop beside a bed that bore a young soldier with both legs cut off above the knee. "Brought you that book I told you about, Thad," he said, smiling. "See how you like it."

"Thanks, Captain." There was no light in the young soldier's eyes, and he put the book down, then closed his eyes.

Clay hesitated, then said, "I'll see you later—before I leave." He felt helpless in cases like this—but always made the attempt. Shaking off the gloom that had come to him, he went to the section where Mark's bed was located and found Matron Pember there, speaking with one of the doctors.

"Oh, this is Capt. Rocklin," Mrs. Pember said. "This is Dr. Jarvis, Captain. He's just been looking at your uncle's wound."

Clay glanced down and saw that Mark was awake. His face was sunken, and his eyes, always so brilliant, were dull and had no luster. "How are you, Mark?" Clay asked quietly.

"All right." Mark's voice was a hoarse whisper, and he had a fever that was dragging his vitality from him day by day.

Dr. Jarvis motioned with his head, and Clay followed him down the hall, saying, "Be back soon, Mark."

Dr. Birney Jarvis was a small man with pale green eyes. He stood there silently, dry washing his hands, then shrugged, saying, "Your uncle is in poor condition. The operation was almost too much for him. None of us expected him to survive it, but we had to try."

"Did you get all the metal out, Doctor?"

"Can't say." There was a clipped brevity in the doctor's voice, and he seemed almost unconcerned about his patient. *Probably got too many of them,* Clay thought. *And he's seen a lot of them die.* Clay judged the man's mannerisms and attitude, and a strong feeling came over him. He disliked and distrusted this man. There was no evidence or proof, but Clay knew that Jarvis would be of no help to Mark, and Clay determined right there to have another physician look at him.

"Our family doctor told me he'd come and see my uncle. Would that be all right, Doctor?"

"If you feel we're not competent, I suppose you can do so."

Clay tried to mollify the man, for he'd be over Mark's case and in a position to do him damage. "It's not that, sir, but Dr. Maxwell has taken care of all us Rocklins for a long time. Even if he couldn't do anything medically, it might make my uncle feel better to see him."

"Do as you please," Jarvis said coolly. "He's not going to make it in any case."

"The Lord can raise him up."

Jarvis sneered at that. "Then you'd better have the Lord come and take over the case."

Clay held a tight rein on his temper, saying only, "Thank you, Doctor," then turned and walked back to Mark's bedside. He found Mrs. Pember still there and drew her aside. "What's wrong with Dr. Jarvis? He's not at all concerned about my uncle."

"I can't comment on that, Captain," Mrs. Pember answered. "All I can say is that we'll do our best for Mark Rocklin."

"I know you'll do that. I've been meaning to compliment you on your excellent treatment of the men. I'm very grateful to you. My son is doing very well."

"Why, yes, he is. He'll be released soon." She looked across at Mark and shook her head. "I'm afraid we'll have your uncle with us for some time."

Clay talked with Mrs. Pember, then sat down and spent two hours with Mark. The sick man could not talk much, but it seemed to comfort him to have Clay there. Finally he took his leave, promising to return the next day and to bring Susanna with him.

Leaving the ward, he moved to the next building, where he found Lowell sitting up in a chair and talking with the pretty young woman Clay had noticed before. When Lowell introduced her, he said, "If my son gives you any trouble, Miss Smith, you tell me. I've had to paddle him before."

"You sure did!" Lowell agreed. He turned to Rooney, who was staring at his father. "Don't cross him, Rooney. He's a bad man!"

Clay saw that Lowell was in excellent spirits, and before he left he said, "Miss Smith, thank you for taking such good care of my boy. He's very special to me."

Rooney almost said, "To me, too" but choked it back. "He's doin' real good, sir."

After Clay left, Rooney said, "Your pa is sure a handsome man!" A mischief came to her and she added, "Too bad you didn't take after him."

Lowell looked down at his hand. "You're right. My brothers, David and Dent, look just like him. I'm the runt of the family."

Rooney was shocked at his answer and put her hand on his. "Don't be foolish!" she said quietly. "God makes us like he wants us."

Lowell looked up quickly. "You believe that?"

"Yes, I do."

Lowell shook his head. "I'm glad, Rooney. I hope you always do."

Rooney changed the subject quickly. "When will you be going back to the army?"

"Not for quite a while—maybe a month. Once I get out of here I have a special assignment to work on for Gen. Longstreet." He shifted on the chair and muttered, "Never could stand to be still. Wish I hadn't caught that bullet." He saw her eyes go to Billy Reynolds, who had no legs, and flushed. "Shouldn't have said that," he muttered. "It's just that I get restless."

"What is it? A spy mission or something like that?"

"Well, I'm going to make a balloon." He saw her look of surprise and quickly related Gen. Longstreet's offer. He grew excited as he spoke—but when he finally finished, he lapsed into a gloom that drew his shoulders down. "Aw, I'm just dreaming. Since I've been lying here, I've realized that it can't be done."

"Why not? Don't you know how to make one of those things?"

"Oh, I could figure it all out," Lowell said quickly. "The

trouble is there's nothing to make the canopy—the big balloon itself—out of. The Federals have lots of silk, but there's none in the South that I know of. That's all I need, Rooney—just a few scraps of silk!"

Rooney stared at him in disbelief. "Why, that's not right, Lowell! There's *lots* of silk right here in Richmond."

Lowell stared at her as if she'd lost her mind. "What in the world—"

"Silk *dresses,* silly!" she said, laughing aloud. "There must be *hundreds* of silk dresses in this town."

"Silk dresses? Why—" Lowell's eyes grew round, and he whistled. "Why, that's right, isn't it, Rooney!"

"Sure it is. Could you use silk dresses to make your balloon, Lowell?"

"I don't see why not—but . . ."

"What is it?"

"How would I *get* the dresses?" Lowell stared at her blankly. "I can't go around asking women to give me their dresses! I'd get shot by a jealous husband."

Rooney smiled, and her eyes were brighter than Lowell had ever seen them. "I can get them for you."

Lowell's face grew very intent as excitement built up in him. "Would you do that, Rooney?" He reached out and took her hand, squeezing it hard and not even conscious of it. "Why, we could do it—you and me!"

Rooney was *very* conscious of his hand holding hers. She had spent so much of her life fending off men that it felt strange to receive a touch from this young soldier without feeling fear.

She smiled, her dark blue eyes shining as she said, "We'll do it together, Lowell! We'll make a balloon together!"

CHAPTER SIX
A Visit to Gracefield

✦

As Lowell turned the carriage into the long sweeping drive lined with massive oaks, Rooney's heart seemed to contract. Every day he was in the hospital, Lowell had *insisted* that she visit his family, and after making every excuse, Rooney finally conceded. So the day Lowell was released, he rented a carriage and then drove up in front of Chimborazo to pick up his new assistant.

Now as the horses drew up in front of the tall white house with massive white columns spanning the front and side, she wished heartily she'd never let him talk her into coming. She'd evaded all his inquiries concerning her home and family, inventing a story that involved an imaginary family in Natchez, Mississippi, and an aging and ailing aunt in Richmond that she'd come to nurse. Lowell had hinted broadly that he'd be pleased to visit her at home, but she told him "Aunt Lillian" was too ill for *any* excitement—even a visitor.

Now as Lowell leaped to the ground and handed the lines to a tall black man, she wanted to cry out, "Take me back to town!" However, it was too late for that. Lowell reached up, and she had no choice but to let him help her to the ground.

"Come on, Rooney," Lowell said happily. "I'm anxious for you to meet my family." He was wearing a fine gray suit, for his uniform was too tight for comfort on his wound. His hazel eyes were gleaming, and his brown hair fell across his forehead, making him look very handsome and youthful. Holding to her arm, he said, "You're going to love my grandmother—everybody does."

Rooney was too frightened to answer. If his hand had not firmly grasped her arm, she felt that she would have whirled and dashed out into the woods that flanked the house. As they reached the top of the steps, the massive front door opened, and a heavy, white-haired black man greeted them.

"Marse Lowell!" The affection in the slave's voice was evident, and he seemed to have trouble speaking. Swallowing hard, he cleared his throat, saying roughly, "Whut you mean gettin' yo'self shot and scarin' Miz Susanna half to death! Ort to be ashamed!"

Lowell laughed and stepped forward to give the man a hard hug. "Don't you start fussing at me, Zander! I'll get plenty of that from Grandmother." Turning to the girl, he said, "This is Miss Rooney Smith, a new friend of mine. And this is Zander, Rooney. He and his wife, Dorrie, are the real bosses here!"

"I'm glad to know you, Zander."

"You come in now, Miz Rooney," the butler said, smiling. "Miz Susanna, she out in the scuppernong arbor."

"Have Dorrie fix the blue bedroom for Miss Rooney, will you, Zander?"

Lowell passed into the house with the girl in tow. She had time only for an awed glance at a spacious foyer and a broad stairway that divided the lower part of the house. She caught a glimpse through a door of walls lined with books, and across the hallway, maids were cleaning the largest room she'd ever seen in a house. "That's our ballroom, Rooney," Lowell remarked. "Maybe we'll have a ball before I have to go. You like balls, don't you?"

The only dancing Rooney had ever seen was of the crude dance-hall variety, so she only murmured, "They're very nice." She followed him out a side door and saw a building made up of white lath and covered with green vines.

"There's my grandmother," Lowell said, and Rooney saw the woman who was moving among the flowers that surrounded the arbor.

"Lowell!"

Susanna Rocklin lifted her head to catch sight of the couple and put down a basket, coming to them at once with her arms outstretched. She embraced Lowell, kissed him firmly, then turned to examine the young woman. "And who is this you've brought to see us?"

"This is Rooney Smith," Lowell said. "She's going to help me build a balloon to fight the Yankees with."

Susanna smiled and put her hand out to Rooney, saying, "I'm so glad you've come, my dear. Clay's told me all about your kindness to Lowell and Mark."

As Rooney responded with her eyes lowered, Susanna studied her carefully. Her visits to Chimborazo had been in the afternoons, so she had never met the young woman, but she'd heard much about Rooney Smith! Not only Clay, but Mark had sung her praises. And Lowell! Well, he'd talked of her with such excitement that Susanna had been very curious. "Lowell interested in a young woman? That's something new!" she had remarked to Clay.

What she saw was a young girl of no more than seventeen, with dark blue eyes shaded by impossibly thick black lashes. Her skin was close to olive and her complexion was smooth and fresh. The girl's hair was in a style that Susanna had never seen—cropped very short, it was a cap of rich auburn curls that framed her oval face. She was not tall, no taller than Susanna herself, and her figure was slender with the curves of young womanhood. She was wearing a simple blue dress and a pair of black shoes, both rather well-worn.

Susanna was surprised at the girl's beauty and at her obvious poverty. But many in Richmond were wearing their shoes and clothing to the point of thinness, so she smiled now and said, "Come into the house." She took Rooney's arm and as they turned and walked toward the house said, "We'll have something to eat, and then you can tell me all about this outlandish contraption my grandson's gone so daft over."

★ ★ ★

Breakfast was served in the "small" dining room—which to Rooney was not small in any way. She had been informed by Lutie, one of the maids who had awakened her by simply entering the room, "Miz Rocklin, she say you come down for breakfus' when you gets dressed."

Rooney had brought no nightgown, but had found one in the top drawer of a polished chifforobe. It was made of pale yellow silk, finer than any garment she'd ever owned in her life. She had worn it only because Lowell's grandmother had said, "Use any of the clothing you find in the room, Rooney." She had washed off in hot water that Lutie had brought to the room, dried on a thick, fluffy white towel, and then— she'd experimented carefully with some of the powder she'd discovered in a china container on the washstand. It had smelled so heavenly that she'd dusted herself with it. Then she'd gone to bed, buried in the huge featherbed. She'd never slept on anything but a rough shuck mattress—and sometimes on worse!—and for a long time she'd lain there clean and sweet smelling and floating on air, or so it seemed.

When Lutie called the next morning, Rooney bounded out of bed feeling like a princess. Quickly she dressed and went downstairs. Mrs. Rocklin was waiting for her, saying, "We'll have a nice breakfast all to ourselves, Rooney. Lowell was up before dawn. He went to his Uncle Claude's to ask about borrowing some machinery of some sort. But he promised to be back by noon."

Rooney had taken a seat at the large oak table across from Susanna. Through high windows she could see the spacious grounds roll away toward the road and the woods.

Rooney said little, letting her hostess do the talking, and when the food came, she was amazed—scrambled eggs, fresh hot biscuits, thick-sliced bacon, grits, white gravy, and four different kinds of jelly.

"This one is made from the grapes in the scuppernong arbor," Susanna offered. "I like it the best."

Susanna Rocklin was sixty-one years old, but there was only a slight graying of her auburn hair. She had a patrician beauty that had only grown more fragile with age. Her eyes were an unusual blue-green that showed intelligence and kindness.

"Lowell kept you up too late, Rooney," Susanna said, a smile on her lips. "I gave up at eleven. Did he talk about balloons all night?"

"Oh no, ma'am." Rooney shook her head, sending her curls into a light dance about her head. "He told me all about how it was when he was growing up here. About all the Rocklins and the people who live here in the country."

"He loves his home, doesn't he?" Susanna said, sipping the strong black coffee in a delicate cup. "He always did."

"Are his brothers like him?"

"Oh no, child! Dent and David are twins, of course. They look like their father. Lowell looks . . . well, more like me, I suppose."

"He really does," Rooney murmured, struck by the sudden realization that the face of Susanna Rocklin had been mirrored in her youngest grandson's face. Except for the color of the eyes, they looked much alike. "What was he like when he was a little boy?"

That question prompted an answer that lasted until the sun was over the trees that lined the road. Susanna spoke of her family for a long time, then blinked and laughed in a half-embarrassed fashion. "Good heavens, Rooney. I've done what I always hated for grandparents to do."

"What's that, Miz Rocklin?"

"Bored you to death talking about my grandson!"

"I wasn't bored," Rooney said, offering a shy smile. "You have a wonderful family."

"What about your own family, Rooney?" Susanna inquired.

"Oh, there's just my ma and my brother, Buck, back in

Mississippi. . . ." Rooney stumbled through her story, little knowing that the sharp mind of Susanna Rocklin was learning more about her than she would have liked for the woman to know.

"You're very fond of your brother, aren't you, Rooney?" Susanna asked gently. "I can tell by the way you talk about him."

"I guess so." Rooney faltered and wanted to tell this beautiful and kind woman how much she was worried about Buck—about his future. But she didn't dare for fear that she might give herself away.

Fortunately for her, Lowell came through the door breezily, saying, "Well, you didn't wait for me to have breakfast! I thought a poor wounded soldier would get better treatment!" He was smiling and went to kiss his grandmother, then sat down. "Dorrie!" He lifted his voice in a loud cry, and when a heavyset black woman came through the door, said, "Dorrie, are you trying to starve me to death? Bring me some of those wonderful biscuits of yours!"

Dorrie laid her severe brown eyes on the young man. She was the wife of Zander and did more toward keeping the Big House running than Susanna Rocklin herself. "If you'd come to the table on time," she said with a sniff, hiding her affection for Lowell behind a stern look, "mebby you'd get breakfus'. I got more to do than wait on lazy menfolks!"

But Lowell charmed the woman, Rooney saw, and soon she brought in a heaping platter of food. He caught at her as she went by and pulled her close. "Do you remember the time I killed your prize rooster with my slingshot, Dorrie?"

"I remembers it. Do *you?*"

Lowell squeezed her, laughing down into her ebony face. "I guess I do! I've still got scars from the pounding you gave me with that peach-tree switch!"

The thick lips of Dorrie turned up into a grin, and her old eyes shone. *"Humph!"* she snorted. "If you don't behaves yo'self, Marse Lowell Rocklin, I jes might do it *again!"*

The three of them sat there for an hour, Lowell eating

heartily, talking excitedly with his mouth full. He was full of schemes for building the balloon and had become very excited after his visit at Hartsworth, the plantation of Claude and Marianne Bristol. Marianne was the only daughter of Noah Rocklin, the founder of the Virginia Rocklins.

"Box can do all the metal work here," Lowell said, "and Uncle Claude's got a wagon I can have to make the gas-making machinery."

"To make what?" Susanna demanded.

"Oh, Grandmother, I've explained all that," Lowell exclaimed. "We have to make gas to fill the balloons."

Susanna had no head for science and shook her head. "I don't understand any of it."

Lowell reached over and squeezed her hand. "You don't have to. All you have to do is give notes to all your friends."

"Notes? What sort of notes."

"Notes asking them to give Rooney their old silk dresses—and underwear."

Susanna stared at him in astonishment. "What did you say?"

Lowell was enjoying himself. He had a playful streak in him that David and Dent lacked, and he loved to tease his grandmother. "I said we've got to have silk dresses to make the balloon. I can't go barging in asking women to give me their dresses, can I?"

"But *underwear*? Really, Lowell!"

"Well, women do wear silk underwear."

"And how do *you* know so much about women's underwear?" Susanna demanded, her fine eyes flashing like fire.

Lowell leaned back and tried to put an innocent look on his face. "Oh, I hear some of the fellows talking. That's what they say, that woman have lots of silk underwear. It's true, isn't it?"

"Rooney, I'm embarrassed for my grandson," Susanna said, her lips pressed tightly together. "He's got no manners at all!"

Rooney had heard much worse talk than Lowell's all her

life, but could not say so. She sat there watching Lowell, amazed at how he could tease his grandmother. *It's nice,* she thought. *How close they are—how much they love one another!*

"I will *not* write such a note, Lowell Rocklin!"

"Aw, now, you *have* to do it!" Lowell grew alarmed, his face falling. "I mean—how else can I get the silk? There's none in the whole Confederacy. And Gen. Longstreet really needs this balloon!"

It took a great deal of persuasion, but Lowell was set on the matter. Susanna felt the business would be undignified. But finally she said, "I'll not write a letter, Lowell, but I'll go with Rooney and introduce her to some friends in Richmond. Rooney can do the collecting and see the things get to you."

"I knew you'd do it!" Lowell stood up, stepped over, and hugged Susanna.

She took the embrace, then stated, "But no underwear! I'm firm on that. I won't have those Yankees staring at the underclothing of Virginia's ladies!"

Lowell winked at Rooney, saying, "See how she is? Can't do a thing with her!"

Susanna laughed and turned her smile on Rooney. "He's spoiled rotten, Rooney! I hope you don't let him get around you the way I do. Make him behave!"

Rooney looked at the two, both so fine looking—and so filled with love. She said, "I don't think I'll be able to do much with him, Miz Rocklin. You've taught him how to get what he wants."

"Right!" Lowell nodded. "After all," he added, "I don't want much—just my own way!"

The two women laughed at his absurd statement, and even Lowell had the grace to blush. "Well, I guess that sounds a little conceited." Then he looked at Rooney, and his eyes were filled with pride as he said, "But with a partner like Rooney, this thing's got to go! Gen. Longstreet, here we come!"

CHAPTER SEVEN
Lowell Fails the Test

Mark Rocklin's world had contracted to a single cot in a ward full of wounded and dying men. Pain was to him what water was to a fish—an element that surrounded him. He slept and awoke, but both states were vague and uncertain so that at times he was confused as to whether what he saw was reality or dream.

Time passed, but it had no meaning for him. Vaguely he was aware that men came and either got well or died. One night he came out of sleep to see two orderlies bundling a stiff body into a blanket. One of them said, "Graveyard's getting crowded. May have to start a new one."

The words of the orderly had taken root in Mark's confused mind. He dreamed of a huge graveyard with thousands of tombstones lined up rank on rank as far as the eye could see. They seemed to stretch out into the blue ether of the skies. But then a sinister figure draped in a robe that covered a specterlike countenance came to him saying, "No room! No room for Mark Rocklin!"

Suddenly the scene faded, and he realized that someone was speaking to him, calling his name. He opened his eyes and saw that it was the young girl that often tended to him. *What is her name? Clay had said she was taking care of Lowell. . . . Rooney! That's it!*

"Mr. Rocklin!" Rooney whispered. Her eyes were wide, and she had placed her hands on his chest. "Are you all right?"

Mark Rocklin blinked his eyes, and the last of the nightmare faded from his troubled mind. "Sure," he muttered through dry lips. "I'm OK, Rooney."

Rooney's gaze reflected her anxiety. "You were having a bad dream. I hate those things!" She studied him, then asked, "Can you eat something?"

"Not hungry."

"You've got to eat."

Mark lay quietly as she turned and disappeared. He was exhausted, and the pain in his side was ruinous. Sometimes it went away, but then it would tear through him unexpectedly, taking his breath and shutting off everything else. At other times it was a dull, throbbing ache, bearable but robbing him of ease. *Like having a toothache in my stomach!*

He'd been an active, healthy man all his life, and the days he'd endured since getting shot down had been terrible for him. *Better to be dead,* he thought bitterly, staring up at the ceiling. *I wish that minié ball had taken me right in the head!*

And then Rooney was back, drawing up a chair and holding a spoonful of hot soup to his lips. Obediently he swallowed it, though he was not hungry. He managed to get down half of it before saying, "I can't eat any more."

"You did fine, Mr. Rocklin." She put the dish down and sat beside him, looking down in his face. "The doctor said you were doing a little better."

"He always says that."

"No, he doesn't." Rooney shook her head. "He tells the truth every time. If he says you're better, he believes it's so."

Not wanting to argue, Mark asked, "How's Lowell?"

"Oh, he went home a week ago. Don't you remember?"

"No. Guess I'm losing my mind."

"Don't say that, Mr. Rocklin!" Rooney was distressed and began to encourage Mark. He seemed better, more alert, and she found herself telling about her visit to Gracefield.

When she paused, Mark looked at her with a peculiar expression. "You went to my home, to Gracefield? How did that happen?" He saw her cheeks glow and listened as she explained about how she was helping Lowell with the construction of a balloon. He was truthfully more interested in Rooney's going to Gracefield—especially with Lowell—than in their project, but he listened as she spoke of the endeavor.

"And we're doin' real good, Mr. Rocklin," Rooney said, her eyes glowing with pleasure. "Mrs. Rocklin, she took me to meet some of her friends, and they got real interested. I go by and collect the dresses every couple of days. And when we get enough, Lowell will pick them up. And I'm going to help sew the balloon together."

"How's the collection going?" Mark asked. "Getting plenty of dresses?"

"Well—we did at first, but things have sorta gotten slow." Rooney bit her lip, then added, "I guess some ladies don't want their dresses up where everybody can see 'em. Then, too, there just aren't as many dresses as before the war. Lots of old dresses have been used for other things—bandages and like that."

"And since no new silk dresses will be coming in," Mark murmured, "lots of ladies want to hold on to those they have."

"I guess so."

The two talked for a long time, and Rooney noted that her patient looked better. She guessed that he was bored like many of the badly hurt soldiers. Finally she said, "I have to go to work now."

"Work? What sort of work do you do? Or did I ask you that?"

"No, you didn't. I'm a cook, and I've got to go get supper on." She hesitated, then murmured, "You sure do have a fine family, Mr. Rocklin." Then she turned and left.

That afternoon Susanna Rocklin came to visit Mark. The two talked quietly, and finally Mark asked about the girl. He listened carefully as Susanna related the visit of Rooney and how she'd gotten involved in the balloon project. Finally he asked, "That Rooney—is Lowell interested in her?"

"Oh, I don't know, Mark. Lowell's caught up in this balloon thing. He likes Rooney, but he's never thought of her as a sweetheart."

"She's not of our class, is she?"

"No, but she's very quick, Mark." Susanna shook her head almost sadly. "She's falling in love with Lowell, I can see that much. I'm afraid it will end badly for her."

"There are more important things than class, Susanna."

Startled at his remark, Susanna looked at him carefully and thought, *I know so little about this brother-in-law of mine! He's the strange one. Something has hurt him dreadfully—and he'll never speak of it.*

Then she said aloud, "I think you're right, Mark. With a little education and love, she could be a real lady."

"Well, give it to her, Susanna!" Mark mustered up a smile. "You could never marry me off, but maybe you'll have better luck with Lowell."

"You should have married, Mark," Susanna said simply, love for him filling her eyes. "You have so much to give a woman and children."

Mark stared at her, then shook his head. "Too late now," he said roughly. Then he made himself smile. "We'll both work on Lowell. He can give you a room full of great-grand-children!"

"I'd like that!" She nodded, and they sat there talking until he grew weary and she left the hospital.

★ ★ ★

"You and Uncle Mark have gotten real close, haven't you Rooney?"

"Why, I guess so, Lowell. I hurt for him so bad sometimes, but he never complains."

Rooney and Lowell were in a small barn that was used for grain storage. Rooney was sitting in the midst of a pile of colorful dresses she was separating. Against the dull grays of the sacks of feed, the yellows, greens, and scarlets of the dresses lent a holiday atmosphere. There had been not so much as a square inch of space to be had in war-crowded Richmond, so Susanna had insisted that they do their work at Gracefield. "You can work on that old wagon with Box, and Rooney and I can do the dresses."

It had worked out very well. Box, the elderly blacksmith at Gracefield, had taken over the construction of the wagon and machinery that made the gas, and it amused both Susanna and Rooney to watch the tall, dignified slave boss Lowell around in a lordly fashion. Lowell didn't care, for he admired Box. "That man's got more sense than Jefferson Davis's whole cabinet!" he had often said of Box.

Rooney had managed to keep her identity and her poor background a secret, but she lived in fear that she would be found out. Buck had been puzzled by her long absences, and she had not enlightened him. Studs Mulvaney had interrogated her, but she had told him only that she was helping with the wounded men at Chimborazo. This satisfied the big man, for he knew the hotel wasn't a place for a girl such as her. But he had given her a warning: "Better take a stick to Buck. He's running with some pretty tough boys."

Now as Rooney sat surrounded by the colorful silk dresses, she thought of her brother. *I've got to stay home more, spend more time with him.* She spoke her thoughts to Lowell, saying, "I've got to stay close to home for a while."

"Your aunt's not doing so well?" he asked at once.

"N-no," Rooney stammered. She had always hated lies and deceit, and it hurt to be dishonest with Lowell. She had come to know the Rocklins enough to know that they were people who put a great premium on truth and honor. But she could not think of another way. *It'll only be for a little while,* she thought. *Then he'll get his balloon made, and he'll never see me again.*

This thought hurt her, and she turned to the dresses,

saying, "I'll have to take all the stitches out of all of these. It's going to be slow, but I'll do the best I can."

"We'll have to get you some help." A thought came to Lowell, and he said, "I know. We'll get Rena. She's due home this afternoon. Been on a visit with Melora Yancy." Suddenly he snapped his fingers. "What's wrong with me? We'll ask Melora and her sister Rose to come and help." Reaching down he pulled Rooney to her feet, saying, "We need a little vacation anyhow."

Rooney protested but was glad to get outside. Lowell took the big carriage, and Susanna was excited by the idea. As they drove out, Lowell said, "Grandmother needs more company. She thinks a lot of Melora and Rose."

"Who are they? Do they own a plantation?"

"Oh no, just a small farm. Father and Buford Yancy are raising hogs together." He hesitated, wondering how much to tell this girl about his father and Melora. It would not do to tell her about the tangled skeins of his family history. He had known of his father's love for Melora Yancy for a long time, but he knew as well that his father had been completely faithful to his mother. The thought of his mother, Ellen, was painful, for she had been a weak woman. Finally he said, "My mother died nine months ago. And now my father and Melora are engaged."

Rooney asked, "Are the Yancys planters?"

"The Yancys are poor, but proud as any princes. Most of the older boys are in the army. Only four left at home now. Melora, she raised the whole bunch after her mother died."

Just before noon they arrived at the Yancy place. Melora came out, and Rooney saw at once that she was much younger than Clay Rocklin. She had never seen a prettier woman, however, and as soon as she got down and was introduced, Melora smiled at her, saying, "I'm glad you've taken this young man in hand, Rooney. His father's about to give up on him." Then she laughed and gave Lowell a resounding kiss. "I guess if I'm going to be your step-mother, I've got a right to do that!" Then she turned to say,

"Don't you do that, Rose, he's a ladies' man." Rose Yancy was a seventeen-year-old image of her older sister. She smiled shyly at Lowell, who laughed at her and gave her a hug despite her protests. Another girl of thirteen named Martha came to greet them, and a boy of eleven.

"Where's Buford?" Lowell asked Melora.

"Down with the hogs." A dimple appeared in the dark-haired woman's face, and she added with a light in her fine eyes, "I think Pa's prouder of any of those hogs than he is of us." She motioned toward the rear of the cabin, saying, "Rena and Josh are with him. Why don't you go take a look at the critters, Lowell? I'll entertain Rooney."

Lowell set off for the hog pen accompanied by the children, and when he was out of hearing, Melora asked, "How is he, Rooney? His wound?"

"Oh, not bad at all, Miss Yancy. It hurts some, but soon he'll be good as new."

"That's good news—and call me Melora." She smiled and shook her head. "That young man has got you in on some wild scheme, Clay tells me. Come on in and have some fresh milk while you tell me about it."

Never had Rooney felt so at ease with a person as she did with Melora Yancy. There was something in the dark-haired woman's manner that made her feel comfortable. At Melora's urging, she related her experience in the hospital, including her care of Lowell and Mark.

Melora had the gift of silence and sat across the table listening carefully, her full attention on the girl. Clay had told her about Rooney, and others had mentioned her, too, so she was pleased to find that they had not exaggerated the girl's simple manners and fair beauty.

Finally Rooney ended her tale. "And so we've got to make this balloon for Gen. Longstreet, and Lowell's come to ask if you and Rose can come and help with it." She hesitated, then added, "I don't think that's really the reason he wants you to come, though."

"No?"

"I think he sees how lonesome his grandmother is since her husband died. She needs some friends around to get her mind off her grief. And since you will be family . . ."

Melora smiled. "Did Lowell tell you how his father and I met?"

"No, he didn't," Rooney answered. Her eyes grew big. "Was it romantic?"

"Oh my, no!" Melora paused. "Well, not in the normal sense of the word. We met twenty-three years ago when I was just a little girl. He was real sick, and my family and I nursed him back to health."

Melora continued for twenty minutes, filling in the details of their lives from that first encounter to Clay's troubled marriage, his life as a wanderer, and his prodigal return to Gracefield. "He joined the army to prove to Lowell that he wasn't unfaithful to Ellen," Melora said. Then she looked full in Rooney's face. "I've been in love with Clay Rocklin since I was six years old, and I always will be. He's the best man I know, Rooney. He and I have nothing to be ashamed of. We're both Christians and have kept our friendship through a lot of trouble. You'll hear gossip, of course, but I can come to Clay as his wife knowing that both of us were faithful to God."

Rooney was entranced. She'd never heard anything like what Melora had just told her. "I hope you'll both be happy," she said quietly. "Will you—" She broke off as voices came from outside and only had time to say, "Thank you for telling me."

She had a fine time, and as she and Lowell left in the late afternoon, they had Melora's promise to be at Gracefield in two days. She smiled at Rena, who was standing beside Josh. "That is, if we can get Rena out of the pigpen. Josh has made a farmer out of her." She added quietly, "Josh is smart—but he stutters so that he hardly says a word. Rena's been good for him."

Rena Rocklin had come as a surprise to Rooney. She was like Clay, but still unique. They had spoken once when they'd gone to the well for water. Rena had asked about Mark, then had said, "Have you seen my father?"

There was a note in the girl's voice that caught Rooney's attention. *She's very close to him, she thought. Guess she's even a little afraid now that she doesn't have a mother.* "I haven't seen him for a week, but Lowell said he'll come when you get there." She saw the relief wash over Rena's face and knew her guess had been right.

Lowell put Rooney in the carriage, and they pulled out, waving good-byes and nodding at the Yancys' promises to be at Gracefield soon.

"That was so nice, Lowell."

"The Yancys are the best there is," Lowell answered. He kept her entertained for most of the journey by telling her tales of hunts and good times the Rocklins and the Yancys had enjoyed.

When they were five miles from home, darkness caught up with them. Lowell stopped at a creek to let the team drink and then turned to her. "Are you tired, Rooney?"

"Oh no. I never get tired."

They sat there, and the silence fell over them like a soft blanket. Far off a dog barked, and in the thicket next to the creek something moved through the thick brush. Overhead the darkening sky was spangled with what seemed to be millions of cold, twinkling lights. Lowell looked up at them in silence, then said quietly, "God outdid himself making all those, didn't he?"

"I've never seen so many!"

They sat there, listening to the faint sounds that floated to them. They spoke rarely and finally Lowell said, "I'm glad you're not one of those talking women, Rooney—one of those who can't bear a minute's silence."

She turned to him, and her large eyes caught the reflection of the moon. "I like it quiet," she said and smiled at him.

He put his arm around her and gave her shoulders a squeeze, much as he might have done with a young male friend. "You've helped me a lot, Rooney. I've been meaning to tell you how much I appreciate it."

"Why, I haven't done anything, Lowell." She was acutely conscious of the pressure of his arm on her shoulder, but felt strangely safe with this young man.

"Yes, you have," he contradicted her. "You took care of me in the hospital, and of Uncle Mark. And you came up with the idea of dresses for the silk. And you've been good to my grandmother." He nodded and squeezed her arm, adding, "That's a lot, Rooney!"

"I like doing things that please you, Lowell."

Her face, glowing in the silvery moonlight, filled his sight—and he became aware that the shoulder on which his hand rested was firm and rounded and warm—not at all like a hunting companion. Her face was only inches away from his, and he thought of Rooney Smith as an attractive and desirable young woman, not as a helper in a scheme!

Her hair was fragrant with soap, and her body lay firmly in the simple dress she wore. A vitality came from her, and her smile had a warmth that had some sort of promise. It was not the easy manner of some young women, for there was a virginal freshness about this girl that was very attractive in his sight. He'd not been much for girls, partly because most of them he'd courted had been too casual and even easy.

But not Rooney. She faced him with open eyes, and he put his free hand on her arm, pulling her around to face him. She watched him with surprise dawning in her eyes, but there was no fear. He drew her in and kissed her, his mouth resting lightly on her soft lips. He felt her innocence, yet there was a response in her lips that told him that she was a woman who had love to give.

When he drew back, he watched the expression pass over her face; he saw the generosity of her mouth, the glow of her eyes, and since he was a young man keenly aware of beauty, he found it hard to speak.

"You're a sweet girl, Rooney," he whispered finally. He

released her at once as she drew back, and he asked, "You're not afraid of me are you?"

"No—never of you." Rooney's voice was gentle and warm in the night air, and though she said no more, Lowell knew that she had been stirred by the kiss—as he had.

Speaking to the team, he drove down the silver ribbon of road, and when he let her out at the front door, she smiled at him, saying, "Good night, Lowell. Thank you for taking me."

He nodded, said good night, then put up the team. It was late and his grandmother was in bed. His wound hurt, but that was not what kept him awake. He thought for a long time about that moment at the creek—and knew that he would never forget it.

★ ★ ★

President Jefferson Davis had proclaimed March 27, 1863, to be a national day of fasting and prayer. When that day came, all over the South men and women met in groups or sought a place of solitude to seek God. Never had the people faced such a crisis, and they responded by calling on God with fervor.

Lowell had found the streets of Richmond relatively bare and was told that most people were home praying. He went at once to Chimborazo where Matron Pember welcomed him into her small office. When he asked about Rooney, she said, "Why, I can't say, Mr. Rocklin. She hasn't been in for three days now." A slight frown crossed her brow, and she added, "It's not like her. She's always been so faithful."

"Do you know where she lives?"

"Why, I don't really. She's never spoken of her home life. I thought *you* might know."

Lowell shook his head. "All I know is that she lives with an invalid aunt. And I don't even know her last name—Aunt Lillian is all I've heard Rooney call her."

Mrs. Pember was sympathetic and even worried. "Your uncle misses her greatly, as do all the men in the ward."

"Maybe she told him her aunt's name," Lowell said hopefully. He bid Mrs. Pember good-bye, urging her to get in touch with him if Rooney came back to the hospital. He went at once to see Mark and found him sitting up in a rocking chair. "Well, you're looking spry as a spring chicken," he said at once.

"I'm better, I guess. But still not able to get out of here."

"Do you know where Rooney lives?" Lowell burst out. "I haven't seen her for nearly a week."

"Why, no, Lowell, I have no idea." Mark's face was drawn with pain, and when he moved, it was slowly and with care. "Do you think something's happened to her?"

"Oh, I've got no reason to think that, but it's got me worried." His uncle, he saw, was concerned, too, and he put the best face he could on the problem. "Maybe Aunt Lillian needs some extra care at home, and Rooney can't get away. . . ." Lowell visited for an hour, then left the hospital.

All the next day he roamed the streets, visiting old friends and always asking if they knew a sickly woman named Lillian. He had no success and on the second day gave up. He was preparing to go back to Gracefield and carry on with the work, but before he left he ran across an old friend, Dan Whitter. Whitter was a reporter for the Richmond *Examiner* and insisted that the two of them have dinner.

"Got to go by the court first, Lowell," Whitter explained. "Got a big case comin' up, my first time to cover one. Won't take long though, then we'll go eat."

Lowell agreed, and the two of them made their way through the streets of Richmond. It was a crowded, bustling place filled with soldiers on leave, businessmen, and workers from the factories. Whitter led Lowell to the courthouse, which was not as crowded as the bars and saloons.

"Wait here, Lowell." Whitter nodded at one of the many empty seats in the courtroom where a small scattering of visitors watched the processes of the court. "Won't be but a few minutes."

"Sure, Dan. Take your time."

Lowell settled down in one of the worn benches, pulled a copy of the *Examiner* from his pocket, and began to read. It was filled with stories of the war and little else. Jefferson Davis, he saw, was under attack—which was not unusual; the president of the Confederacy was a man who made firm friends and hard enemies. Vicksburg continued to resist Union naval attacks. Lowell thought, *As long as Vicksburg stands, we still can get supplies. If it falls, the Federals will have control of all of the Mississippi River—and cut our Confederacy in half.*

A woman's angry voice interrupted the stillness of the courtroom, and Lowell looked up to see a hard-faced woman with dyed hair being brought in forcibly by one of the officials. The judge said angrily, "You just behave yourself, woman! You're in trouble enough."

The woman screamed an obscenity at the judge, who shouted, "I hold you in contempt of court and sentence you to pay a fine of ten dollars! Now, set her down and gag her if she don't shut up!"

The bailiff took the judge's words literally, forcing the woman to sit down and stating loudly enough for everyone to hear, "If you don't shut, I'll shut you!"

Lowell shook his head, for the sordid scene displeased him. He had lifted his paper and was about to begin reading when another bailiff entered with two prisoners, a young woman and a small boy.

The world suddenly seemed to stop—for the young girl was Rooney Smith! Lowell had been stunned no more by cannon fire at Malvern Hill than he was by the sight of Rooney! He dropped the newspaper, and his face grew pale as the judge began to read out the charge of attempted homicide. Clara Smith had been involved in a knifing at the Royal.

After reading the charges, the judge asked, "Do you have a lawyer, Clara Smith?"

"No, I ain't."

"Well, the court will have to appoint one." He looked at

the young people. "Who are these children?" he asked. The bailiff coughed and said, "Children of the accused, Your Honor."

"Well, the case is put off until a lawyer can be found. Put it down for two weeks from today. The woman will remain in custody."

Clara Smith began shouting but was taken out at once by the heavyset bailiff. Rooney turned to follow her, but the bailiff said, "You can visit her in jail, miss."

Rooney turned and spoke to Buck, and the two of them walked slowly down the aisle toward the door. When they were halfway there, Rooney saw Lowell—and stopped dead still. Her lips began to tremble, and her eyes were tragic.

Lowell stared at her but could not bring himself to say a word. He was shocked so deeply that all he could do was stare at the two. He saw her waiting, and for one instant he was on the verge of going to her. She looked so tiny and so vulnerable! Then he thought of what it would seem like to the citizens of the court, and word would get back to his family. Of course his unit would hear of it—there was no secrecy in this sort of thing.

Rooney saw the struggle going on in Lowell, saw his face draw with shame and anger. Her heart beat faster as he seemed almost ready to come to her.

But he dropped his head—and Rooney knew it was over. "Come on, Buck," she whispered, and led him away. She held her head high, and her eyes were dry—but sorrow and shame were cutting her inside like a razor!

★ ★ ★

"And you didn't go to her? You let her walk out of that courtroom without speaking?"

Lowell blinked his eyes in shock as Mark Rocklin's words slashed at him. He went to Chimborazo the morning after the trial, and when he reported the event to his uncle, fire burned in Mark Rocklin's eyes. Scorn dripped from his pale lips as he gave Lowell Rocklin a tongue-lashing such as that young man had never received!

"You're so *holy* aren't you!" Mark stabbed with his voice as he might have lunged with his fists if he'd been able. "You've never done anything wrong, not the great and pure Lowell Rocklin!" On and on he spoke until Lowell was pale and his hands trembled.

When his uncle stopped speaking, Lowell cleared his throat and blurted, "Well, I just couldn't *think*, Uncle Mark!" He hadn't slept a wink, and all night long he'd wrestled with anger at Rooney—and guilt for doing just what Mark accused him of. Now he took out his handkerchief and wiped his brow. "I mean, why didn't she *tell* me what kind of—"

"And you've shown *exactly* what you would've done if she had, haven't you, Lowell." Mark had been a rough man, and now his eyes were deadly. He loved the young man who stood trembling before him, but he was angry to the bone. The pain struck his stomach and he paused, holding his breath as it tore through him.

Lowell saw the face of the older man stiffen and asked, "Is it bad?" knowing that it was. When Mark didn't speak, he sat down on a chair and twisted his hands, his brow knitted. "I—I was wrong, Uncle Mark."

Mark saw the trouble on the boy's unlined face. *He's still young. He thinks everyone is just what they seem to be.* The pain subsided, and Mark took a slow breath. "You made a mistake, my boy. But we all do that." Bitterness twisted his lips and he said, "I've done much worse. But the difference is that I can't do anything about mine—you *can!*"

Lowell looked up hopefully and, seeing the compassion in Mark Rocklin's dark eyes, said, "I will, Uncle Mark! I'll find her and help her all I can!"

"Do it quick, boy! That girl needs help!"

Lowell stood up and left almost at a run, leaving Mark exhausted and wrestling with the pain. *Don't run from your woes, my boy!* he thought. *I found out a long time ago, that's*

81

a sure way to ruin your life—and the lives of everybody around you!

★ ★ ★

"I need to see Miss Rooney Smith."

Studs Mulvaney looked down at the young man who'd come into the saloon and asked for the manager, took his cigar from his thick lips, and demanded, "What for?" It was only ten in the morning, and the saloon was empty—only Bugs was up and moving slowly around.

"Why . . . I-I'm a friend of hers," Lowell stammered. "She's in trouble, and I want to help her and her brother."

Mulvaney considered the fine clothing and the clean-cut face of the young man. He knew that Clara would be in jail for some time, and he had worried about Rooney and Buck. *This young fellow,* he thought, *could give some help.*

"Come on," he said abruptly.

Feeling as self-conscious as he had ever felt, Lowell followed the big man up the stairs. They passed several women who stared at him hard eyed, but he ignored them as best he could.

Mulvaney opened a door leading into what appeared to be a closet, called out, "Rooney, come down here." He turned to glare at Lowell, his cigar making a circle as he shifted it. "Be careful with these kids, sonny," he said quietly. "I wouldn't like them to get in no trouble. They got enough of that as it is."

Then Rooney appeared, and her face grew still as she saw Lowell. Studs glanced at her, saying, "This a friend of yours, Rooney?"

"I . . . know him."

As soon as Mulvaney moved away, Lowell said hastily, "Rooney, you can't stay in this place!"

"Buck and me don't have anyplace else to go."

Lowell had made no plans for helping the pair. He had come out of shame heaped on him by his uncle. Now that he stood there, he found himself with a blank mind. "I . . .

didn't mean to ignore you—at the court, I mean." When she didn't answer, he hastened to add, "I had no idea you were in trouble."

"There's no way you could have known." Rooney was confused, but said the one thing she wanted to say to the young man. "I lied to you . . . about my family. I'm sorry for that."

Lowell blinked and said instantly, "Oh, don't worry about that!"

"I never wanted to lie to you, but . . ."

She looked very young and helpless, but Lowell couldn't forget that she *had* lied to him. *I'll help her—but it won't be the same* was the thought that came to him.

"Look, you can't stay here. This is no place for you—nor for your brother." Desperately he tried to think of something. "I know! You can stay at Gracefield."

"No, I can't go there!"

The vehemence of her reply startled Lowell. "Why not?"

"I—I couldn't face your family!"

Lowell said, "Rooney, it was Uncle Mark who told me to come and find you. My grandmother loves you, and so will the others."

Rooney was in a terrible position. She hated the thought of staying in the hotel, though Mulvaney had assured her she could. It was Buck she feared for the most, not herself.

If I could just get Buck out of here and on a farm, just for a little while!

"You and I could finish the balloon," Lowell said quickly. "It might not be forever, but for now you and the boy ought to get out of here."

"I'll have to do it," Rooney whispered. "When do you want us to come?"

"Why, right now!" Lowell answered. He wanted to get the two out of the Royal as quickly as possible. "We can be at Gracefield a little after noon."

Rooney looked startled but knew that it might be best. "I'll get Buck," she said.

When she turned to the ladder, Lowell said quickly, "I guess we'd better understand one thing, Rooney." She turned to look at him, and he knew he had to say the thing clearly. "About us—you and me—we'll just be working together. You know what I mean?"

Rooney looked at Lowell. "Yes," she said quietly, "I know what you mean, Mr. Rocklin."

She left him then, and somehow there was a rebuke in her words. *Mr. Rocklin.* Why was her use of that name so hard? She was back soon with the boy. "This is my brother, Buck. This is Mr. Rocklin, Buck."

Lowell nodded to the boy, forced a smile, and said, "You'll be staying with us for a time, Buck. I hope you'll like it there."

"Yes, sir." Buck said nothing more, but just watched Lowell very carefully.

Lowell led them to the buggy he'd brought to town, and they rode out of town at a fast trot. None of them spoke, and the silence grew heavy and uncomfortable.

Lowell glanced at Rooney and saw that her cheeks were pale as she stared straight ahead. *I've hurt her, but she's hurt me, too!*

But the thought didn't give him any comfort, and as the team carried the buggy out of Richmond, Lowell was filled with uncertainty.

Got to get that balloon built and get back to the real war, he thought as he sat awkwardly on the seat trying not to touch the girl who sat beside him.

PART TWO
Lowell

CHAPTER EIGHT
Dresses for the Cause

★

Rooney would never forget the day she and Buck arrived at Gracefield. The trip from Richmond had been strained and silent, with Lowell speaking only briefly. Buck, Rooney knew, was gripped with apprehension, and as she sat beside him, she took his hand and squeezed it. He gave her a worried smile, but said nothing all the way to the Rocklin plantation.

When they pulled up in front of the house, Rooney felt the boy stiffen. "It's all right, Buck," she whispered as Lowell got out and handed the lines to Highboy. "These are real nice people—you'll see!"

Lowell hesitated, wondering how to break the news of these two guests to his grandmother. *I hope she's not going to be too mad,* he thought. *I have to see her alone.*

"Rooney, you might like to show Buck around the place while I go find Grandmother."

"All right." Turning to Buck, she said, "Come on. I'll show you the horses." As they walked away, Buck looked fearfully over his shoulder as the man disappeared into the house.

"Rooney, they won't let us stay here!"

Now that they were actually on the grounds, Rooney privately thought the same. She let none of her doubt show, however, but made herself say cheerfully, "Don't worry. You'll like Miz Rocklin, Mr. Lowell's grandmother. Come on, now, let's look at the horses. I'll bet Mr. Lowell will let you ride one of them."

Buck shook his head doubtfully, saying, "I don't think they'll let us stay. We'd better go back to the Royal." His thin face grew tense, and he asked, "What if Ma comes back and we're not there?"

She won't come back—she'll be in jail, Rooney thought. Rooney had spoken with Studs who knew about such things, and he'd told her that Clara would be sentenced for a short term. "Not too long," he'd added, seeing the stricken look on her face. "Jail's too small, and she didn't actually kill the fellow. You can stay here, Rooney. Don't worry about that."

Rooney set out to convince Buck that they would keep in touch with their mother, but the burden was heavy on his thin young shoulders. "Mr. Mulvaney promised to send word when Ma gets back," she said, then added brightly as they came to the pasture, "See that big black horse? That's King. Isn't he something. . . ."

Inside the house Lowell had found his grandmother sewing in the library. Without preamble he said, "Grandmother, I've got something to tell you."

Susanna looked up quickly and, seeing the worry on her grandson's face, put her sewing down and said quietly, "Sit down, Lowell, and tell me about it."

Lowell was too tense to sit down, but walked up and down as he related the history. From time to time he cast a worried eye at the woman, but saw nothing but serenity there. Finally he got to the end. Drawing his handkerchief out, he wiped his brow, saying nervously, "I—I didn't know what to do, Grandmother. I hated to leave them in that terrible place, so . . ."

When Lowell broke off, struggling for words, Susanna said calmly, "Well, Lowell, I hope you had sense enough to bring them here. I would love to have them."

A look of relief swept across Lowell's face. "I did, Grandmother. But I was sort of afraid to tell you." Now that the worst was over, he came over and sat down beside her on the horsehair couch. "I mean—it's asking a lot to take in two youngsters for I don't know how long—"

"Nonsense!" Susanna said firmly. Placing her sewing basket to one side, she reached over and took Lowell's hand, pressing it warmly. "I'm proud of you, Lowell. You have a good heart."

Lowell flushed, thinking of how he'd turned from Rooney in the courtroom. "Well, I-I'm not sure about that," he muttered. Then he shrugged his shoulders, asking, "Do you want me to bring them here?"

"No, I'll go with you." She got to her feet, and compassion shone in her eyes. "The poor things! What a terrible thing for them to go through! We'll have to be very kind to both of them, Lowell."

The two of them went out on the porch, and Lowell said, "They're looking at the horses, I think." He led the way, and turning the corner of the big barn, he said, "There they are."

Susanna studied the pair who turned to face them. The boy was thin and tense, with a look of defiance in his dark brown eyes. When Lowell introduced her, she said at once, "My, how nice it'll be to have some new faces around! I get so lonesome on this old place." Smiling at Buck, she said, "Most of my menfolk are gone to the war, Buck. Do you think you could learn to drive me to town in the buggy?"

Buck blinked with surprise, and some of the tension left him. "Oh yes, I can drive some, Miz Rocklin!" he replied eagerly.

"Well, you and I will be going quite a bit, I expect." Susanna turned to Rooney and, seeing the humiliation in the girl's dark blue eyes, set herself to put the girl at ease. "Rooney, Lowell tells me you're going to have a long visit with us?"

"Y-yes, ma'am."

"Well, I think that's grand! And I know just the place for

89

you." Turning to Lowell she said, "The old summerhouse, Lowell."

"Why, that's just the thing!" Lowell felt a wave of relief come over him and turned to say to the girl, "It's real private, Rooney. You and Buck can fix it up however you want. Come on, I'll take you there."

"I'll just go along. Rooney and I can see what the inside needs," Susanna said. "You and Buck here can do the man's work." She smiled at Buck, saying, "It's down that little lane there. Suppose you drive us all there?"

Buck nodded eagerly, "Yes, ma'am!" he said, color tinging his pale cheeks. When the four of them returned to the buggy, Lowell helped his grandmother into the front, then gave Rooney a hand into the back. She kept her eyes from him, saying quietly, "Thank you."

Buck scrambled into the driver's seat, unwound the lines, and looked at the lane. "Down through them trees, Miz Rocklin?"

"Yes. Now don't go too fast," she said, smiling at him. She complimented him on his driving skill and was pleased at the way she found to make him feel more comfortable. *Poor little chap,* she thought as they passed through the lane formed by huge oak trees. *How little he has! But he's got good stuff in him—and so has Rooney!*

At the end of the lane, Rooney saw a small frame house nestled under a grove of pines. Buck pulled the horses to a stop and turned to Susanna. "Did I do all right?" he asked anxiously.

"Why, I should say so! I don't know of a man who could do better! I'd trust you to take me to Richmond right now!" Susanna patted his arm, then Lowell leaped to the ground and helped the women down. Looking around, Susanna shook her head. "Grounds need work—and the inside might be a mess."

At that moment a big dog dashed out of the woods, barking excitedly. "Get down, Buck!" Lowell snapped as the huge animal reared up and pawed at his shirt with muddy paws. "Now look at the mess you've made!"

"His name is the same as mine?" Buck asked Susanna with surprise.

"Yes, he's my granddaughter's dog."

"Can I pet him?"

"Of course, but he'll worry you to death."

Buck loved animals, and when he put his hand on the big dog's broad head, that was all it took. The dog leaped up, licking his face and pawing at him frantically.

"You two can do some hunting together," Lowell said. "He's a pretty good coon dog when he wants to be." Still feeling awkward with Rooney, he suggested, "Maybe you and I could tag along, Rooney."

"That would be nice!" Rooney was so pleased at the place and at Buck's pleasure that she forgot some of the painful interview she'd had with Lowell at the Royal.

Then they entered the cabin, and Rooney gasped. "Oh, this is so *nice!*" she exclaimed. It was small with only one main room. It housed a small kitchen off to one side and had a door leading to a bedroom. The main room was well furnished with a couch, a table, and several bookcases. "This is where Clay lived for a while," Susanna said. "He and Rena made it over like it is now. It's been pretty much empty since the beginning of the war, but Rena still comes here from time to time to read."

"Oh, I wouldn't want to put her out!"

"She'll be glad to have you. She and the dog will be with you half the time. You two girls will have a good time, and you'll have to look out for them, Buck—and take care of your namesake, that pesky dog!"

"I'll take care of him!" Buck spoke up at once. "Can I go outside and play with him?"

"Of course! Lowell, you go with them. Show Buck . . . well, I guess we'll have to rename one of you." Susanna smiled. "When I call for Buck, I don't want that old dog coming to answer me."

"I'll be Buck Number One," Buck said. He smiled happily, the first smile Lowell or Susanna had seen from him. "That ol' dog can be Buck Number Two!"

Susanna and Rooney went over the small cabin after Lowell and the boy left. Susanna said nothing about the circumstances that brought them, speaking only of practical things about the summerhouse.

But when they had gone over the place, Rooney slowly turned to Susanna, saying, "Miss Susanna—I lied to you and Lowell."

Susanna knew better than to cut the girl off. People, she knew, had to get things out sometimes, so she stood there listening as Rooney struggled through her confession. *Better to let her get it all out—then we can put it behind us.*

When Rooney finished, saying miserably, "I didn't want to lie, but it just—it just came out that way," tears came to her eyes, and she whispered, "Maybe you don't want a liar livin' on your place!"

Susanna moved forward and took the girl in her arms. At once Rooney threw her arms around the older woman and began to weep. Susanna held the slight form of the girl, patting her shoulder and murmuring sympathetic phrases. Susanna Rocklin was a strong woman, but part of her strength was her compassionate heart. Now as the girl's body was racked with sobs, she thought, *She's never had a mother to love her. I'm glad she's come here. She needs me!*

Finally the sobs diminished, and Susanna took a handkerchief from her pocket. "Now, that's over!" she announced firmly, drying the girl's face. "We women have to do things like that once in a while, don't we?" A wry smile touched her lips. "I wish men had sense enough to cry things out!"

"Nobody ever was so kind!"

"No more of that!" Susanna turned the mood quickly. "What do you think about these curtains? I've got some in the attic that will look a lot better than these. Come along, and we'll go see what we have. . . ."

★ ★ ★

"But—but, Father, think what it *looks* like!"

Clay stared at Lowell, who had appeared in the study of the Big House. "I don't see any problem," he said shortly. He had been assigned recruiting duty and had found it almost worse than battle! But it did enable him to get home, so he didn't complain much. He'd come into the study to work on the books when Lowell had burst in, anxiety on his face, saying, "Do you know what Rooney's doing?" Then without waiting for an answer, he'd exclaimed, "She's going around to the dance hall girls in Richmond asking for their dresses!"

That was when Clay had stared at Lowell. "Well, you have to have them, don't you?"

"Well . . . yes, sir, we do, but not from—from *those* women!"

Clay put his pencil down, leaned on the desk, and studied the agitated face of this son of his. Lowell, he knew, had more family feeling than the twins—that is, he was more concerned about the position of the Rocklin family. *He worries too much about how things look,* Clay thought, hoping Lowell would be able to cease thinking about what other people thought, just as he had eventually learned to do. He was tempted to tell Lowell he was too fussy but knew that wouldn't do.

"Look, Lowell," he said calmly, "in a war we have to do all kinds of things we wouldn't think of doing in better times." He saw the stubbornness on Lowell's face and said a little more stridently, "You ever think your grandmother would be digging up old outhouses?"

This was being done all over the South, for niter for gunpowder could not be imported, and there was no other source. Noting the embarrassed look on his son's face, Clay said gently, "Do you think I *like* having my mother involved in things like that?"

"No, sir, of course not!"

"So Rooney is just doing what you asked her to do, isn't she? Getting silk for your balloon?" Clay leaned back in his chair, his face lined with fatigue. He took his job as a captain in the Richmond Grays seriously and had missed many hours of sleep trying to put C Company back together after battles. "I think you ought to commend her for finding a way to make the project happen," he commented quietly.

Lowell dropped his eyes and after standing silently looked up. "I suppose you're right, sir—but it's humiliating!"

Clay rose and came to put his hand on Lowell's shoulder. "I know, Son, but it's for the Cause. Try to think of it like that." He smiled, his teeth very white against his tanned skin. "I'm proud of you doing this. Most wounded men just sit around and wait—but you've worked hard on this idea."

The praise brought a flush to Lowell's cheeks, but he said only, "Well, guess I'll go tell Rooney to go ahead with the crazy scheme." A wry smile touched his lips, and as he left Clay heard him mutter, "Doesn't matter much—that stubborn girl's going to do it anyway!"

As the two men were talking, Rena and Rooney were in the barn, sitting among billowing silk. Assisted by Rose and Melora, they had cut the dresses carefully into the patterns laid out by Lowell. Now with the Yancy women back home, the sewing fell to Rena and Rooney. Rena looked up from a seam she was working on and put her gaze on Rooney. "Do you think Lowell will let you go get more dresses from Richmond? He was awful mad at you for going to those places!"

"We have to have the silk, don't we?"

Rena studied the face of Rooney thoughtfully. She had grown very fond of her but was puzzled by her at the same time. "What's it like in those places—the bars and saloons, Rooney? Do you ever see any of the bad women?"

Rooney's hand slipped and a flush came to her cheeks. "Didn't you know, Rena? My mother is a dance hall woman."

A gasp came from Rena's lips, and her face contorted with

94

embarrassment. "Why, Rooney!" she whispered in agony. "Nobody told me!"

"I should have told you myself," Rooney said. She looked up and saw Rena's face. "Oh, Rena!" she cried and then leaped up and went to the girl, for tears were running down her cheeks. "Don't cry! It's nothing to cry about!" She sat down beside Rena, assuring her over and over that she wasn't hurt. "I'm used to it, you see. It's the only life I've ever known." Then to avoid future problems she quickly sketched her family history for the girl, ending by saying, "I'm so grateful to your brother for helping Buck and me. So don't you be sad, you hear?"

Finally Rena calmed down, and the two girls sat there working on the silk that slipped through their fingers sibilantly. Rooney was aware that Rena was troubled but waited quietly for her to speak of it. Finally Rena said with her eyes dropped to her hands, "My . . . my mother wasn't a good woman!"

"Oh, Rena!"

"She had . . . men friends," Rena said, and when she did lift her eyes, there was misery in them. "And I hated her—and now she's dead!" This was a thought that never completely left this girl, and no matter what anyone said, a heavy guilt lay deep inside her spirit.

"Do you want to tell me about it, Rena?" Rooney asked gently. And then, perhaps because Rooney had the same problem, Rena opened herself, speaking of her miserable childhood. She'd never been able to talk to anyone fully—they were all too close. But Rooney was her own age, and she talked for a long time. Finally she said, "Do you think God will ever forgive me, Rooney?"

"Oh, Rena, I don't think God holds it against you!"

"I hope not," Rena whispered. Then she heard someone coming and said quickly, "Thanks for listening to me, Rooney—it's a help!"

And then the door opened and Lowell entered. He saw the expression on his sister's face and thought, *She's been crying,* but said nothing. *She's probably been thinking about Mother again.* Then he saw that there was a light expression on Rena's face that had been absent, and it came to him that it was good for her to have a girl her own age to talk to.

"Well, you can go get the dresses, Rooney," he said, then blustered, "but I'm going with you!"

Rooney stared at him, knowing how angry he'd been at her actions. "Why, you don't have to do that, Lowell," she said. "Buck and me can do it."

"No, if it's got to be done, I'm going with you. Get ready, and we'll go this morning."

Lowell turned and left, and Rena said, "Lowell's about as stubborn as a man can get. I didn't think he'd ever change his mind about those dresses." A smile touched her lips and she nodded. "I'll bet Daddy shamed him—or maybe Grandmother."

"I guess so." Rooney dropped a bright green section of silk, rose, and said, "It makes me feel bad, Rena. I hate to humble him, going to all those places."

"He wouldn't do it if he didn't want to, not Lowell." Rena stared at the girl across the table and nodded. "He likes you a lot, Rooney. I can tell."

Rooney looked up at the girl quickly, then shook her head. "No, I don't think so, Rena." Then she turned and left, saying, "We'll get enough to finish it—and he'll be glad when I'm gone!"

CHAPTER NINE
Rooney Takes a Ride

⭐

"I hope the Yankees don't have any spies around here," Susanna Rocklin remarked. "If they do, they won't have any trouble getting a report on this contraption of yours, Lowell."

The field in which Rocklin stood was crowded with spectators, so many of them that Lowell had been forced to beg them to move back so that they wouldn't interfere with the launching of the balloon. There had been no announcement of the event, but somehow word had gotten out so that even before Lowell and Rooney had appeared, neighbors had arrived.

Lowell, who was working on the gas-generating machinery, looked around at the onlookers, then muttered to his grandmother, "I wish they'd all go home!"

"That's not very likely. People around here, they've been talking about my eccentric grandson for days now. None of them's ever seen a man fly, and they wouldn't miss it for anything." She stared at the wagon with its maze of iron pots and winding coils of copper tubing, adding laconically, "To tell the truth, I'm about as skeptical as the rest of them."

"It's got to work," Lowell said stubbornly. "We've tried it on those small balloons. You saw them fly, didn't you?"

"Well, yes, but that's different from all *this!*"

Lowell turned to look at Rooney and Buck, who were carefully spreading the canopy on the ground as if it were a monstrous bedspread. *Come to think of it,* he thought, *it looks like one of Grandmother's quilts!*

Made completely of small pieces of silk dresses, the canopy in the sparkling sunshine seemed to glitter with every color of the rainbow: scarlet, green, blue, yellow—every hue imaginable! Since it was finished, he thought of the long arduous hours that the women had put into the project—especially of Rooney, who had worked tirelessly on the canopy. She had insisted on examining every seam, always insisting on double stitching them for strength, and often had rejected some of the work, insisting, "It's got to be *stronger!*"

Lowell shifted his gaze to Rooney, who was wearing a light blue dress trimmed with white lace, and a white straw hat. Excitement made her dark blue eyes flash, and she was chattering like a magpie to Buck as they moved around, pulling and tugging at the colorful material. *Couldn't have done it without those two,* he thought—and regretted the coolness that had come between him and Rooney. He missed their early camaraderie, and a vague sense of regret came to him as he studied her happy expression. *I've got to try to make it up to her* was his thought, but then he turned his mind to the business of filling the canopy.

"Rooney! Are you and Buck ready?"

"Yes, I think so."

"All right—let's get started."

Lowell checked his gauges, then nodded to Josh, who was standing a few feet away. "All right, Josh, take that hose over and help Rooney and Buck."

"Y-yessir!" Josh exclaimed and, leaping forward, picked up the free end of the flexible tube used to carry the gas from the generating machinery to the canopy. As the lanky boy went into action, Lowell said to his grandmother, "That's a real smart young man. He invented that hose himself."

"Did he now?" Susanna stared at Josh Yancy and shook her head. "Clay's always said young Josh could make anything under the sun. We'll have to see about giving him some more training, Lowell."

"I think that'd be good. He's got too much potential to spend his life raising pigs." As he watched the boy bend over to insert the end of the tube into the opening in the lower section of the canopy, he chuckled. "That hose has to *bend*, and I couldn't figure out a way to do it. We were talking about it at the Yancy place, and Josh finally came up with the idea of using silk and stiff cord. So I figured he earned himself a spot on the balloon team."

Susanna stared at the six-inch tube that twisted like a snake as the boy maneuvered it into position. "How in the world did that work?"

"Josh got the idea of building it around a small tree. He cut down a six-inch pine and took all the bark off. Then he put some lard all over it and took some pieces of silk that Rooney had left over and covered it with them. Then he wound baling twine around the silk and covered that with glue, and he laid strips of silk over that." Lowell shook his head with admiration. "I never thought it'd work, but when it dried, we grabbed the end and it just slipped right off! Easier than skinning a catfish!"

"He *is* a clever young fellow," Susanna exclaimed. "What happens now?"

"We fill the canopy," Lowell said. Taking a deep breath, he called out, "All ready?"

"All ready!" Rooney answered. She and Buck stood beside the brilliant silk, ready to hold it into place as it filled with gas.

Lowell reached out and moved the lever that allowed the gas to escape from the chambers and felt the tube give a sudden jerk. "Here it comes, Josh!" he called out. Steadily he kept the valve open, watching the gauge for a moment, then turned to look at the canopy.

"It's working!" he exclaimed, seeing the quiltlike layers of silk suddenly rising in the center. A mutter went around the people who were watching, and Lowell grew tense. *Got to be just right—can't go too fast or too slow.*

Rooney and Buck moved quickly around the edges of the canopy, lifting folds to make the inflation easier. Josh held the entry port tightly affixed to the exhaust tube, his face intent as he tried to let none of the gas escape. It had been the best time of his life, working with Lowell and Rooney on this balloon, and he now knew that he would never be happy as a farmer. As the canopy swelled and grew like a small mountain before him, he struggled to his feet, aware that somehow he was going to do things like this—not feed pigs!

"Look at that thing!" A cry went up from Buford Yancy, who had brought his whole family over to watch the show. Tall, lanky, and stronger than most young men, Buford's mouth dropped open as the balloon swelled before his eyes. "I never seed such!"

Neither had the crowd, for a babble of voices filled the air as the balloon grew larger. They were all simple people, accustomed to only the simplest machinery, and they stood there mystified. And the slaves! Superstitious to the bone, they moved back with fear, one elderly woman muttering, "It's de *debbil!* Dat's whut it is!" But she was not frightened enough to leave, for this was far too exciting to miss, so she moved back a few feet, her eyes fixed on the sight before her.

"Watch the harness!" Lowell called out. He'd seen that as the balloon began to rise, the ropes that held the observation basket were getting tangled. "Grandmother—hold this handle right here!" he ordered.

"What's that?" Susanna was so startled she could hardly speak, but Lowell gave her no chance to object, so she gingerly grasped the handle, staring at it as if it might blow up in her face.

Lowell leaped to free the lines and, seeing that his grandmother seemed to be doing the job, called out, "Hold it right there! I'll help with getting it up!"

Rooney, her heart beating with excitement, ran around

freeing the silk. The folds were now free, and she could see that the seams were holding well. "It's working, Buck!" she cried out, and the two of them grinned at each other wildly.

Now the silk canopy was rising, swinging to an upright position. It was not round, but fuller at the top than at the bottom. Lowell had figured out that such an arrangement would give more lift, and there would be less opportunity for the gas to escape.

The slight breeze caught the flowering canopy, and Josh yelled, "I c-can't hold it!" He held on desperately, but was losing his hold, Lowell saw.

Lowell yelled, "Highboy! Box! Give a hand!" He'd given careful instructions to these two, who in turn had enlisted ten of the huskiest men on the work force, and at once they ran to grab the suspension ropes. "Hold it down!" Lowell yelled, wild with excitement. He waited until Josh cried, "She w-won't take any m-more, Mr. Lowell!"

"All right!" Lowell leaped back to the wagon, reached around his grandmother, and shut the valve. Then whirling, he leaped back to grab one of the ropes. Rooney and Buck, he noted, were hanging on to ropes along with the slaves.

"Let it go up—slowly, now!"

As they played out the ropes, the balloon rose ten feet into the air, and the small gondola made of woven willow limbs was jerked aloft.

"Let me go up, Lowell!" Rooney cried, her face alive with excitement.

"No!" Lowell had decided that on the first flight there would be no passengers. Instead, he had placed four fifty-pound sacks of feed in the gondola. "Nobody's going up the first flight—and I'll be the first one to fly! Now, let it go—real slow, now!"

At Lowell's direction, the men played out the suspension ropes. Cries went up from the crowd, and Lowell himself wanted to shout as the balloon rose slowly into the air.

It works! he thought, and he'd never in his life had such a feeling of exaltation. The rope slipped through his hands,

101

and he kept the men steady as the balloon rose. Finally it was over a hundred feet in the air and would have gone higher if he had not called out, "That's high enough! Hold it there!"

Carefully, he tested his rope and discovered that the slaves held it with ease. Dropping the line, he moved back and stared up at the graceful shape of the balloon as it swayed in the breeze. He discovered that he'd moved close to Rooney, who was staring upward, and without thinking, he suddenly put his arm around her and gave a squeeze.

"We did it, Rooney," he breathed. "We did it!"

Rooney was startled by the sudden hug, and for one moment, she surrendered to it. Looking up, her eyes sparkling, she whispered, "We did, didn't we, Lowell!"

For that one moment, he forgot the balloon, the crowd, and everything else. He was only conscious of the firmness of her shoulder as his hand lay on the thin dress she wore and of the creamy smoothness of her cheeks. Her lips were parted slightly, and her dark blue eyes were enormous.

And then she pulled away, her expression changing, and Lowell felt the wall that was between them—and knew that he was the one who had built it. Hastily he turned his attention to the balloon, and Rooney moved quietly back to stand away from the little group.

Only one person had noticed the scene between Lowell and Rooney—Susanna Rocklin. Her sharp eyes had taken it in, and she had not missed the manner in which Rooney Smith had moved away from her grandson's embrace. She said nothing, but on an impulse went to stand beside the girl. When Rooney looked at her, she smiled, saying, "You must be very proud, Rooney."

"Oh—"

"Lowell told me this morning that he could never have done it if it hadn't been for you."

"I didn't do all that much."

Sensing the hurt in the young woman, Susanna said quietly, "He's a very different sort of young man, Lowell is.

He's trying to find his way, and that's never easy, is it, Rooney?"

Rooney sensed that Susanna was trying to tell her something. She bit her lip and dropped her head for a moment, then lifted her eyes to face the older woman.

"No, it's not easy," she murmured, and then her eyes went to Lowell, who was staring up into blue sky. "I guess growin' up is never easy—for anybody!"

★   ★   ★

"You're not going up in the balloon—and that's *final!*"

The argument about who would make the ascent in the balloon began immediately after breakfast. Lowell had gone outside to study the wind and the weather, and he had come back to announce with satisfaction, "Everything is good. Just a little breeze, not enough to matter."

Rooney had said almost nothing during breakfast, but she followed him so that the two of them were standing on a small patio just outside the dining room. It was very early, the crimson rays of the rising sun casting a glow over the landscape. She looked across to the field where the balloon wagons were outlined and said abruptly, "Lowell, I should be the one to go up."

That was when he'd stared at her and stated flatly, "You're not going up in the balloon, and that's final!"

Rooney shook her head, the action swaying her curls. "I thought about it all last night. If you're up in the gondola, what would happen if something goes wrong on the ground?"

"Nothing will go wrong!"

"Something went wrong yesterday."

Lowell flushed but shook his head stubbornly. "That won't happen again." He thought of the end of the flight, when the slaves had grown confused as a gust had shoved the balloon to one side. Several of them had dropped their ropes, which caused the remaining slaves to be dragged off their feet. The balloon would have gotten away if Lowell had not acted quickly to get extra help on the lines.

"It might," Rooney insisted. "And what if something happens and you get hurt?"

"What if *you* got hurt?"

"Why, if I got hurt, the balloon can still be used for the army to help Gen. Longstreet. But if *you* broke your leg or something, it's all over. It'll all have been for nothing."

Lowell stared at her with consternation. He was a logical young man and realized that there was some logic to what she was saying. But he had set his heart on going up, and he didn't give up easily.

The argument went on in one fashion or another until ten o'clock, the time for the launch. At one point Lowell had said flatly, "Rooney, I don't want to hear any more!"

He spoke roughly and saw that his tone hurt her, but she had merely said, "I think you're wrong, Lowell. When you get somebody trained to do the work on the ground, you should go up. But you haven't done that."

The balloon was filled, and the crowd, much smaller this time, was composed of the slaves, who would work the ropes, and the family, who stood watching. They knew this flight would be with a passenger, and there was a tension in the air as Lowell put his hand on the basket and stood there for a moment.

Rooney stood beside Buck, saying nothing, and was shocked when without warning Lowell turned and said, "All right, Rooney. You win. Get into the basket!"

Susanna gasped. "He's sending that . . . that *child* up in that thing," she said angrily to no one in particular. "What's he thinking of?"

Rooney looked at Lowell's face, saw the disappointment etched on it, and said, "I know you want to go, Lowell," she whispered so that only he could hear, "but I think this is best."

Lowell shrugged, saying only, "Well, you got your way. Now get into the basket." She thought he was angry, but as she slipped inside he suddenly grinned. "I'm a bad loser, Rooney!" And she felt a warm feeling for him.

She would have spoken, but he stepped back and nodded at Josh, who stood beside the gas machine, calling out, "Let her go, Josh!"

Rooney stood in the fragile wicker basket, watching as the bag began to swell. Soon it was a small mound, and then it swung upright. She stared upward at the swaying canopy and then heard Lowell call out, "Let go—slowly, now!"

The basket jerked, causing her to grab wildly at the rim, but then there was a smoothness, and she knew she was separated from earth!

Fascinated, she watched as the figures grew smaller. She could see the anxiety on the faces of the Rocklins—and the envy in the countenances of Buck and Josh.

Up, up she went, until the people looked very small. *They look like dolls!* she thought with pleasure. There was no fear, and when Lowell called out, "Are you all right?" she leaned over and waved at him.

"I'm fine!" she called back. "Let it go higher!"

For the next hour Rooney was ecstatic. She called out what she could see, her voice faint but clear to those below. "I can see the river—and there's the Chapman farm—and, oh, there's a mail rider coming! He must be five miles away, but I can see him!"

When Lowell finally brought the balloon down, Rooney leaped out and in her excitement grabbed his arm. Her eyes were flashing as she cried, "It's wonderful! You can see *everything!*"

Lowell stood there with the rest, listening as Rooney spoke, and when he finally was able to get a word in, he said wistfully, "It sounds great, Rooney."

Rooney stared at him, realizing what a sacrifice it had been for the young man to let her take his place. Instantly she said, "I know how much you wanted to go up, Lowell. Now, let's get everything straight about what to do on the ground."

She wanted to please him and added, "I'll bet we can settle that today, then you can go up last thing this afternoon!"

Lowell's face brightened, and he laughed out loud. "Lord help the man who gets you, Rooney Smith! You'll have him jumping through hoops!"

Susanna had moved closer, and now she saw the two young people standing close together. She noted the sweet expression on Rooney's face and saw Lowell suddenly laugh and reach out to pat her shoulder.

A smile touched the lips of Susanna Rocklin, and she nodded to herself as an idea touched her mind. As she turned away, she thought, *I wish you were here to see this, Thomas.*

CHAPTER TEN
Camp Meeting

⭐

Gen. Silas Able looked up at the young private who'd somehow managed to get past his aide. "Well, Private, what is it?"

Lowell Rocklin said quickly, "General, I know you're busy, but I've been working on the balloon that Gen. Longstreet wanted to see made."

"Oh . . . yes, I remember. The general mentioned the balloon to me in a correspondence when I came to the corps." Gen. Able's division had been serving in Tennessee, but Lee requested his presence in Virginia. Gen. Longstreet had been sent southeast to lay siege to Suffolk, Virginia, and Able was his replacement. He resembled Longstreet in appearance, being a blunt man in form as well as manners. He had heavy features, a high domed forehead over a pair of level blue eyes. A full beard and heavy mustache covered the lower part of his face, and he looked durable as stone. "What's your name, Private?"

"Pvt. Lowell Rocklin, General. My father, brother, and I are in the Richmond Grays, serving under Gen. Jackson."

Gen. Able nodded and demanded bluntly, "And this balloon—you've actually got one?"

"Oh yes, sir. It's ready to go. And I'd guess that there'll be a chance to use it pretty soon."

The general's eyes glinted with humor. "You don't have to be very smart to see that the army's getting ready to move out."

"No, sir."

Chewing on the stub of a cigar, Gen. Able considered Lowell. His mind was filled with the ten thousand details that generals must attend to. But Able tried to put those things behind him as the prospect of what a balloon would mean to the Army of Northern Virginia played in his mind. "I'd like to see what you've done, Private. Where is it?"

"Outside the camp, sir," Lowell said eagerly. "I wasn't sure if you wanted the troops to see it. It's down by the east road, near where the cavalry's stationed."

Able nodded and turned to his aide. "Jenkins, I'm going with this man. I should be back in a couple of hours." He mounted his large bay, and the two men rode through the center of the camp. It was a beehive of activity, and Lowell kept silence, awed by being in the company of such a high-ranking officer. But Gen. Able began asking questions, and soon he'd discovered a great deal about Lowell. Able was an officer who liked to know his men as well as possible and was impressed at the ingenuity and drive of this young private.

"Your wound still bothering you, Private?" he asked, his sharp eyes taking in an artillery unit being prodded by a loud lieutenant.

"No, sir, hardly at all," Lowell said quickly. "I'm able to rejoin my regiment, but I thought I might do more good working with the balloon."

"If you can give us the Yankees' position, you'll certainly be useful. What's it like up there?"

"Oh, General, it's *fun!*" Lowell flushed, then said, "I know that's not what it's for, but it's the closest thing to flying there is, and I guess all of us have watched the birds and wished we could do what they do."

"I suppose so. Can you see a long way?"

"Why, sir, it's amazing!" Lowell began to describe the things that could be seen, and Gen. Able listened carefully.

One of the most difficult problems of a commander was finding out what was happening. The only method available was the courier, but that was slow and often inefficient. The courier had to make his way to some point of the battle, where he might get killed. If he didn't get killed, he had to be intelligent enough to grasp the details of the battle. He often had to find an officer who was wounded or dead or who had moved to another part of the field. Then, after gathering his information, he had to make his way back to his commander and deliver the message. But by that time the situation usually had changed completely.

"God knows we need some help with intelligence," the general said when Lowell paused. "We're going to have to do all we can to stop the Yankees."

"We can do it, sir!"

Gen. Able glanced at the open face of the young man and hoped that the rest of the army was as confident. "That's the way to talk, Private," he said with a nod.

As the two rode along, the general spoke of the importance of getting information in battle, and Lowell absorbed it all. By the time the two of them pulled up beside the two wagons, Lowell had learned more than most knew about the battle to come. "I know we can help you, General!" He swung off his mount, followed by the general, and gestured. "There it is, sir!"

Gen. Able stared at the wagons, which looked much like any other wagons—except for the solid high sides on one of them. Turning to Lowell, he said, "I guess I expected to see the thing all ready to fly. How long will it take to get it up in the air?"

"Oh, about an hour, sir, but we'll have to have some men to hold it down."

"I can commandeer whatever you need. I'd like to see how the thing works."

"Yes, sir!" Lowell motioned to Rooney, saying, "Let's get started—" And then he realized that Able was staring at the girl, as were many of the soldiers who were in the area. "Oh, this is Miss Rooney Smith. Miss Smith, Gen. Silas Able."

Able removed his cigar, then his hat. "I'm happy to meet you, Miss Smith." He studied the girl, noting that she was wearing a man's clothing—a pair of brown trousers and a white shirt. They fit her loosely, but her slim figure left no doubt as to her sex. "I didn't know we'd have such an attractive young lady on our staff."

Rooney colored and said, "I'm just a helper, General."

"Don't believe that, sir," Lowell stated quickly. "There wouldn't even *be* a balloon if it weren't for her!"

Gen. Able listened carefully as the young soldier related how getting the silk had been the young woman's idea and then said, "Well, now, that's the way our Southern ladies are, always able to find a way to do what has to be done."

Lowell and Rooney quickly prepared the balloon. Gen. Able simply pointed at ten cavalrymen, and they leaped at the chance to help Rooney spread out the canopy. As she kept them from trampling on it in their eagerness, Lowell worked on the gas-generating machinery. Gen. Able stood right beside him, his sharp eyes taking in every move.

Finally Lowell called out, "Rooney, let's fill it." Then he directed the cavalrymen, showing them how to hold the ropes. He turned the valve, saying, "General, would you hold this valve open so I can give a hand with the balloon?"

"Of course."

Gen. Able stood there, his hand on the valve, watching carefully. *If this thing would only work!* Finally he saw the balloon right itself and rise ten feet into the air. Lowell called out, "Shut the valve, General." And when the general shut the valve, Lowell grinned. "Be glad to have you come with me, sir!"

Gen. Able was tempted but knew that Lee would have a heart attack if one of his officers did such a risky thing. "I'll stay here, Private," he answered, a smile hidden behind his beard.

"You fellows do just what Miss Smith tells you," Lowell

said. As he got into the gondola he heard one of them say, "Thet little lady kin tell me to do *anythang!*"

Then at Lowell's command the balloon rose, with Rooney directing the men. It soared high into the air, and when it was about seventy-five feet in the air, Lowell called out, "I can see your camp, General! And there's a long line of wagons coming in from the south."

Gen. Able was convinced. He stood there listening as Lowell described everything within a five-mile radius. When the young man called for Rooney to bring him down, Able was standing right beside the gondola. A cheer went up as he shook Lowell's hand, and he turned to see what seemed to be Jeb Stuart's entire cavalry surrounding them. They were waving their hats and calling out, "Just show us where the Yankees are, Soldier!"

"Come along, *Sergeant* Rocklin," Gen. Able said and saw the surprise in the young man's face. "Gen. Longstreet informed me that he promised to make you a sergeant if this contraption worked. You've done a great thing, and I want to let Gen. Lee hear about it."

"Yes, sir!" Lowell suddenly remembered Rooney and said, "But I'll have to help Miss Smith put the balloon to bed."

"Looks like she has plenty of volunteers," Gen. Able remarked. "But you come to camp tomorrow—and bring her with you. Bring this thing with you, too. I want Gen. Lee to see it in action."

As Gen. Able rode away, Lowell made his way to Rooney. She was surrounded by a close-packed ring of rangy, sun-burned troopers who were all trying to speak to her.

"Now, men, let Miss Smith get her work done," Lowell said firmly.

A tall sergeant turned to him scowling. "Hey, jine the cavalry, you duck-footed infantry!" Lowell bristled and would have made an argument out of it, but Rooney intervened.

"Thanks, Sergeant, for your help. I hope you'll be around when we go up to spot the Yankees."

Dazzled by the bright eyes of Rooney, the soldier capitulated. "Wal, now if you ever cut loose from this feller, Miss, you can be *our* balloon lady, can't she, boys?"

A shout went up, and finally the sergeant herded his squad back to their campground. "Blasted fellow didn't have to be so—so *familiar!*" Lowell fumed. "You better watch out for these soldiers, Rooney. They're a bad lot."

"You're a soldier," she replied. In fact, she had enjoyed the teasing of the men, for they were nice, not like others she had known. A thought came to her, and she gave him a quick glance. "You're not *jealous,* are you, Lowell?"

"Jealous! Why, don't be silly!" Lowell threw his head back and drew his lips tightly together. "I'm responsible for you, and I'm going to see that nothing happens to you. Jealous!" He snorted and turned to begin taking the balloon down. She watched him for a moment, then her lips turned upward as she smiled.

They camped that night where they were. Lowell told Rooney, "Better get a good night's sleep. No telling how hard we'll have to travel when the army moves against the Yankees."

But they didn't get an early sleep, for the tall sergeant came over to say, "You two religious folks?"

Lowell was surprised and grunted half angrily, "You think we're heathens? Of course we're religious!"

The sergeant grinned at Lowell's indignation. "Revival goin' on. Stonewall's sure to be there. Pretty good preacher, too—just a little heavy on the fire and brimstone." He looked at Rooney and said innocently to Lowell, "If you're too busy, I'll be happy to escort the lady to the meetin'."

"I'll see to the lady, Sergeant!" Lowell said stiffly. After the cavalryman left, he turned to Rooney and asked, "Do you want to go?"

"Yes, but not in these clothes." Rooney turned and disappeared into the wagon. Lowell secured the gear in the gas-generating wagon and, when he was finished, found that Rooney was waiting for him.

"You . . . you look very nice," he said abruptly. She was wearing a light green dress with a white collar and lace on the sleeves. It fitted her snugly, and he added, "Pretty dress."

"It's one of Rena's," Rooney said, smoothing the sleeve with her hand. "I didn't think of bringing a dress, but she told me I might need one. She's so nice!"

"Sure is. Well, let's get to the meeting."

They were soon among the crowds of soldiers hurrying to an open field where they found a place near the wagon that had been converted into a pulpit of sorts. The soldiers formed ranks around the speaker's platform, and Lowell suddenly nudged Rooney, whispering, "There's Stonewall!"

Rooney turned to catch a glimpse of the famous warrior, and as chance would have it, he turned at that moment. His eyes were the palest blue that she had ever seen, and they fastened on her. Able was standing beside Jackson, and seeing Stonewall looking at Rooney, he leaned closer and said something to him. Stonewall nodded and said something to a young major beside him. Instantly, the young officer turned toward Rooney and started across the open space.

"Miss Smith, Gen. Jackson would be pleased if you and the sergeant would join him for the service."

Rooney gasped and looked wildly at Lowell. He took her arm firmly, saying, "Thank you, Major. We'd be honored." Stepping out, he towed Rooney toward the officer, whispering, "Come *on*, Rooney! We'll never get a chance like this again." When they reached the generals, he dropped Rooney's arm and saluted smartly. "Sgt. Lowell Rocklin, General, and this is Miss Rooney Smith."

Jackson removed the old forage cap that had been pulled down over his eyes. He had an unusual face, rather youthful, and his voice was pleasant as he replied, "Gen. Able has been telling me about the work you two are doing. I commend you for it." When the pair responded, Jackson asked about Lowell's family and was delighted to find out that they were in his command. "A father and *two* sons—what a testimony for the Southern Confederacy!" he exclaimed. Then he turned to Rooney and thanked her for her efforts. He was about to inquire into her family when the service began, and he said quickly, "You'll enjoy the service. The Lord is moving mightily among our men."

The service began when a heavyset young lieutenant began with a prayer, then led a song service that lasted for half an hour. Lowell knew all the songs, having heard them from his childhood, but they were all new to Rooney.

The men sang loudly such songs as "All Hail the Power of Jesus' Name," "Amazing Grace," "How Firm a Foundation," and a host of others. As song after song pealed on the soft April air, Rooney felt very peculiar. The words of the songs moved her, and as she looked around at the joy on the faces of some of the young soldiers—and of the older ones, as well—she wondered, *How can they be so happy when they may be dead in a few days?*

The last song began, and Stonewall Jackson, who had kept time with his hand, though not singing much, leaned over and whispered, "This is my favorite hymn, Miss Smith!" The words were clear, and Rooney listened hard as the song floated over the assembly:

> *There is a fountain filled with blood*
> *Drawn from Immanuel's veins;*
> *And sinners, plunged beneath that flood,*
> *Lose all their guilty stains.*

The words caught at Rooney as no words from a song ever had. She had no understanding of their meaning, but she was filled with grief and fear—and at the same time with a faint conception of joy such as she'd never known. Closing her eyes, she strained to catch each word as the song went on:

> *The dying thief rejoiced to see*
> *That fountain in his day;*
> *And there may I, though vile as he,*
> *Wash all my sins away.*

Dear dying Lamb, Thy precious blood
Shall never lose its pow'r,
Till all the ransomed Church of God
Be saved, to sin no more.

E'er since by faith I saw the stream
Thy flowing wounds supply,
Redeeming love has been my theme,
And shall be till I die.

Rooney heard Jackson say fervently, "That's it! That's it! Redeeming love!" Hot tears suddenly burned her eyes, and her sight was so blurred she could not see except in wavy images. She had no handkerchief, but a hand touched her shoulder, and Jackson's voice said, "Here, daughter—use this!"

Blindly Rooney groped for the handkerchief, but no sooner had she wiped her eyes and looked up into Jackson's eyes, than her own filled again.

"Do you know the Lord Jesus, my dear?" Jackson leaned forward to ask. When Rooney shook her head, he asked, "Would you like to know your sins are forgiven?"

Rooney thought of her life, how awful it had been, and whispered, "I-I'm too bad!"

"We are all sinners," Jackson said. The preacher had mounted the wagon, and Jackson said, "After the sermon I would like to have a talk with you. Perhaps I can help point you to Jesus."

Rooney never forgot the next hour. The preacher, a tall, gangling man in the uniform of a chaplain, preached on the love of Jesus for sinners, and by the time the sermon was over, Rooney was weeping freely. When the preacher asked for those who needed salvation to come forward so that he could pray with them, Jackson spoke to Rooney quietly. He quoted a few simple verses that seemed to go straight to Rooney's heart like swords, and then he asked if she would let him pray with her. She had nodded at once, and the general began to pray—not loudly, but very quietly.

Lowell was uncomfortably aware of all of this. He looked worried, but Able touched his arm, whispering, "Don't worry, Rocklin. Stonewall is doing what he loves best." Lowell nodded and watched as Rooney moved her lips and then lifted her head. He saw that her cheeks were stained with tears, but her eyes were brilliant as stars.

Jackson peered into the young woman's face, and a smile touched his thin lips. "You've been touched by Jesus," he said. "Never forget this moment, daughter. It's a holy time."

Much later Lowell and Rooney arrived at their wagon. The stars were out and the moon was full. Rooney had said nothing all the way back to their wagon, and when they got there, Lowell hesitated, then said, "Well, that was something, Rooney."

"I've never been to church, Lowell, never once in my whole life."

The announcement shocked Lowell. He had been brought up with church being such a part of his existence he couldn't imagine life without it. True, it had made no big impact on him, but it was *there*. He turned to Rooney, saying, "I never knew that."

"It's wonderful, isn't it, Lowell?" She took a deep breath, expelled it, and then said, "Why didn't you tell me being a Christian was so good?"

Lowell stared at her, unable to say a word. He had taken his religion for granted, but now he saw such a peace in Rooney that he became uneasy. "I don't talk much about it," he mumbled.

Rooney looked at him for a long moment, then nodded. "Nothing will ever be the same for me, Lowell." Then she turned and entered the wagon, leaving the young man as disturbed as he'd ever been in his life!

CHAPTER ELEVEN
A Time to Fight

★

Lowell was chomping at the bit for a chance to see action, dreaming about the moment when he could prove the effectiveness of the balloon. Finally Gen. Able sent word that scouts had reported enemy movements. "Keep that machine of yours ready, Sergeant. I'll be taking a force out to meet the Yankees. I think it's some sort of diversionary movement, but it'll be a good chance to test your balloon out before we get into a really big fight." Two days later word came to Lowell and Rooney that Gen. Able was pulling out with a rather small force. When Lowell got to the general's tent, Able said brusquely, "Sgt. Rocklin, stay close to me. Chances are I won't have time to waste when I need your balloon."

"Yes, General!"

Lowell and Rooney took their place in the short line of supply wagons, almost suffocating with the fine dust raised by the feet of marching men and plodding mules. They were dead tired when they pulled off the road with the rest of the weary drivers to rest briefly for the night. They cooked a quick meal and afterward wandered to Gen. Able's headquarters, hoping for news. They didn't see the general; however, they did speak with one of his aides, who told them, "The enemy was sighted by scouts, Sergeant. We'll engage them tomorrow."

"Better get some sleep, Rooney," Lowell said when they'd returned to their equipment wagon. "I think we'll be seeing some action tomorrow."

Rooney sat down by the fire and stared into it silently. Lowell came to sit across from her, saying, "I can never sleep before a battle." He looked at her curiously, then asked, "Are you afraid?"

Rooney looked up, and the yellow blaze sent a reflection to her eyes. "Why—I don't think I am." This seemed to puzzle her, for she poked at the fire with a stick, lost in thought. Finally she said, "I'm not very brave, you know. I've been afraid of things all my life. But somehow I'm not afraid of what's going to happen tomorrow."

"That's good," Lowell said, nodding. "No sense worrying about what you can't help."

But Rooney shook her head. "I don't understand it, but I know it's got something to do with what happened at the revival." She suddenly smiled at him, her face serene and happy in the glow of the fire. "I was always afraid to die. I had bad dreams lots of times. But now if I die, I'll be in heaven, won't I, Lowell?"

"I guess so."

She seemed fascinated by the thought—and pleased. She gave the hot glowing coals a poke with her stick, sending tiny yellow sparks flying. "What's heaven like, Lowell?"

He stared at her blankly, then shook his head. "I don't know. Never thought about it much." Her words seemed to disturb him, and he knew that he had never had the sort of experience that Rooney had. *Grandmother's got it—and father. And Dent and Raimey. But I've never had any sort of . . . of feeling like Rooney's got.*

"Good night," he said and, rising from the ground, went to his blankets and rolled into them under the wagon.

Rooney was surprised at his abrupt manner and disappointed. She wanted to talk, but Lowell was obviously troubled. She rose and got into the wagon. She slipped off her boots and went to sleep fully dressed, but first she prayed for Buck, then for all the Rocklins and the Yancys. She was not used to praying, but somehow she found the words flowing from her lips. And finally after she had asked God to keep all of them safe, she began to thank God. She had so little to thank him for, but now it was as if a river were loosed inside her, and she whispered her thanks to God and her praises until they seemed to fill her spirit with joy. She fell asleep, her lips uttering praise and thanksgiving—and she felt very close to God!

★ ★ ★

The noise of cannon was deafening, and Lowell could hardly hear Gen. Able. "Sir—I couldn't hear you!"

Able lifted his voice. "I said, we've got to know what sort of force is over that hill. Can you get that thing up in the air and have a look?"

"Yes, sir!"

"I'll send Maj. Hankins, my aide, with you. Tell him what you see—and be sure you count the battle flags. That way we'll know how many regiments we're facing. Take ten men with you to help."

Lowell turned, and Able's aide and the men he had selected followed him. When they reached the balloon, Lowell called, "All right, Rooney. Let's get going!"

Rooney had everything ready, and soon the balloon was ten feet in the air. As Lowell got into the basket, Rooney leaned forward, her face pale. "Don't stay up too long," she said.

Lowell laughed at her, excited by the chance of helping in the battle. "Just don't let those fellows turn me loose," he said. "The wind's blowing toward the Yankee lines, and I don't want to report on their supply lines! Now, let's get up there."

The balloon began to rise, and Rooney watched anxiously as the men played out the lines. Higher and higher it rose, and then the aide said, "They'll spot this thing, those Yankee gunners. Makes a perfect target."

Lowell watched avidly as the balloon rose above the tops of the trees, and when he saw what seemed to be a sea of blue, he yelled, "Major, I see them!"

"Where are they massed? How many are there?" Maj. Hankins yelled back. As Lowell called down the positions of the Federal troops, the officer jotted the information down in a brown notebook with a pencil.

"Cavalry over to the west—maybe two troops," Lowell yelled. "And they're moving four batteries of guns up over that little ridge. They'll have the range of our headquarters when they get there!"

"I'll take all this to the general," Hankins yelled, his voice almost blotted out by the sound of cannon that seemed to be growing stronger. He turned and left at a run, dodging among the men who were coming up to meet the enemy.

Just as he disappeared, a shell exploded not twenty feet away from where Rooney stood. She was deafened by the explosion and saw men blown into the air. She closed her eyes against the blast, but when she opened them, she saw the lower part of a man's body up against a tree where it had been blown.

"Lowell! You've got to come down!"

"No, I'm all right!" he shouted.

One of the men holding a rope said, "Miss, they've got the range. We'd better get out of here."

Rooney hesitated, then looked up to where the balloon was swaying in the breeze. "Lowell, we've got to pull out of here—"

But even as she called out, she saw with horror the gondola take a hit.

"Reel him in!" she cried, and at once the men began hauling the balloon down. But even as it came down, another shell exploded just above the colorful canopy. The silk was rent in a hundred places, and the men found the ropes limp in their hands.

"Get out of the way, lady!" a sergeant cried and came to pull Rooney to one side. She fought him, and then the gondola hit the ground and was covered at once by yards of tattered billowing silk.

"Lowell!" Rooney cried out, and jerking away from the soldier, she leaped to the fallen balloon and began tearing at the silk.

"Let me help you!" The sergeant fell in beside her and, pulling out a knife, slashed at the thin material.

Rooney seized the silk and pulled at it in a frenzy. She tore her fingernails and felt nothing. Then she saw a patch of gray uniform. "He's here! Help me get him out!"

The two of them pulled the silk away, and Rooney saw that Lowell was crumpled up in the bottom of the basket. His face was turned up, and she saw his eyelids flicker. "He's alive!" she cried. "Get him out!"

The soldier took a look inside, and his hand suddenly fell on Rooney's arm. She stared at him, tried to pull free, but he said, "His leg—it's bad!"

Rooney looked down and saw that Lowell's right leg was shattered above the knee. Scarlet blood was pumping steadily in a fine mist that had already made a puddle on the floor of the gondola.

"Let me get him!" The soldier reached down and pulled Lowell out of the basket, gripping him under the arms. He laid him down and stared at the leg. Without a word, he whipped off his belt and wrapped it around the wound in the leg. "He's lost a lot of blood," he muttered, shaking his head. "Got to get him to the doctor, but I can't let go of this belt."

Rooney leaped up, ran to the wagon, and got a blanket. When she returned, her face was pale as death, but her voice was strong. "You men, put him on this, then get three on a side. Sergeant, you hold on to that belt while we're moving him!"

"Do what she says, boys," the sergeant ordered. The men leaped to it, and almost at once they were hurrying away toward the field hospital. They passed new troops coming in but paid no heed to them, and in ten minutes the sergeant said, "There it is."

Rooney had been walking beside the sergeant, but now she ran ahead. An officer standing beside an ambulance stared at her, exclaiming, "A woman! What in the name—"

"Doctor, we've got a badly wounded man," Rooney broke in. "Where do you want him?"

The doctor stared at her, then at the soldiers carrying the bloodstained blanket. "On the table—here. Give them a hand, Lester, you and Tyrone!"

Rooney stayed as close to Lowell as she could. His eyes opened, and he muttered, "Rooney. What—"

"Here, get out of here, young woman!" the surgeon snapped. He was glaring at her, and then he looked at the leg. "Got to come off," he said gruffly.

"No!" Rooney whispered. "Please!"

The doctor stared at her. "This your husband?"

"N-no, sir."

He gave her a closer inspection and saw the fear in her eyes. In a more kindly voice he said, "I'm sorry, but the bone is shattered. Actually there *is* no bone right here." He indicated the terrible wound above the knee. "It's the only way to save his life," he said, then without more ado, he said, "Tyrone, take this young lady out for a walk."

"But I want to stay!"

"No, you don't," the doctor said firmly. "You can be of help to him afterward—but for now, he needs me."

Rooney stared at the doctor, swallowed hard, then nodded. She felt the touch of the man called Tyrone, who led her away. She found the sergeant waiting and went to him at once. "Thank you, Sergeant," she whispered. "You saved his life."

The sergeant shook his head, saying, "Well, I hope things go good for him—and for you, too, miss." He turned and called loudly, "All right, let's go get into this here fight!"

Rooney said to the man who stood waiting for her, "I'll

go wait over under those trees. Come and get me when it's over!"

"Yes, ma'am. And don't worry. He'll be all right."

"Yes."

Rooney moved leadenly across to the grove. When she got there, she found herself praying. She was so stunned by what had happened that she found it almost impossible to think, and her words seemed strange and disjointed. The sun was hot, and the noise of the cannon throbbed, accompanied by thousands of muskets being fired.

Finally a voice said, "He's fine, miss. You can see him now."

Rooney whirled and followed the man to where Lowell lay on a cot. He was covered by a blanket, and the surgeon was looking down on him. When Rooney came to stand beside him, he said gently, "I did a good job. He'll have a good stump, with lots of muscle on it." He didn't say anything about the gangrene that killed many men who were wounded, for he was a kindly man.

"Your man?" he asked softly.

Rooney looked down at Lowell's face, so still and white. "He doesn't know it yet," she said, "but he's going to be."

The surgeon grinned and patted her shoulder. "You know what I think? I think he's a *very* fortunate young man!"

CHAPTER TWELVE
"I'll Never Believe in Anything!"

After the engagement, the road to Richmond was jammed with wagons loaded with wounded. Men with major wounds were placed on the hard boards without even blankets, and as they were tossed from one side to the other, cries began to be heard, "Put me out—let me die! I can't stand this!"

Rooney had left the gas-generating wagon where it stood on the battlefield and had made a comfortable bed in the other one. She'd gathered the shredded balloon canopy and used the silk to make a thick mattress.

The second day after the amputation, she'd faced the surgeon, whose face was gray with fatigue, asking, "Doctor, can I take him to the hospital?"

"Yes. Get him there soon." His eyes were bitter as he looked at the men lying under trees with no cover at all. "Most of these will die before they get there—and some of them even afterwards."

"If you'll have the nurses put him into the wagon, I'm ready to start," Rooney said. She ran at once to the wagon and drove it back to the hospital. Going to Lowell, she said brightly, "Lowell, we're going home!"

Lowell was lying on a cot with a blanket over him, pulled up to his chin. A pallor had drained all the natural color from his cheeks, and his eyes were dull and listless. He looked up at her and gave a brief nod but said nothing. The shock of the operation had been great, and he had lost far too much blood. After he had regained consciousness and looked down at the stump of his right leg, he'd clamped his lips together and said nothing. When the surgeon had tried to cheer him up by saying "You'll be up and around on a brand-new leg before you know it," he had stared at the man with bitterness.

Soon Rooney was on the road, which was crowded with marching men; now and then a troop of cavalry rode by, sending clouds of choking dust into the air. She stopped after an hour of this and pulled off to the side. Holding a canteen, she stepped into the wagon and knelt beside Lowell. Taking a handkerchief, she soaked it and removed the film of dust from his face. "This dust is bad, but we ought to be out of it soon," she said. When his face was clean, she asked gently, "Does it hurt much, Lowell?"

"No, it's all right." His tone was flat and spare, and his features were fixed as he stared up at the top of the wagon cover.

Rooney wanted to do more, but there seemed to be no way to comfort him. Pouring some of the water from the canteen into a cup, she said, "Drink more water, Lowell. The doctor said for you to drink as much as you could." He lifted his head and drank half the water, then muttered, "That's enough."

Rooney put the canteen beside him, then returned to the wagon seat and spoke to the horses. They resumed their plodding journey, and Rooney kept them at it all day. She paused at noon, pulling the wagon off to the side of the road, beside a muddy stream. The horses were thirsty, but she didn't let them drink too much. She fed them a little grain, then climbed into the wagon. Lowell looked at her blankly, and she tried to show a cheerful spirit. "I need to check your bandage, Lowell," she said.

"It's all right."

"Now, don't be that way. The doctor said to check it often." She ignored his argument and looked carefully at the bandage. It was caked with dried blood, and she said, "I think it's all right. The bleeding's stopped."

It was hot under the wagon cover. Lowell's face was oily with sweat and plastered with the fine dust that fell over everything. She poured some water into a basin, soaked a square of cloth, and cleaned his face. "It'll be cooler when the sun goes down," she encouraged him. "I'll pull off the main road to make camp." She paused for his reply, but he closed his eyes without speaking, and she left and resumed the journey.

In midafternoon she crossed a wooden bridge and saw that the creek under it ran into a grove of hickory trees. A dirt trail followed the stream on the far side, and it looked solid, so she turned the team to follow it. Sixty yards from the main road, the trail entered the trees, and at once she found a spot beside the brook wide enough for the wagon and shaded by the towering trees.

Jumping to the ground, she unhitched the team and took them to a small meadow intersected by the creek. The grass was dry but would do for forage, and she tied the horses separately by long ropes to sturdy trees. They could reach food and water easily and would be fresh in the morning.

Returning to the wagon, she pulled the bolts that held the back section of the main frame and lowered it. Lowell, she saw, had pulled himself to a sitting position and was watching her with listless eyes.

"Lowell, this is a good place to camp. I'll make you a bed, and then we can get you out and you'll be more comfortable." She pulled several of the blankets from the floor and made a neat pallet not five feet from the back of the wagon. Moving him would be difficult, but she knew he needed to get out into the cooler air. *Don't let him see how scared you are,* she told herself fiercely. Hiding her apprehensions, she moved to the rear of the wagon.

"Can you pull yourself over here, or should I get in and help?"

"I can do it."

He twisted around and carefully pushed himself forward with his hands until he was on the edge of the wagon bed. She took his good leg and carefully lifted it over the edge, then said, "Now, you hold on to me and let down—be careful you don't bump your wound."

Lowell stared at her. He had fever and was filled with bitterness at the loss of the leg. But the intense heat of the wagon had been terrible, in addition to the pain the rough ride sent through him. He glanced at the stream with its cool shade and nodded. Through pale, tense lips he muttered, "I'm too heavy for you."

"You're only going right there. Just come down and put your arm around my shoulders."

Lowell had a fear that if he moved he might tear the stitches free—but at the same time didn't much care. He shrugged and slowly moved over the edge. It proved to be easier than he had thought, for he held himself carefully, bracing against the bed of the wagon, and his single foot touched the ground. Then she was against him, her arms bracing him tightly, and he moved one arm around her neck.

"That's it! Now, let's just move right there to those blankets—just two steps. . . ."

Lowell let go of the wagon and the world seem to reel. But Rooney held him tightly, saying, "That's it—just one step—good! Now another—now, let yourself down."

She handled him very well, but it was with a grunt of relief that he sank down on the blanket. Looking up, he grunted. "Good to be out of that wagon."

"I know. Why don't you sit with your back against that tree? I know you're tired of lying down."

Lowell agreed, and it felt very good to be sitting up on solid earth without the jolting of the wagon. As soon as he was comfortable, she ran to the wagon and found a cup. Going to the creek, she filled it with fresh, cool water and brought it back to him. "This will be better than what we've had," she said with a smile.

His mouth was parched, and the cool water was the best

drink he'd ever had. He sipped it slowly, letting it drain into the dried tissues of his mouth. He'd heard the wounded who couldn't be brought in cry for hours for water, and now he knew what torment they had been going through.

The coolness of the water—and of the slight breeze that came through the trees—refreshed him, and he sat there sipping the water and watching Rooney work. Procuring a hatchet, she chopped some dry wood from a fallen hickory, built a quick fire, and then began to throw together a meal. She worked rapidly and efficiently, and once when she looked up and met his eyes, she smiled, saying, "I'm going to fix us a *good* supper!"

When the meal was ready about an hour later, she carefully ladled some of the rich stew she'd made into a bowl and brought it to him. "No white tablecloth and silver tonight," she said cheerfully. "No time to make biscuits either, but we've got half a loaf that's not too bad."

Lowell accepted the bowl of stew and the spoon, and took a bite. It was very hot and he sputtered. Blowing on a fresh spoonful, he tasted it and looked at Rooney, who was watching him. "Good," he said briefly. "Real good!"

Rooney was pleased. "I made lots of it, so eat all you can."

The two of them sat there eating slowly, and Lowell found that he could not eat more than half of his portion. "Just not very hungry," he muttered.

His face was flushed and Rooney thought, *He's got fever.* It was what the doctor had warned her of, but she said only, "You can have some more later. Let me get you some fresh water. We've got plenty of that."

The sun went down slowly, and after Rooney cleaned up the dishes and stored the stew in a closed pot, she said, "I'll just take a little walk—see what's down the creek."

"All right."

She walked away and followed the creek for two hundred yards. There she stopped to wash her face and tend to her personal needs. It was growing darker, and she stood beside the stream, praying for God to take the fever away.

Finally she turned and made her way back to the small camp and discovered that he was lying down and had fallen asleep. She moved softly to the wagon, got a blanket, and made a bed for herself across the fire. It was early and she was not sleepy, so she sat there quietly. She could hear the traffic on the road, but it was muted and did not disturb Lowell.

Overhead the leaves of the hickory trees rustled, seeming to whisper secrets to each other, and through the leafy fringe she could see the star-spangled sky that covered the earth.

Once she got up and moved to kneel beside Lowell. Touching his cheek lightly, she was shocked by the heat of his body. *Bad fever! I've got to get it down like the doctor said.*

She went to the wagon and grabbed some of the silk scraps. Finding a gallon bucket, she went to the creek and filled it with cool water, then went back to Lowell, who was tossing now with a fitful mutter.

"Lowell. Wake up." She had to call his name several times, and when his eyes opened, they seemed blank. "I've got to get your fever down," she said. He only stared at her, and she began taking off his shirt. He blinked but made no resistance. When his shirt was opened, she took a square of the silk, dipped it in the cool water, and then removed it. Wringing some of the water out, she opened the cloth and spread it over Lowell's body. He jumped at the touch of the cold material, and she murmured, "Be still, Lowell. It's all right."

For two hours she kept up the treatment, getting cool water from time to time. His body was so hot that the cool, wet fabric was heated almost at once, but she worked on doggedly.

At one time he grew delirious, calling for his grandmother. "Is that you, Grandmother?" he would mumble and try to reach for her.

"Yes, Lowell, this is your grandmother," Rooney would whisper. "Lie still now, and Jesus will take care of you."

He would peer at her through fever-bright eyes and then

seem to be reassured, only to go through the same thing a few minutes later.

Finally the fever went down, and Rooney breathed a shaky prayer of relief. "Thank you, Lord!" she said, then dried Lowell and put a dry shirt back on him.

She went to her pallet, tired as she had ever been, and fell to sleep at once. Time passed over her, and she had no sense of it. Finally she heard Lowell speak and came awake at once.

"Yes, Lowell?" Rooney was groggy, but got to her feet and went to kneel beside him. "Are you all right?"

Lowell's head was down, but as he lifted his face to her, she saw the despair in his eyes by the light of the stars and the moon. He had always been a young man with a cheerful air, but now he was filled with bitterness.

Glancing down at his stump, he stiffened, then looked at her. "I wish it had killed me!" he stated flatly.

"No, that's not right, Lowell!"

"Right? What does that mean? Is it *right* for a man to creep around for the rest of his life a hopeless cripple?" His eyes were deep wells of anger as he whispered bitterly, "Don't talk to me about what's *right!*"

Rooney reached out to touch him, but he shoved her hand away roughly. "Leave me alone!" he said, his voice thick with anger.

"Lowell—don't be like that!"

"I'll be what I please—and I'll tell you one thing, Rooney . . ."

When he paused and looked down at his leg, he seemed to have forgotten what he had meant to say, so that Rooney asked, "What is it, Lowell?"

Lifting his head, he clenched his right fist and shook it at the heavens above. Then he said in a grating tone, "I'll never believe in anything again!"

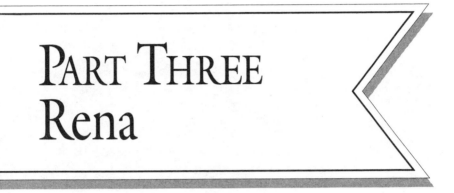

PART THREE
Rena

CHAPTER THIRTEEN
Clay Goes Recruiting

In 1863 spring came to Virginia so suddenly that it caught people by surprise. The sullen cold that had lain over the land seemed to leave overnight, bringing warm breezes. So sudden was the change that it was almost like walking out of one room into another. The grass that had been touched by September's frosty hand emerged in short emerald tongues. The woods put on their summer greenery, and the rivers ran clear within their banks.

But if relief had come to Virginia in the form of warm weather, wounded and dying men from old battles filled the hospitals and many of the homes of the land. Death became as familiar as birth, and almost every family struggled with the loss of a young man, cut down by the bloody scythe of war.

The Confederate army had enjoyed a brief respite, for the Northern army had withdrawn to Washington—but only to prepare for another onslaught as soon as the problems of winter warfare were behind them and thinned ranks could be filled by the new recruits. Lee well knew that the Army of the Potomac would be back in greater force than ever— and he knew also that such tactics could only end in defeat for the South. He began to think of forcing the war, of leading his Army of Northern Virginia north. He well understood that he would have to fight the politicians who would scream that he was leaving Richmond unprotected— but there was no greater gambler in Virginia than Robert E. Lee. As the crippled army began to rebuild, more and more he turned his mind toward the North, hoping that one successful attack would carry the message of total war to the people who had never heard a shot fired.

But as Lee began to move in his mind toward launching an attack, the South had to go on. It was more difficult now, for they were cut off from their supplies. The sea route was closed by a vigilant U.S. Navy, which had thrown a tight net around most of the coast. Only a few fleet clipper ships were able to run the blockade, and they could not bring in the enormous supplies required to keep the South fed and clothed. Coffee and tea were gone—many were drinking "Richmond coffee," which might be made from roasted acorns. Household stores vanished, and only what could be grown locally was found in the almost-empty stores of Richmond.

The Southern army had to depend on a very few factories—and on captured arms. The cavalry did good service here, and Gen. Jeb Stuart captured so many Federal supply trains that he was insulted when some of the mules he captured were of poor quality. He sent a message to President Lincoln:

> President Lincoln:
> The last draw of wagons I've just made are very good, but the mules are inferior stock, scarcely able to haul off the empty wagons; and if you expect me to give your lines any further attention in this quarter, you should furnish better stock, as I've had to burn several valuable wagons before getting them in my lines.
> (signed) J. E. B. Stuart

But humor was not common in most of the South, for the war had become a long, drawn-out affair that was not going to the Southern advantage.

In the wards of Chimborazo, packed to the walls with wounded men, the doctors and nurses worked so hard that it was difficult to keep a cheerful face. Mrs. Pember was one who managed to achieve this, for she understood that the wounded needed more than physical care. She spoke of this once to Rooney during a brief respite one evening. Rooney left Buck at Gracefield and had come to the hospital to offer her services again now that the work on the balloon was sadly behind her. She shared a tiny room with another nurse, and her presence helped relieve the overworked staff.

"I'm glad you've come, Rooney." Mrs. Pember nodded, a tired smile on her thin face. "You're always so good for the men."

"They're so scared—most of them," Rooney answered. She took a sip of the sassafras tea, then shook her head. "Lots of men would rather die in battle than come to a hospital."

"I know. They're young and many of them have never been sick nor away from home. Now they're thrown into this big place where they get very poor care, though we do our best!"

"Some of them cry when they think no one is watching."

"Yes. And so do I." Mrs. Pember saw that the girl was surprised and asked, "Don't you, Rooney?"

"Why . . . yes ma'am, I do," she confessed. She was tired after a long day, but there were still things to do. "Billy Rosemond died last night. I've got to write his mother, and I don't know what to say."

"That's always hard," the older woman said heavily. "All we can do is tell them their men died easily."

"Billy didn't!"

"I know, but what good would it do to tell his mother that?" Mrs. Pember laid her dark eyes on Rooney and said gently, "Sometimes kindness is better than the truth."

The two women sat in the small office, quietly drinking the strange-tasting tea, and speaking from time to time. Finally a knock at the door caused them to look around. "Come in," Mrs. Pember said.

The door opened, and both women were startled to see Clay Rocklin enter. "Why, Capt. Rocklin, come in!" Mrs. Pember said, rising to greet him. "I didn't know you were back in Richmond."

"Good evening, Mrs. Pember. Hello, Rooney. I came in to try to get supplies for the company." Clay nodded, and they saw that he was worn thin, his eyes weary. "I hate to bother you at this time of night, but I've got a problem."

"Sit down, Captain."

"No, I can't stay," Clay said quickly. He looked at the two women, then shook his head. "I've just come from my home, and I'm worried about my mother."

"I thought it might be about your uncle Mark or Lowell." Both men had been taken to Gracefield for extended care. The hospital was so crowded and nourishing food so scarce that Mrs. Pember had suggested to Susanna Rocklin that they would get better care at home.

"Well, Matron, I guess I really have come about them." He took a deep breath, and Rooney could see how worried he was. Fine lines had appeared around his mouth and eyes, and he was keeping himself upright only by a concerted effort. "I think it was the right thing for both of them to come home, but it's more than my mother can handle." He shook his head, adding, "She's not young anymore, and with the shortages and us Rocklin men in the army, it's about all she can do to manage the home."

"What do you need, Captain?" Mrs. Pember asked quickly.

"Well . . . ," Clay hesitated, then turned to Rooney. "I guess I need Rooney Smith," he said. Then he added, "I know you need her here, too—"

"Of course we do," Mrs. Pember broke in. "But your mother must have help as well. As you know, Miss Smith is only a volunteer here, and I cannot force her to stay—or to leave." She turned to Rooney. "Would you be willing to go, Rooney?"

"I hate to leave you and the men here, Matron, but the

Rocklins have done so much to help me and my brother. I just can't say no."

Clay expelled a deep sigh of relief. "I'm glad to hear that!" he exclaimed, and Rooney saw that her words had indeed lifted a load from his shoulders. His smile lightened the heaviness of his drawn face, and he added, "I'll be leaving tomorrow for a time with the company, but I can take you now—if that's not too soon for you."

"I'll get my things."

Clay spoke with Mrs. Pember for five minutes, expressing his appreciation for the fine treatment the men of his company had gotten from her, and then he and Rooney left the hospital and were on the road toward Gracefield.

"Will there be more fighting soon, Mr. Rocklin?" Rooney asked. She glanced at him as he sat loosely on the seat beside her, thinking of how tired he looked.

"I'm afraid so, Rooney."

"Will your company be in it?"

"Well, nobody knows for sure," Clay answered slowly. He was drowsy, but the cool air was like wine, and as they moved into the country he felt the pleasure that always came to him when he was in the open. He turned and smiled at the young woman, adding, "Some regiments have gone through the whole war and never heard a gun fired. Others, like ours, have had so many losses they're only a fraction of their size at Bull Run."

Rooney looked very pretty, the fresh air making her cheeks rosy, and her blue eyes were enormous—or seemed to be. She considered what he said, then shook her head. "That doesn't seem fair," she commented.

"No, I guess not. But wars are never fair."

"I wish it were all over," she said quietly, her lips growing tight. "One of my patients died this morning—Billy Rosemond. He was seventeen years old—the same age as me." A brooding came into her expressive face, and her voice was tinged with both anger and grief. "His home was in Arkansas, in the mountains. He had a sweetheart there he

139

talked about all the time. Her name is Sue Ellen Grantly, and they were going to be married when he got home."

A battery of field artillery came thundering down the road, sending up a cloud of dust. Clay drew the wagon off to the side of the road and waved a salute at the youthful officer who rode before the guns. He waited until the unit passed, then spoke to the team and moved them back onto the road. "That young fellow had better save his horses," he commented.

Rooney, however, was still thinking of the young soldier. "He won't be going home now, Mr. Rocklin. They took him out and buried him in that big graveyard close to the hospital." Dropping her head, she stared at the floor of the wagon, fingered the material of the brown cotton dress she wore, then looked at him to ask, "Will she remember him in five years—or twenty-five?"

"I think so, if she really loved him."

Rooney was caught by Clay's reply and pondered it as the wagon rumbled along. Finally she said, "She'll be alive and she'll marry—have children, maybe. But Billy's missed it all. He'll never be a husband or a daddy. In a few months he'll be nothing but bones. He won't ever have anything."

"He will if he was saved, Rooney," Clay said gently. He had learned to love this young woman, admiring her courage and her steadfast determination to keep herself pure in a terrible world. "Death seems like the end of everything to us who are left. But to those who die, it's not that way." He sat in the seat, tired to the bone but suddenly anxious to bring some of the faith that was in him to the heart of Rooney. Clay Rocklin had been an impetuous young man, but time, grief, and experience had tempered him. He had passed through a crucible of hardship that had fashioned him into a mature man of wisdom.

"You're not the only one to think as you do, Rooney," he said, his voice even and steady. "Most people do, I guess. I know I've spent a lot of my life wondering about God and trying to figure out how there can be a world that's such a mess with God able to do anything. And I don't have all the answers. Nobody does. But I've studied the Bible, I've listened to men and women of God, and I've come to understand that most of our grief for the dead is wrong."

"How can it be wrong to grieve?"

"It's not wrong like it's wrong to hate or hurt someone," Clay answered. "It's—well, it's more of a *mistake,* I guess you'd say. I'm talking now about grieving for those who died believing in Jesus Christ." A frown passed over his face, and he shook his head sadly. "Those who die lost . . . well, I don't know how to speak of that, Rooney. It's the worst thing I can think of. But if a person is saved, what happens to him when he dies?"

"He goes to heaven, doesn't he?"

"That's right. And what is heaven?"

Rooney shifted uncomfortably on the seat, for she had some doubts on that subject. "Well, from what I understand, it's a place where there's no pain and no problems— where people never die."

"That's part of it," Clay agreed, "but there's more to it. I may get in trouble here, Rooney," he said, smiling at her. "Don't tell the preacher on me, but I'm not sure that heaven is exactly like most of them preach. I mean, most people take their ideas of heaven from the book of Revelation, and it tells about heaven like it's a big city, full of gold streets and high walls with gates of pearl."

"You don't believe that?" Rooney was shocked, for she had gotten the idea that good Christians believed all the Bible.

Clay held up his hand quickly, saying defensively, "Hold on now, don't shoot!" He was amused at her reaction and assured her, "It may be like that, Rooney. I don't really know—and don't really care. The important thing to me about heaven is not what the streets are made of, but who's there."

"You mean Jesus?"

"Yes! If Jesus is there, I don't care if the streets are made out of gold or dirt! He's the center of that place, and he never made anything that wasn't good, did he?" Then Clay waved his brown hand in an expressive gesture that swept the rolling fields and the low foothills. "As for me, I'd rather heaven looked like Virginia in the spring—like this! I wouldn't give one spoonful of Virginia dirt for any big city in the world!"

"Why, I never thought of that!"

Clay laughed and suddenly reached out and grabbed Rooney's hand, so that it was almost swallowed. "Don't let me lead you astray," he said. "Believe every word in the Bible, Rooney. It's the Word of God without error. I believe that with all my heart; it's just that I don't understand all of it."

Rooney liked his ease in holding her hand. Once she would have fought like a wildcat if a man in this isolated spot had done that, but she had learned from Lowell and Clay Rocklin that not all men were evil. It was a good feeling to let herself trust the big man beside her, and when he released her hand, she said thoughtfully, "I guess you mean that we'll miss Billy Rosemond, but he's in a better place."

"Have to think that, Rooney," Clay said. "I've seen lots of good men die in this war, but I'll see them again someday. That's what it is to be a Christian."

"Then . . . Christians never say good-bye, do they?"

Clay was struck by the words of the young woman. "Why, I never thought of that! But by heaven, it's *so*, Rooney!"

The two of them moved in a leisurely fashion all evening, stopping once to rest the horses, and then continued their journey. Rooney had never enjoyed a trip more, for she had a tremendous affection for Clay Rocklin. She had admired him for some time, but now she thought, *He's the best man I ever met! I wish every man in the world was like Mr. Clay Rocklin.*

Finally as they moved into the driveway of the Big House, she asked, "How are Mr. Mark and Lowell doing?"

"Not very well, either of them. Mark isn't getting any better, and there's nothing much a doctor can do."

"And Lowell?"

"He's doing well physically, Rooney, but . . ."

Rooney glanced at him sharply, then said, "I know. He's real bitter."

Clay noted how quick the girl was, then said slowly, "He'll survive the loss of the leg, but I'm worried about him in other ways. I've seen it before, Rooney. Some men get so angry when they take a bad injury that they never have any joy or peace in them." He bit his lip and added in a whisper, "I pray to God that doesn't happen to Lowell!"

Rooney, without knowing it, reached over and put her hand on his arm. "We won't let him, Mr. Clay! You and me and Miz Susanna, we'll pray and pray for him!"

Clay felt a warmth go through him, and his eyes suddenly burned with unshed tears. He'd seen so much misery and so much selfishness in his world—and now the gentleness of Rooney Smith touched him.

"God bless you, girl!" he whispered huskily. "That's exactly what we'll do. And God will help us!"

★ ★ ★

Melora came out of the house when she heard a team and wagon approaching. When she stepped onto the porch, she paused at the sight of Clay Rocklin driving up to her front door. She was a strong woman, but for years the very sight of Clay had brought her a peculiar weakness. She had loved him for so long! First as a small child, she'd loved him as children love some adults. Then as she'd made the passage from childhood into adolescence, she'd fought against the confusing emotions that had warred in her bosom, knowing that she could never have him, for he was married, and yet she was drawn to him in a powerful fashion. Finally as a mature woman, she'd come to know that she'd never have another man. *If I can't have Clay, I'll live alone. I love him too much, and I couldn't rob another man of his right to a wife's love!*

For years now, she had carried this love locked away from everyone. While Clay's wife was alive, Melora and Clay had remained close friends, each knowing of the love in the other, but both aware that God would never let them have one another. Now that Ellen was dead and Clay was free, Melora was aware that he was now hers. The sight of him brought a pleasure to her, and she called out, "You must have smelled my pies baking all the way in Richmond."

Clay laughed, hauled the team to a stop, and leaped out of the wagon. For a big man he was agile and light on his feet, and now he tied the team, then came to her, his face lightened at the sight of her. He had spent years mourning the fact that he'd thrown away the best part of his youth married to a woman he didn't love and knowing that he could have had Melora. But he'd learned to accept that, and now he came to stand before her, admiration for her dark beauty in his face.

She was twenty-eight now, but looked no more than eighteen. Her large almond-shaped eyes were green, and her black hair hung down her back to her waist. As always, he wanted to touch her but refrained. "Well, you may have an exalted idea about those pies of yours, Miss Yancy," he said. "A man might have other reasons for coming this way."

Melora's eyes sparkled as she shot back, "Oh, you don't want any pie, then? Well, I suppose Pa and the children can finish it off." She smiled demurely, adding, "It's only blackberry cobbler anyway."

Clay's jaw dropped, and he held up his hand in alarm. "Wait now—don't be so blasted quick!" He nodded and tried to look unconcerned. "Maybe I could eat just a *small* portion of that cobbler!"

Melora burst into laughter, a pleasant sound in the afternoon air. "You liar! I'll never believe another word you say!"

Clay shrugged his shoulders, looking crestfallen. "Well, I guess I wouldn't blame you. I can resist anything except temptation—and Melora Yancy's blackberry cobbler!" Then he grinned and put his hand out, taking hers and saying, "I'm a man in a poor condition, woman."

"Really?" She loved these games he played with her and waited for him to come out with the thought that was to be plainly seen in his dark eyes.

"Yes. And you'll never know if I love you for yourself—or for your pies!"

Melora grew still, her form straight and her face clean and strong in the fading light. "I know already." She spoke simply and without any reservation. It was the way with this woman to be so open with her feelings, and Clay loved her for it. He stepped forward and took her in his arms, and she came willingly. When his lips fell on hers, there was a wild sweetness in the kiss, and the touch of her strong body pressing against him brought strong hungers. Her hands pressed the back of his neck as she pulled him closer, and all of the years of waiting seemed to evaporate. Now there was nothing to keep her from loving him with all the ardor that she had repressed for so long. Melora had long known that there was a fierce side of her nature, and now she loosed it, clutching Clay with her strong arms, savoring the strength of his lean, muscular body and the roughness of his caress. Then she felt her control slipping and pulled her head away, whispering, "Clay—I want you!"

Clay felt with Melora as he had never before felt with any other. "We'll be married, Melora! I have to have you!"

"When, Clay?"

"I can't say for sure, Melora. As soon as this war ends." They stood there, looking into each other's eyes, thinking of what had passed—and what each knew was to come.

"The others are in the field, but they'll be back soon." She spoke quietly, then asked, "Can you stay for a while?"

"Yes."

"Then we've got time for a walk. Let's go down to the creek before supper."

They had their walk, Clay telling her of the family, she

listening quietly. Always they had enjoyed each other's company, even when she was a child and he a full-grown man. The years had ripened this union, so that now there was complete ease and trust in each of them. They both knew that the love of the other was so true that nothing could change it, and the security of this warmed them both.

Finally they went back, and Clay was greeted by Buford and the children with enthusiasm. He was, to the children, more or less a favorite uncle, for he had always been good to them. To Buford he was a good friend, and the older man looked often at Clay over the supper table with affection in his greenish eyes. Most men, Yancy realized, would have taken advantage of a girl like Melora, but Clay Rocklin had been true as steel.

Finally when supper was over, they sat around the cabin, Clay enjoying the time immensely. After the tension and rigors of battle and bloodshed, it was a haven where he could rest and forget.

Finally the younger children left, but Clay said, "Josh, I'd like to talk to you."

Josh had turned to leave but now wheeled and asked, "M-m-me? Why, s-sure, Mister Clay." The children all called him that, for it was what Melora had called him for years—still did on occasions.

Buford and Melora turned to Clay, not knowing what to expect, and Josh looked startled.

"Josh, we're short of help at my place. I'd like for you to come and help—if your father can spare you."

Buford said at once, "Why, shore, Clay! One of my nephews is coming to stay with us, my brother's boy. He's 'most sixteen now, and he can do the spring plowing while the others take care of the hogs."

Clay nodded, then looked at Josh. "I'll pay you full-grown man's wages, Josh. Our overseer is gone for a time, so you'll have to work hard to fill in until he gets back."

"I c-couldn't oversee n-nobody!"

Clay laughed, then rose and clapped the boy on the back,

noting the strong muscles that lay on Josh's lean frame. "Didn't expect that," he said. "Just pitch in with the animals—you're real good with that. And you can help Box with the blacksmith work."

"I'd l-like that!"

"Thought you might," Clay said, grinning. "Just don't forget there's other work to be done. You'd stay in there fooling with some invention or other the whole day long, I think."

Josh idolized Clay Rocklin and nodded his head. "I kin g-go right n-now, can't I, Pa?"

Buford gave his consent, and Josh scooted off at once to get his clothes. "Sorry to rob you of a hand, Buford," Clay apologized.

"Ain't no nevermind," Buford replied with a wave of his hand. "Do the boy good to be there." He got up then, saying, "I'll git his tools from the barn."

When he left the room, Clay rose and went to Melora. "This was good," he said simply. Pain came to his eyes and he said briefly, "I wish I didn't have to go back."

"Someday you won't have to leave me."

Clay stared at Melora, then nodded. "That'll be the best thing in the world, won't it?" He took her hands in his, held them gently, studying her face, memorizing it, she knew, for the time ahead when he would be gone.

Swiftly she lifted her face, and he kissed her. His lips were firm as he held her in his arms, and she felt again the desire in him. She felt it in herself, as well, but she had long ago learned that her longing for Clay Rocklin had this element. She was not ashamed of it but was proud that he was strong enough to release her.

"Some day soon, Mister Clay," she whispered, "you won't have to go!"

CHAPTER FOURTEEN
"You Learn a Lot on a Coon Hunt"

★

Josh Yancy liked and respected Lowell Rocklin deeply. Indeed, except for his own father and Clay, there was no man he thought more of. For this reason he had jumped at the chance to go back to Gracefield—so that he could spend more time with him.

But it hadn't worked out that way. Clay had taken him to the room that would be his, a snug room built off the barn. Then Clay had taken the tall young man around and lined out his work. Afterwards Josh had said, "C-can I go see M-Mr. Lowell now?"

"Yes, Josh, I wish you would." Clay held the boy's eyes adding, "My son is pretty depressed. He needs all the friends he can get. I'd appreciate it if you'd spend a lot of time with him."

"Why, s-sure I w-will!"

Josh went at once to the Big House, and Susanna had greeted him warmly. "Why, Josh, I hear you're going to be taking over some of the work around here. That's good to hear. We need a good man on the place!" She had smiled at his embarrassment, then asked, "Did you come to see Lowell?"

"Y-yes, ma'am."

"Come right along. I'll take you to his room."

Josh had yanked off his floppy hat and held tightly to it as he followed Susanna down the hall. He had been in the Big House before, but it always made him feel awkward and out of place. Susanna turned through one of the doors, and when Josh entered, he saw Lowell sitting in a wheelchair staring out the window.

"Look who's come to visit with you, Lowell," she said brightly.

Josh stepped forward and was shocked to see how pale and thin Lowell Rocklin was. He hid his thoughts, however, and said, "H-hello, Mr. L-Lowell. I'm g-glad to see you."

Lowell looked up, but he didn't smile. "Hello, Josh," he said briefly. His eyes were flat, and his mouth was pulled tight as if he'd tasted something sour. His attitude was more of a shock to Josh than his physical appearance, for Lowell Rocklin had been one of the most cheerful people the boy had ever seen.

"Now, Josh, you sit down and you two can talk," Susanna said quickly. "I know you must be hungry, so I'll have Dorrie fix up something for you both."

"Don't fix anything for me," Lowell said flatly.

Susanna hesitated, then left the room. Josh stood there uncomfortably, for Lowell hadn't invited him to sit down. Finally he eased into the chair facing Lowell and said, "I'm g-gonna be w-working here, Mr. L-Lowell."

Lowell glanced up at the boy without interest, nodded, and muttered, "That's good."

Josh was not good at small talk—his speech impediment kept him quiet with most people. But in the past he'd been so excited working with Lowell that he'd talked as much with that young man as he ever had with anyone. But for the next half hour, he was absolutely miserable. Lowell sat in his chair silent as a stone, not even answering the questions the boy asked him—merely nodding as if it didn't interest him much.

Josh grew desperate and finally asked, "What w-was it like . . . the b-battle, I m-mean?"

Lowell had glared at Josh, and for the only time in the conversation, some life showed in his eyes. He gestured down at his stump, then said acidly, "It was like that!"

Josh had been crushed and fell silent. The two sat there, Josh longing to leave but not knowing how. When Susanna came to the door to say, "Come along, you two," he was on his feet in an instant. He looked at the wheelchair and asked, "C-can I help you to the d-dining r-room, Mr. Lowell?"

"No! I don't need any help!"

Susanna saw the boy's head move as if he'd been struck. She touched his arm, saying, "Go along to the kitchen, Josh. I'll be there soon." He went with a gust of relief.

When he was in the kitchen, he found that Dorrie had put a plate of hot food on the table and a big glass of cool buttermilk. He began to eat, and she stood at the end of the table for a time. Her eyes were dark and brooding, and she finally said, "Mr. Lowell, he bad off. Gonna take the hand of Gawd to help dat boy!"

Josh looked at her, startled, then nodded. "I r-reckon, so, D-Dorrie," he said slowly. He was thinking, *This ain't gonna be as much fun as I thought,* but he kept that thought to himself, and when Susanna entered, he saw she was troubled.

"You'll have to be patient with Mr. Lowell," she said quietly. "It's very hard for him."

"Yes, m-ma'am."

"He's always been so strong and able . . . the best horseman in the country, the fastest at the races the boys ran." She shrugged her shoulders, then turned to face the boy. "You two were very close, Josh. He thinks a lot of you . . . as if you were a younger brother. Please try to help him all you can."

"I sure w-will!" Josh nodded. He hated to see the Rocklins so torn by the tragedy and said hopefully, "H-he'll be f-fine, you'll s-see!"

Susanna gave him a thankful look, then began to speak of other things. But after the boy left, she and Dorrie sat down.

The black woman knew Susanna well. "Doan you be frettin' now, Miz Susanna," she said firmly. "Gawd is gonna bring us through dis . . . lak he done brought us through befo'."

Susanna felt the force of the woman's love and loyalty and put her hand out. When the hard, work-worn hand of Dorrie closed around hers, she felt a rush of gratitude and said, "I don't know what the Rocklins would do without you, Dorrie."

★　★　★

Rena missed her father more than ever. Ever since he'd come back from his wanderings, she clung to him fiercely, and when he'd gone to the army, it had been terrible for her. Susanna had done her best, but her need for a strong man was something that no woman could give. Her own mother had given her so little love, and now even she was gone. Rena felt more alone than ever.

She visited Melora and had gotten very close to Rose, but the visits were rare. So Rena was left with much time on her hands. She did her best to help with the nursing and spent many hours with Uncle Mark. He was cheerful at times, but his wound was a constant drain on his strength, and she could only sit beside him, reading to him a great deal.

As for Lowell, after a few determined efforts to pull him from the despair that was eating his life away, she gave up but helped with his food and other slight chores. She longed to talk to Lowell, for the two had been close once, but now he was closed off behind some sort of wall that Rena could not penetrate.

When Rooney came, Rena was happy, for she got along well with the girl. But Rooney was busy helping Susanna and Dorrie and taking care of Lowell. Buck spent much time in the fields learning about crops, so Rena was alone.

She read for hours, the same books that Clay had read with her when he'd first come home. She loved to remember those days when she'd had him all to herself! They had been the best days of her life—just she and her father alone in the summerhouse, with books and a fire and lots of time in the crisp nights and then in the cobwebby mornings. How she longed for those days!

But they were gone. And now dark thoughts pushed aside the good memories. She no longer dreamed of days past, but rather had terrifying nightmares. They were always the same, and they always woke her with a fright that made her heart beat like a trip-hammer.

They were brief dreams, lasting only a few seconds. She was in the summerhouse when a horse came down the lane. She would rise from her chair and go outside—and fear would sweep over her. The horse was black as night, and the rider was dressed in dark clothing. A black hat was pulled over his eyes, and his face was concealed behind a black neckerchief. Rena would stand there as this frightening horseman drew close, fear crawling though her mind. When he arrived, his great horse drawn up before him, he leaned forward, and Rena saw that he had no face, just a skull-like feature with burning eyes that seemed to scorch her skin and shrivel her where she stood.

She would try to run, but she was paralyzed. Then he would speak in a voice that rattled like chains, and his breath was like an open grave as he said with a vile laugh, "Your father is dead!"

Then Rena would scream and come out of her sleep, gasping and weeping. It would take hours for her trembling limbs to grow still, and she came to dread the night for fear of the nightmare coming again.

She'd had the dream the night before she went downstairs to find Uncle Mark sitting at the table. He could move around very little and always with great pain, but he covered his discomfort by saying, "Good morning, Rena. Come and eat some of these good pancakes Dorrie fixed for you and me."

"I'm not very hungry," she said, but sat down, and when Dorrie put a golden brown pancake on her plate, she cut it into neat morsels and began to eat. Mark noted her wan face, but said nothing. *Missing her father*, he thought and set out to take her mind off Clay.

"Gracefield has a new hand, did you know that?" he said, smiling.

"A new hand?"

"Yes, young Josh Yancy. You know him, don't you?"

"Oh yes. He helped Lowell with the balloon."

"He's quite an interesting boy. Clay was telling me how handy he is with tools." Mark forced himself to eat another bite of pancake, then added, "Ought to be company for you. You're about the same age."

"He's very shy," Rena remarked. "I guess because he stutters so bad."

"I think he might get over that," Mark said. "Some people do. Has he always stuttered?"

"Oh yes. I've known him for a long time—all my life, really. But he's a strange boy." She sipped the cocoa from the china mug, then said thoughtfully, "You know, Uncle Mark, now that I think of it, he's always avoided me. Every time I've gone to visit Melora, he always stayed out hunting. And he'd come in late, after I was in bed. The only time he'd talk to me was when we were out with the pigs—and then he only talked about those dirty animals!"

"What does Melora say?"

"I asked her about Josh once, and she talked about him a long time. I could see she was worried about him." Rena chewed a bite of pancake thoughtfully, then said, "She told me some people seem to be born feeling they're not as good as other people. She said Josh was like that. Even though he could do so many things so well, like making things and hunting and shooting. But she said she thought he stuttered because he felt like he was inferior."

"I've heard of things like that," Mark murmured. "But if he ever finds out he's not inferior, he might not stutter at all."

"I guess so." Rena looked at her uncle, then asked, "Do

you think Lowell will get better, Uncle Mark? I mean—the way he acts?"

Mark frowned, for he had put this question to himself many times. He hesitated, not wanting to discourage the young woman, and finally said, "His problem is sort of like the one Josh has, Rena. He thinks because he lost a leg he's not the equal of other men. That's not unusual, I believe. Not true, of course, but with a strong young man like Lowell, it must seem that way. He's thinking nobody will ever love him—no woman, that is. And that's hard on a young man."

The two sat there talking, and Rooney joined them, and finally Susanna. They talked carefully around the subject of Lowell's condition, and finally Rena rose, saying, "I'm going riding if it's all right."

Her grandmother agreed, and she went at once to change into a riding habit that Clay had bought for her, one with a divided skirt that had made her the object of considerable gossip. But she loved to ride the horse Clay had gotten her and could not bear the sidesaddle most women used.

When she got to the stable, she found that all the stable hands were gone and set out to saddle the mare herself. But Candy was a difficult horse to manage, and finally after half an hour, Rena was exhausted and furious.

"You dumb ol' horse!" she cried angrily. "I ought to beat you with a stick."

"C-can I h-help you, M-miss Rena?"

Rena whirled to find that Josh had come across the field and was watching her. Suspecting that he might be laughing at her, she snapped, "No! I'll get this saddle on if it kills me!"

Josh started to leave, but he couldn't just leave Rena to struggle with that all day.

He was, in fact, more afraid of Rena Rocklin than he was of almost anything—and always had been. Clay had brought her to his home often when she was only a child, and Josh remembered every visit! He didn't remember, however, the moment when he'd grown so tense around her that he avoided her. All he knew was that she was so beautiful and so far above him that he could not bear the thought of being humiliated by her. She'd never made fun of his handicap, but he was terrified that she might—and he didn't think he could stand that!

But now he forced his timidity to one side, came forward, and picked up the saddle. Ignoring her protests, he moved toward Candy, murmuring her name. The mare watched him suspiciously but allowed him to grasp her bridle. He tied her to the rail fence, then slapped the saddle on her. He tightened the cinch, then turned to say, "Y-you just h-have to let her kn-know who's boss."

Rena smiled suddenly and said, "Thanks, Josh." She mounted and took the reins. But instead of riding away, she asked, "How do you like living here, Josh?"

Josh had turned to leave, but at her question, stopped and turned to face her. "F-fine, Miss R-Rena," he replied. As always his mind went into some sort of paralysis, and he cursed himself. *After she's gone, I'll think of all kinds of stuff to say!*

Rena waited for him to say more, then when she saw that he was silent, she said, "You ought to go hunting. I know you and your father love that. My father said the woods are stiff with coons this year."

At once Josh's face brightened. "I'd l-like that! I'll f-find me a d-dog and go t-tonight!"

A whim came to Rena, born perhaps out of the boredom of her life—or perhaps out of a desire to spend her night free of the nightmare. "Take me with you, Josh," she said impulsively.

"Why, I c-can't do that!"

"Why not?"

"B-because. . . ." Josh wanted to say that aristocratic young ladies didn't go running through the woods with poor white boys, but he couldn't manage all that. He stood before her helplessly, not knowing what to say. Finally he shook his head. "Miz R-Rocklin—she wouldn't like it!"

Rena grinned at Josh. "You haven't been here long enough to find out how spoiled I am! I can get anything I want out of my grandmother." While not far from the truth, Rena knew that she would have to maneuver carefully to do anything as wild as this! "I've even got a dog," she said. "The slaves borrow Buck sometimes to go coon hunting. You have to take me, though, to get Buck." Rena laughed at the shocked expression on Josh's face, then added, "Buck and Rooney will probably want to go. They don't know any more about hunting coons than I do, so you'll have to teach us all. What time do we leave?"

★ ★ ★

They left at dusk, Josh still in shock. He had never for one moment believed that the Rocklins would let Rena go on a coon hunt, but Rena had produced her grandmother with a flourish, bringing her to the blacksmith shop, where Josh was helping Box.

"My granddaughter tells me you fancy yourself a coon hunter, Josh," Susanna Rocklin had said at once. "Is that right?"

Josh had blinked in surprise, appalled. *That fool girl has got me in trouble right off,* he'd thought. "W-well, I've g-got a few, ma'am."

"Well, it's not very ladylike. But I can't think of a better reason than that for her not to go, so you take her along. Take Rooney and Buck, too." Susanna had smiled fondly at Rena, then instructed Josh, "Don't let them get chewed up by a bear or some other wild creature, you hear me?"

Josh had been too surprised to do more than nod, but at dusk he was joined by the three, who were all happy at the thought of spending the night in the woods.

Josh had said at once, "Go put on warmer c-clothes, and bring a bl-blanket!" He had gone to the kitchen and gotten enough food from Dorrie, who glared at him.

"Boy, you watch out fo' dem young folks!"

"I w-will, D-Dorrie," he muttered, then left the kitchen

to go to the barn. He tied the sack on a mule named Revelation, and when the others came with blankets, he strapped them on.

"We can't all ride one mule, Josh," Buck piped up.

Josh grinned suddenly. "Nope. We w-walk, just l-like he does."

Rooney laughed at Buck, saying, "You wouldn't know a coon if you saw one!"

"Would too!"

Rena was happy as she said, "Let's go, Josh. Buck's ready!"

The big dog sensed the excitement and ran ahead as they left the grounds. Josh spoke to him, and Buck came at once to his call. Rena was surprised. "Buck won't mind most people like that," she said. "How do you do that—make him mind?"

"Don't know." Josh shrugged. "M-most dogs seem t-to mind me."

Josh had been careful to talk to some of the slaves who hunted and had gotten good instructions. He led them to a spot about five miles from the house and then said, "Here w-we are."

Buck looked around, asking, "Where's the coons, Josh?"

"More to c-coon hunting th-than you might think," Josh said with a grin. "Let's m-make a fire."

The three of them ran to find wood, and by the time Josh had unloaded Revelation, they had enough to build a large fire. "Can I start it, Josh?" Buck asked. "I know how to build a fire."

"Fly at it, B-Buck!"

Josh let the three do the work, and when the fire was crackling, he pulled out a blanket and sat down on it close to the fire. Rena stared at him. "When do we get the coons?" she asked.

"Not for a l-long time," Josh said. Clasping his legs, he looked at the three who were all ready to start killing coons with both hands. "The b-best part of a hunt is sittin' around the f-fire," he said mildly.

The three looked rather foolish, but joined Josh. They slowly unwound, and finally they began to talk freely. Josh said almost nothing, but Rena found it pleasant to talk and to listen. The darkness closed in, and there was something cozy about the flickering fire that scored the darkness. She was wide awake and happy, glad that she'd organized the hunt.

After two hours, Rooney said abruptly, "I'm hungry!" Rena and Buck echoed this, and they scurried around getting the food out of the sacks. There were potatoes and steaks—but nothing to cook in.

"We can't eat these raw, Josh!" Rena said reproachfully.

"I'll show you." Leading them to a small creek nearby, Josh showed them how to wrap the potatoes in mud, then how to bury them in the hot ashes. Then taking his sheath knife, he cut four saplings with forks on the end, peeled them, and showed the others how to attach the steaks to the forks. They went to the fire, and soon the smell of cooking meat filled the air.

They ate the steaks and the biscuits that Dorrie had donated like famished sharks. Later they dug the potatoes out of the ashes, but the three looked doubtful. "Eat those old black things?" Rena asked.

But when Josh opened them with his knife and dug the firm, white, steaming flesh from the blackened hulls, they devoured them with relish.

Finally about midnight, Josh rose, saying, "Buck! Go!" The big dog bounded into the darkness, and Josh yelled, "Well, you w-wanted to hunt c-coons, didn't you? C-come on then!"

Rena would never forget that wild chase! She plunged through the woods, stumbling into holes, running into saplings that struck her across the face, out of breath and half afraid. But always she was aware that Josh was beside her, grabbing her arm to keep her from falling. "How can you *see*, Josh?" she gasped. "You must have eyes like an owl!"

Rooney and Buck were floundering through the thickets, both afraid of getting lost, but having the time of their lives. Finally Josh called, "He's treed!"

Not five minutes later he led them to an open spot with one huge tree in the middle of it. By the light of the moon, they could see Buck clawing at the tree, baying in a hysterical fashion.

"Persimmon t-tree," Josh informed them. He peered upward, then said, "Big 'un!"

"How do we get 'em down, Josh?" Buck cried out, his eyes big with excitement.

Josh was staring up into the tree. "Go up and shake h-him down, B-Buck!" he commanded. "We'll l-let the d-dog take him!"

Rooney protested, but Buck went up the tree like a squirrel. As he moved upward, he sensed the coon moving and cried out, "He's goin' out on a limb, Josh! I'll shake him down! Get ready!"

Standing beneath the shadowy form of the animal, Josh waited, and soon the limb began to move violently up and down. "Watch out!" he yelled to the girls—and at that moment he saw a dark mass falling right at him!

Rena could not see clearly, but she saw the coon hit Josh, knocking him to the ground. She screamed, "Josh!" but all she could see was the blurred form of Josh rolling on the ground. He was shouting, "Git off me!"

After a few moments of frenzied action, part of the bulk scooted into the dark pursued instantly by the dog.

"Josh, there's another one up here!" they heard Buck yell. "Want me to shake him down?"

"No! That was a bobcat you shook out on me—not a coon!"

"Oh, Josh!" Rena cried out and ran to where he was coming to his feet. She misjudged the distance and ran into him, upsetting him so that he fell down—and she with him.

For one moment her face was close to his, and she whispered, "Are you hurt bad?"

"No!" Josh said, terribly conscious of Rena as she was crushed against him. Struggling to his feet, he pulled Rena up, then shouted, "Buck, don't shake *nothing* else out of that tree! It might be a grizzly bear!"

Rena and Rooney found that extremely funny and began giggling hysterically. Buck came scooting down and stopped to stare at the two, then he, too, began laughing. "I'll bet you looked funny when that ol' bobcat landed on you!" he said.

Josh stood there, embarrassed and ready to put up his wall of silence, but he found that he could laugh with them. All four of them laughed until they cried, and finally Josh said weakly, "Well, I g-guess we scared every c-coon away for t-ten miles!"

He led them back to the fire, and they stayed awake for hours, talking and singing old songs. Rooney sang one of the songs she'd heard the soldiers sing in camp:

> *Soft blows the breath of morning*
> *In my own valley fair,*
> *For it's there the opening roses*
> *With fragrance scent the air,*
> *With fragrance scent the air,*
> *And with perfume fill the air,*
> *But the breath of one I left there*
> *Is sweeter far to me.*
>
> *Soft fall the dews of evening*
> *About our valley bowers;*
> *And they glisten on the grass plots*
> *And tremble on the flowers,*
> *And tremble on the flowers*
> *Like jewels rich to see,*
> *But tears of one I left there*
> *Are richer gems to me.*

The sweet voice of the young woman seemed to lay a charm on the dark woods, and a quietness followed. Soon

Rooney and Buck rolled up in their blankets and were fast asleep.

Josh thought that Rena was asleep, too. He sat staring at the fire until Buck came out of the woods, his tongue hanging out. Rena spoke, breaking the silence, saying, "Come here, Buck." The dog moved to her, flopped down, and then Rena said, "Josh, I never had so much fun in all my life!"

"Well, it is f-fun."

"You know something?" When Josh looked at her, she said softly, "You never stuttered when you were fighting with that bobcat."

She had never mentioned his impediment, and Josh's face reddened. He stared into the fire without answering, and she came out of her blankets and moved to sit beside him. "Don't be afraid to talk about it, Josh," she said. "It's nothing to be ashamed of, and someday it'll be gone."

"No, it w-won't never!"

He turned his face from her, but she wouldn't be denied. "You have to believe things, Josh. I do anyway."

"B-believing won't m-make nothing happen!"

"I think it will." She hesitated, then found herself telling him about her dream. She had never told a soul, but somehow the darkness and the quietness seemed to make it easy. The fire sputtered as she spoke, and when she was finished, she was embarrassed. Half rising, she muttered, "Guess you think I'm crazy!"

He turned and caught her arm, pulling her back. "No, I d-don't," he said faintly. "You're the s-smartest girl I kn-know, 'cept for M-Melora."

She smiled at him, and he felt an odd feeling go through him. He was suddenly aware that he was holding her arm and dropped it abruptly.

"Josh—are you afraid of me?" Rena asked abruptly. "I mean—you've always avoided me. Don't you like me at all?"

Josh dropped his head and cleared his throat. "S-sure I l-like you, but. . . ."

When he didn't finish, Rena knew what he was thinking. "Don't be afraid to be friends, Josh," she said quietly. "I told you about my nightmare, and I haven't told it to anyone else. I thought I could tell you, and you wouldn't think . . . that I was silly."

"I would never th-think that!"

He turned to her and smiled, a full smile that she'd never seen, and she said, "Will we be friends, then? Real good friends?"

Josh swallowed and nodded without speaking. He was too full for speech and finally cleared his throat. "What did y-you mean about b-believing something?"

"I have to believe Daddy will come home and not get killed." She shivered at the words and fear came to her, but she shook her head and said, "It's like—as long as I believe it, it'll happen, but if I stop . . ."

She broke off, and the two of them sat there in the flickering light of the fire. Finally she said, "Josh, let's both try to believe that my daddy, Dent, and your brothers will come home safe and that some day soon you won't stutter anymore."

Josh Yancy had never met anyone like this girl! For years he'd watched her, but shyness had kept him from approaching her. Now he was sitting beside her, looking into her dark eyes—and she was asking him to be her friend!

"I-I th-think that would be . . . r-real nice," he managed to say.

The two sat there, conscious that they had been given to one another. Finally Josh smiled at Rena, shaking his head. "You learn a lot on a coon hunt, d-don't you, R-Rena?"

CHAPTER FIFTEEN
"I'll Never Be a Man Again!"
★

After the coon hunt Rena continually pressured Josh to take her again. He put her off on that, but took her several times after small game—rabbits and squirrels. She was never able to hit much, and she hated it when Josh did. The first time he knocked over a plump rabbit and picked up the limp, bloody carcass, Rena had taken one look and cried, "Oh, the poor thing!"

Josh had given her an astonished look, then asked, "W-well, did you think I was g-gonna *kiss* it, R-Rena?" She had refused to look at it and begged him not to shoot another one. "What about th-that bacon you had for b-breakfast?" Josh had grinned slyly. "You think that p-pig died of old age?" But Rena had prevailed, and they had spent the afternoon tramping through the woods.

David had noted that Rena was constantly begging Josh to do something or other and one morning commented on it to Susanna. The two of them were walking along the lane that led to the main road when Rena and Josh appeared at the edge of the woods, the girl's clear laughter sounding on the fresh April air. "She keeps that boy hopping, doesn't she?"

Susanna glanced at the pair and nodded. "He's been very good for her, David," she said. "She's been lonely for a long time."

"I know. Glad Dad thought of hiring the boy. He's as hard a worker as I ever saw—and he can make anything under the sun, I do believe!"

They ambled down the lane, enjoying the brilliant colors of the oaks and maples, then turned at the edge of the woods and made their way slowly along the split-rail fence. Abruptly David said, "Lowell's no better." His face was lined with pain, and he shook his head with desperation. "Just sits in that room and broods. You'd think he'd at least talk to his brother about it."

"He won't talk about his injury to anyone, David."

"I know, and that's bad. You know how some of the men are at Chimborazo? They make a joke about their wounds."

"Lowell will have to learn to accept this, but he's all shut up in himself. Your father is worried sick, and I guess I am, too."

David looked at her, and a startled expression came to his face. *If Grandmother's worried, things are even worse than I thought!* He took a few more steps, then halted and turned to her. "I wish I were a stronger man," he said, a sad note in his voice. "More like my brother Dent."

"Don't you ever say that!" A fierce light came to Susanna's eyes, and she seized his arm and shook him angrily. "I won't have you talk like that, David!"

He blinked at her in astonishment, for she was not given to such outbursts. He smiled suddenly, then reached out and wrapped his hands around hers, holding them tightly. "Always take up for me, don't you, Grandmother?"

"You're who you are, and God made you that way, David. I don't want to hear you put yourself down again!" She saw that her sudden outburst had stunned him and made herself wait until she grew calmer. "I'm not Belle Boyd, the glamorous Rebel spy, but you don't want me to be, do you?" When he burst into laughter at the absurdity of her statement, she touched his arm saying, "God made you, and he made Dent. He needs both of you, so let's hear no more foolishness!"

★ ★ ★

"Oh, come on, Josh!" Rena begged. She had nagged him into taking her into the woods to look for the eggs of wild birds for her collection, but as they emerged, she'd asked him to take her fishing.

"I don't have t-time, Rena," Josh had protested. Looking across the field, he spotted Susanna and David Rocklin and said guiltily, "Now l-look, there's y-your grandmother and your brother!"

Rena gave a careless look at the two, then shook her head, her long dark hair swinging over her back. "They don't care what I do." She tugged at his arm and turned her eyes up at him—a tactic that she'd discovered would make him do almost anything she asked. "Come on, Josh, let's go!"

But Josh shook his head stubbornly. "No, I c-can't do it. I g-got work to do!" But when she continued to hold his arm and plead, he said finally, "W-well, we can go l-late this afternoon, I guess."

"Good!" Rena's eyes gleamed with victory, and she turned and ran away, saying, "I'll go dig some worms, and we can get some liver from Dorrie for catfish bait!"

Josh stared at her, then shook his head, mumbling, "I got t-to quit g-givin' in to that g-girl!" Then he hurried after her, turning to go to the forge, where he spent an hour working on various chores. Box, the elderly blacksmith, grinned at him as he worked, saying slyly, "Glad you fin' a little time to work, Josh." He was seventy-two and had been the blacksmith for the Rocklins since he was a young man. His hair was white as cotton, but his upper body was as powerful as ever from years at the forge. His world was no larger than Gracefield, and he wanted it that way. "Guess making a wagon wheel ain't as much fun as runnin' around with a purty gal, is it, Josh?"

Josh looked up from the forge, his face glowing from the heat. He knew Box was teasing him, but he didn't mind. Box was his teacher, and he had become fast friends with the slave. He looked at the piece of steel critically, then took it over to the anvil and picked up a hammer. Box watched as the boy began to strike the white-hot metal, nodding with approval. *He's a good one. Don't nevah waste his strength none. Always hits jes' right.*

When Josh finished the job, he put his tools away, saying, "I've got to go see Miss Rooney, Box. See you later."

He left the shop and went to the Big House, where he found Rooney in the kitchen shelling peas with Susanna. "Hello, Josh." Rooney smiled at him as he entered. "Come on and help us shell peas." She knew how he hated that kind of work and said quickly, "Just teasing." She rose and put the peas on the table, saying, "Something's wrong with Lowell's wheelchair. It's hard to roll."

"I'll t-take a look."

"I'll go with you. I'll be back to help with the peas, Miz Rocklin."

The two of them moved out of the kitchen, and the boy asked, "How is he?"

"His leg is healing well, but . . ." Rooney didn't finish, and Josh understood her anxiety. The two of them entered the room and found Lowell in the bed. Several magazines were scattered on the coverlet, but he was simply staring out the window.

"Josh has come to fix your chair, Lowell," Rooney said. "You need to get outside and get some of this good spring air in your lungs."

Lowell merely looked at her, then said, "Hello, Josh."

"Hello, M-Mr. Lowell," Josh answered quickly. *He looks better than the last time I saw him,* he thought. He let his eyes drop to the brightly colored spread that covered the injured man, and marked the flatness where Lowell's leg should be. Quickly he averted his eyes, turned, and walked to the wheelchair. As he examined the chair, he listened as Rooney tried to carry on a conversation with Lowell. But it was hopeless, and Josh thought of how miserable it had been trying to speak with him.

He looked at the chair, then turned to say, "N-needs a new axle."

"Can you fix it, Josh?" Rooney asked.

She was wearing a yellow dress that Josh had never seen before—one of Rena's he guessed. *She sure does look nice,* Josh thought. *If lookin' at her don't pick up Mr. Lowell's spirits, I don't know what will!* "Oh, sure," he said. "Have to t-take it with m-me, though."

Lowell had been looking down at his marred outline. Now he lifted his head and said bitterly, "Go on, take it. I'm not going anywhere."

"You will be, Lowell," Rooney said quickly.

"Where would I go, to a ball? I could charm all the ladies with my new one-step waltz!"

There was such anger in Lowell's voice that Josh wanted to help him. "Aw, Mr. Lowell, you'll b-be gettin' around soon."

"In a wheelchair? No, thanks!"

Josh spoke before he thought, but he had grown very fond of Lowell during the days they had worked together. "You can g-get a new leg. L-lots of men—"

"Shut up!" Lowell glared at the boy, his eyes hot with anger. He had kept to his room, refusing to leave except on rare occasions, and his nerves were ragged. Night after night he had lain awake, hoping to die, and when that hadn't happened, he had searched for something to do with his life.

But there was nothing—or so he had decided. All his life he'd been active riding, hunting, and fishing. And none of those things could be done by a man with one leg. Sometimes he'd have a quick, vivid memory of a dance, of gliding around the room easily, looking into the eyes of a young woman, and a terrible fury would come, sweeping over him like a red tide. He'd taken his health for granted, and now that he was crippled, there was nothing in him, no resources to fall back on.

And so he lay in his bed—or sat in a chair—and stared out the window. And he treated people miserably! He lashed out at his grandmother, at Rooney, and at the slaves, shouting with a rage that rose in him unbidden. He let the loss of his leg turn him into a monster.

Now he stared at Josh, who had dropped his head, and felt shame. But he could not apologize, so he said, "Go on, fix the chair. I can sit in it and look out the window."

Josh left without a word, and Lowell glanced at Rooney, expecting her to berate him for his shameful outburst. But she merely began cleaning up the room, and finally her silence grated on him. "Well, go on and say it!" he growled.

Rooney turned to face him, her voice gentle. "Say what?"

"Tell me I'm an ingrate!" He ground out the words. His lips were contorted in an expression of self-loathing, and his eyes were filled with misery. "Say it! I could have been killed. Or tell me that other men have lost their legs without turning into . . . sullen beasts!"

Rooney's eyes filled with compassion, and she sat down on the edge of the bed. "You mustn't think such things, Lowell," she said gently. She wanted to put her arms around him and hold him as she'd held Buck when he was small and had come to her with his hurts. But she was wise enough to know that this was not the time—not yet. "You've had a bad time—worse than most men. Nobody can blame you for . . ."

When Rooney halted, Lowell suddenly grinned—the first sign of any humor she'd seen! "Acting like a spoiled brat?" he said. "Oh, don't be afraid to say it, Rooney. Don't you think I know how ungrateful I've been?"

"You mustn't—"

He waved his hand impatiently, cutting off her words. "I know what you've done, coming here and nursing me and Mark. But Mark's easy to take care of. I'm the one causing all the trouble." He had been sitting up, his back braced against the pillows. Now he slumped, and the anger and bitterness seemed to fade—at least for a time. He sat there silently, then looked up at Rooney, saying in a tightly controlled voice, "Other men have handled this, Rooney, but I can't. I never will."

"You will, Lowell!" Rooney could no longer refrain from touching him. She took his hand in hers, looking directly into his troubled eyes. Hope glowed in her eyes, and her lips parted softly as she spoke. "I know it'll be hard. There'll be some things you won't be able to do as well, but some things you'll learn to do better than before!"

Lowell stared at her. "What could a one-legged man do better than one who's got both legs?" he demanded.

"Why, Lowell Rocklin, I expect you could do just about anything you wanted to do!"

Her statement shocked Lowell, and then he demanded again, "What could I do better with only one leg?"

Rooney was very quick, and she at once replied, "Why, you could invent something." She read the surprise in his eyes and rushed to say, "I know you don't like to talk about the balloon, but it was wonderful, Lowell, the way you made it! Gen. Able told Mister Clay that he wished you'd make another one. He said it wasn't your fault that it got hit by a shell!"

"Not enough silk in Richmond for another one—even if we used ladies underwear!"

His faint attempt at humor encouraged Rooney, and she squeezed his hand. "I guess not. But you could make something else for the army. And Josh and I would help!"

Lowell's eyes grew thoughtful, and he was very much aware of the firmness of her hand, which held his tightly. He could smell the faint lilac perfume that she used, and the sun shone on her hair, catching the gold glints in the auburn tresses.

For a moment she thought he was about to agree, and her spirit soared. But then he sighed and turned his head away from her. He pulled his hand free and muttered, "No, I'm just a cripple."

His words destroyed the brightness of her smile, and she whispered, "No, Lowell!"

But he turned to face her, and she saw that his eyes had gone dead. He shook his head slowly, saying, "I'll never be a man again, Rooney—not a whole one anyway."

"You can try, Lowell!" she pleaded.

"No! If I can't be a whole man, I don't see any use in anything." He rolled over, turning his back to her. Slowly she rose and without a word left the room.

Lowell lay on his side, sick at heart. Outside his window he could hear a group of blackbirds making their raucous cries. He kept his eyes tightly shut, trying to shut out the world. A vision of Rooney's face rose before him, and he heard her whisper, *You can try, Lowell!*

But he lay there facing the wall and knew that he would never be what others wanted him to be. *I can't do it!* he cried silently. *It'll all be pity, and I can't take that!*

CHAPTER SIXTEEN
Mark and Rooney

★

"Look, Buck, the army's like a pyramid," Clay explained to the boy who sat beside him in a weathered cane-bottomed chair. The two of them had come in from a quick tour around the plantation and now were waiting for Josh to bring the buggy up from the barn.

Buck had been asking Clay question after question about the army, and Clay had answered them patiently. He was looking rested now, all the strain of battle that recent skirmishes had etched into his face was gone. A notebook was on the seat of an empty chair beside him, and he tore a page out of it, fished in his pocket for a pencil, then began to draw a diagram of a pyramid.

"Right here at the top is Gen. Lee. He's the commander of the Army of Northern Virginia. But that army is divided into two parts, what we call *corps*. Gen. Longstreet commands one and Gen. Jackson the other."

Buck studied the page, then asked, "Which corps are you in, Captain?"

"Jackson's corps," Clay said. "But a corps is divided up into *divisions*—usually two or three, each one commanded by a general. A division's usually got somewhere between two to four thousand men."

"That's a lot!"

"Yes, it is—too many for one man to keep up with. So each division is divided into *brigades.* See?" Clay drew on the paper and watched the boy follow it intently. *He's a bright boy—reminds me of David.* He drew more lines, saying, "And each brigade is divided up into what we call *regiments,* usually about five hundred men."

Buck glanced up at Clay, admiration in his sharp features. "It's really complicated, ain't it?"

"Sure is, but it has to be this way. Sometimes the army has to move quick, Buck, and it can only do that if the privates know what to do." He leaned back and smiled at the bright-faced youngster. "Now Gen. Lee can't come and say to every private, 'Soldier, get ready to march!' No, that wouldn't do. So he tells his corps commanders, and they tell the division commanders under them, then they pass the word along to brigade commanders, and they yell at the officers of the regiment—that's the next unit on the pyramid. Every regiment has ten *companies.* And I think, Buck, the company is the most important unit of all."

"Why is that, Captain?"

"It's small enough so the captain over it can know every man. He's like a father to them, sees after them, you know? And most of us, when we're asked which unit we're with, will name our company—like I'll say, 'I'm in C Company.'"

"And what does a lieutenant do in the company?"

"Look here, Buck," Clay said, pointing at the pyramid.

"Here's C Company, and there are two platoons. My son Lt. Denton is over the First Platoon. He leaned back and watched the boy study the chart, then nodded. "That's pretty well the way all armies are made up, Buck. Think you understand it?"

"Sure!"

Clay smiled and tore out a fresh sheet of paper. "All right, let's see you draw that pyramid." He took the pencil sketch, folded it, and watched as Buck fell to drawing, his whole attention on the paper. Josh pulled up in the buggy, and Clay

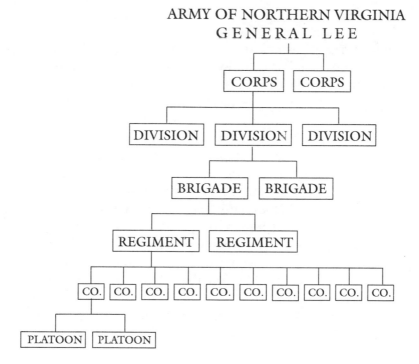

ARMY OF NORTHERN VIRGINIA
GENERAL LEE

said, "I'll go up and say good-bye to Lowell, Josh. Wait for me."

Josh nodded, then slipped out of the buggy and mounted to the porch as Clay stepped into the house. Clay walked quickly down the hall, opened the door, and entered. "Came to say good-bye, Son," he said to Lowell, who was sitting in his wheelchair holding a book. Not wanting to tower over Lowell, he sat down quickly in the straight-backed chair, studying the boy's face. *He's pale as a ghost, and he's lost too much weight* was his thought, but he said only, "Hate to leave, but the army's moving right away."

Lowell said, "I wish you didn't have to go."

"Well, it'll be over someday, Lowell." Clay leaned back and sighed deeply. "The world's upside down, but it's been that way before and it'll be that way again. The thing to do when that happens is just to hang on until it comes right again."

"I guess so."

Lowell's reply was without energy, and for the entire ten minutes that Clay sat there, he replied to questions but offered nothing of his own. Finally Clay despaired, hating to leave but knowing that he must. Leaning forward, he said intently, "Son, I know this has hit you hard, but you've got a lot of life ahead of you. You can't hide in this room for the next thirty years." He spoke passionately and with compassion, but it was useless. Finally he saw that he was speaking to a man who'd given up on life, so he rose and moved to stand over Lowell. He bent down, embraced him, and said huskily, "God keep you, my son!" Then he waited, but Lowell only stared at him, saying nothing except, "I hope you come back safe—and with both legs."

Clay turned and walked from the room defeated and frustrated. He found Buck on the porch holding out his sheet of paper, asking, "Is this right?"

Clay stared at it blindly, then made himself focus on the drawing. "Yes, Buck. Exactly right. You'll make a good soldier someday."

"Maybe I can go with you now," Buck piped up eagerly. "Some of them drummer boys ain't no older than me!"

Bitterness came to Clay as he stared at the boy's youthful countenance, but he mustered a smile. "Stay here and take care of your sister, Buck. You're only a boy once, and there's no going back to live it again." He reached out and shook the boy's hand, then turned to say, "Let's go, Josh."

"Yes, sir!"

The two men got into the buggy, and Josh slapped the reins, startling the team into an abrupt trot. Getting to the main road, he turned their heads toward Richmond. For several miles neither man spoke. Finally Clay pulled himself together and turned to say, "I appreciate your driving me to camp, Josh." When the boy muttered that it was no trouble, Clay studied him more closely.

All the Yancy boys look like copies, he thought, then said, "I think Lonnie will make sergeant pretty soon. He's a fine soldier, but so is your other brother." Lonnie was in Clay's company, and Bob had just rejoined the company after recuperating from the leg wound he received at Fredericksburg.

"I g-get to thinkin' I ought to b-be in with them, C-Captain."

"No, you're too young! And besides, you're doing an important job."

"Raising p-pigs?"

"Doesn't sound like much, but the army will starve if it doesn't get food. And some fools are so busy raising cotton they won't have a thing for the soldiers!" Clay had made a cause of this, trying to get his fellow planters to see that the docks were full of cotton that could not be sold. *Why grow more?* he'd asked but had been ignored. All most Southern planters could think of was cotton, and they'd plant it until the bales reached the heavens.

Shrugging off his anger, Clay leaned back and thought about his family. Finally he said, "You've been good for Rena, Josh." He noted the boy's nervous glance and chuckled, slapping him on the shoulder. "You afraid I'd be a mad father, jumping all over you for taking my girl hunting?"

Josh colored but turned to face the big man squarely. "Y-yes, sir, that's about w-what I expected."

"You should know better," Clay said. "You've known Rena since you were children. And you know that since her mother died, and since I'm gone, she gets lonesome."

"I seen that." Josh wanted to say more but felt decidedly awkward. The distance in Southern society between a poor white farmer and a plantation owner was much like the distance between stars.

But Clay said, "You're an honest young man, Josh. I didn't hire you just to do the work." He was amused at Josh's look of astonishment and added, "I wanted you to be there to help Lowell. And now I see I was wiser than I knew. Because now it's pretty clear that Rena needs someone, too."

"I-I think the w-world of both of 'em, Mister Clay!"

"I know that, Josh, and it takes some of the pain out of leaving just to know that you'll be around." He hesitated, then said, "Lowell isn't easy to be with, but I hope you'll try to spend time with him. Get him interested in something—anything! He's got to get out of that room!"

Josh nodded sharply. "Miss Rooney and m-me talked about th-that."

"That's a bright young woman, Josh. What'd she say?"

Clay listened carefully as Josh slowly spun out the scheme that he and Rooney had put together. It took some time, for Josh halted often, angered by his impediment. The words were there, but they seemed to get lodged in his tongue. Finally he said, "So we h-hope it'll help him, C-Captain."

"You know, it just might!" Clay sat up, his back rigid with excitement. "It just might work!" He slapped his thigh hard and shook his head angrily. "I hate to go! By heaven, I do!" Then he caught himself and took a deep breath. Expelling it slowly, he said evenly, "But nobody wants to go off and fight—unless he's a fool!"

"Where w-will you be f-fighting, Captain?"

"I don't know for sure, Josh," Clay said slowly, then his eyes turned north. "Somewhere north of here. Maybe even Maryland again."

Josh looked in the direction Clay had indicated, then shook his head. "Tell Lonnie and B-Bob to be c-careful." He paused and added shyly, "And you t-too, Mister Clay!"

"It's in God's hands, Josh," Clay said heavily. "All we can do is pray!"

★　★　★

The good days were full of dull, throbbing pain—something a man could bear. One could bear a toothache for a day, and if Mark thought of it like that, it seemed easier: *A toothache in the side, that's all it is.*

But the bad days were different. The pain came at unexpected moments, such as when he was lifting a spoon of hot chicken soup to his lips. He'd never been stuck with a bayonet, but the pain was like that—or so he thought—a sliver of hot steel stabbing without warning into his side! There was no controlling it—his whole body would arch in protest, sending the soup spoon flying. *If it would only begin easy, I could get ready for it!* Mark would think, but it never did. Always it was unexpected, and it never failed to send him into a gasping spasm.

Some days they didn't come—and the day that Clay came to say good-bye was one of his good days. The pain gnawed dully at his side and stomach, but he could bear that and covered it with a smile on his pale lips. He'd talked with Clay, urging him not to make a fool of himself by rushing into danger, then had halted abruptly. "But it does no good to warn you, Clay. I know you better than to think you'll take care of yourself." He'd spoken of Lowell, promising to do what he could, but neither man had much hope.

After Clay had left, Mark had gotten out of bed and moved carefully to the window, where he'd watched the two men leave for Richmond. Carefully he straightened up, and a surprised look crossed his thin face as there was little pain.

"Well, you're going to behave yourself, are you?" He had gotten into the absurd habit of speaking to his wound, addressing it as if it were a familiar enemy. "Well, then, I'll just take advantage of your good behavior by getting dressed and getting about a bit."

He walked into the kitchen half an hour later, and Dorrie stared at him with a startled expression. "Whut you doin' outta dat bed!" she snorted. "Miss Susanna ain't said nuffin' 'bout you gettin' up!"

"Had to have some of your good cooking, Dorrie," Mark said with a smile. "My sister-in-law won't bring me anything but soup with weeds in it."

"Dem ain't weeds!" Dorrie snapped. "Dat's *parsley,* and it's good fo' you!"

Mark had been fond of Dorrie for years and had always loved to tease her. "Now, Dorrie, I know a weed when I see one," he insisted. "I'm not here for soup with weeds in it, anyway."

"Well, whut *does* you wants?" Dorrie demanded.

Mark closed his eyes as if thinking and counted off the items on his fingers: "A chicken-fried steak with lots of mushrooms. Some hush puppies and fried catfish, with lots of hot sauce to go on it. Oh yes, some oysters covered with black pepper—"

"Mr. Mark! You done los' yo' mind?" Dorrie stood in the center of the floor, staring at the tall man aghast. "Why, dat stuff would kill you daid!" At that moment Susanna and Rooney entered, and Dorrie informed them of the demands the sick man had made. She didn't see the wink he gave the two women, but was outraged and refused to have anything to do with it!

"I'll fix something for him, Dorrie," Susanna said, smiling, and Dorrie huffed off breathing dire prophecies about what would happen if the patient was allowed to eat such things!

"It's wonderful to see you're feeling better, Mark," Susanna said with a bright smile. "Sit down, and I'll fix you something good. Rooney, you eat with him." When Rooney started to protest, she said firmly, "Am I the mistress of this house? Do as I tell you!"

Rooney sat down but was not afraid. She had learned that there was nothing to fear from Susanna Rocklin. And she was quick enough to know that Susanna wanted her to spend time with her brother-in-law, so she began speaking at once, and soon Mark was resting in a chair, listening as Rooney related the tale of the coon hunt.

"I'd like to have seen that bobcat and Josh rolling around on the ground," he said when she had finished. "Did Rena like it?"

The two sat there until Susanna brought a plate of fluffy eggs and dry toast with the crust removed. "You can't have anything with grease, Mark, but I've got some fresh dewberry jam, the kind you like so much."

Mark ate only a little but enjoyed the company. He said so later when he and Rooney went out for a short walk—orders of Mrs. Susanna Rocklin.

"I'm glad to get outside," he said, breathing the fresh warm air. "Didn't know how much I liked the outdoors until I couldn't have it."

"It is nice. I've always loved spring best of any time of the year," Rooney said. "I grew up in the city, so I never really got to enjoy all the flowers and budding trees." She thought briefly of those days, then said shortly, "I hope I never have to go back there again!"

They were passing the scuppernong arbor, and Mark was growing tired. "Let's sit and rest here." When they were seated, he said idly, "You didn't like the city, Rooney?"

"Oh, I hated it! But there wasn't anyplace else for me to go. . . ." Without meaning to, she began to speak of her life. She was not aware of how skillful the man who sat beside her was at drawing people out, and it was with a shock that she suddenly realized that she had told him more than she intended.

"Oh, I didn't mean to go into all that!"

Mark smiled at her, saying, "I'm glad you told me about yourself, Rooney." His cheeks had some color in them, and the pain was mild—for the moment. "It was a difficult life—for you and for Buck, too. And I'm sure you'll never have to go back to that sort of thing."

But his words caused Rooney's brow to crease, and her eyes grew cloudy with doubt. "I worry about that," she said quietly. She had not confessed this to anyone else, but somehow the man sitting beside her was so kind! "We can't stay here always," she added. "I love my mom, but when she's out of prison, I don't think we can go back to living the way we did. This place has been so good for Buck. Who knows what would happen if he started hanging around those bad men again. But I don't know what else we can do."

Mark began to offer her reassurance. "Maybe when your

ma gets released, she'll see how much better this place is for you than a saloon. And Susanna needs you, Rooney. Even after the war, she'll need you. I think . . ."

He spoke quietly and was rewarded by seeing that his words were giving comfort to the girl beside him. But just as she seemed to be fully at peace about her future, the pain came to Mark. He was saying quietly, "And Buck will be able to go to school—"

Then it hit him, like a white-hot saber driven to the hilt into his side. He gasped and grabbed at his side, his face drained white as paste.

"Mr. Mark!" Rooney saw him falling to one side and quickly leaped to hold him. At first she was afraid he was dying, but he managed to gasp, "Don't . . . worry! Just a . . . bad spell!"

Rooney saw Highboy working on a window of the house and cried out, "Highboy, help me!" When he came galloping up, she said, "Help me get Mr. Rocklin to his room!"

Highboy practically carried the stricken man up the steps, and Rooney moved ahead, opening doors. When they got to Mark's room, Rooney said, "Be easy, Highboy. Put him on the bed."

The two of them eased him down, and Highboy asked nervously, "You wants me to fetch Miz Susanna?"

"No, Highboy. Thank you, but it's all right now."

The slave left, and Rooney pulled off Mark's shoes, then began to loosen his clothes. Then she looked at his contorted face and turned at once to the washstand. Taking a brown bottle from the shelf, she poured a few ounces into a small glass, then returned and placed it to his lips. He swallowed it, and she replaced the bottle. She had grown efficient in taking care of large men and soon had his clothing off. Carefully she removed the bandage on his side and saw that his wound was draining an unhealthy stream of yellowish fluid. Quickly she cleaned the wound, dressed it, then sat down beside him, saying, "Are you feeling better, Mr. Mark?"

The opiate was taking effect, and he moved his head slowly toward her. The searing pain had subsided, dulled by the drug, and his eyes were heavy lidded.

"Yes," he whispered. "Thank you, Rooney!" He licked his lips, then shook his head. "That was . . . a very bad one!"

Rooney rose and got a pan of cool water and a cloth and bathed the sweat from his face. He lay still with his eyes closed, and she thought he had passed out. But then he opened his eyes and stared at her. She could not read the expression in his dark eyes, and finally she asked, "What is it, Mr. Mark? Can I get you something?"

He didn't answer but continued to examine her through drug-dulled eyes. Finally he whispered, "How old are you, Rooney?"

"Why, I'm seventeen."

He found that interesting and after a long pause whispered, "Seventeen . . . and a fine young woman."

The clock on the wall tolled the seconds, and once again he began to slide away into unconsciousness. But again the eyes opened, and his lips moved.

"I was in love with a young woman once."

"You were, sir?"

"Oh yes. . . ." His eyes began to droop, and he forced them up with an effort. His lips were dry, and she gave him a drink, then put his head down.

Rooney knew a little of the Rocklin family history. She knew that Lowell had told her that Uncle Mark had never been married. *Maybe he married her and kept their marriage secret from everyone,* she thought. Rooney asked, "What was her name?"

"Her name was . . . Beth." Mark gazed at Rooney through haze-filled eyes. "You . . . you remind me of her. . . . So beautiful."

"What happened to her, sir? Did you marry?" Rooney asked quickly, for she could see Mark slipping away again.

"She . . . she . . . so beautiful." And then Mark was unconscious.

183

Rising, she slipped out of the room and went to find Susanna, who was alarmed over the incident. "Oh, he's asleep now," Rooney assured her. She and the older woman spoke about the care he'd need, and then Rooney asked, making her tone casual, "Did Mr. Mark ever marry?"

"No. We all hoped he would, but he never did."

"That's too bad," Rooney said. "He would have made some woman very happy."

CHAPTER SEVENTEEN
"Let Us Cross over the River"

Gen. Robert E. Lee led the Army of Northern Virginia, determined to hit the Union army such a blow that the Peace party in the North would force Lincoln to end the struggle.

Clay Rocklin and the members of C Company of the Stonewall Brigade saw him as he rode by on Traveler. "Look at him. That's Bobby Lee!" Lonnie Yancy breathed. "Ain't he somethin' now? And look at that hoss!"

The horse was iron gray, sixteen hands high, with a short back, deep chest, and small head. His delicate ears moved constantly as he bore his burden proudly. He was the jewel of his master's hands, guided by word and not by rein.

The rider, too, was iron gray, his hair and beard now frosted. Lee had a broad forehead, deep-set eyes, straight nose, firm lips. He was all grace and symmetry, and unlike Stonewall Jackson, whose strength was hammered, his was beneath the surface. He was loved and idolized as no other general on either side, one of those men who can cause other men to follow them to their death. He was a firm Christian, believed in his country with all his soul, but he could not lift his sword against his native state. Virginia was home and family, and he threw himself into what he knew was a losing struggle because of his love for this land.

Clay watched Lee ride past with his staff, then turned to Lonnie Yancy, saying, "Yes, he's something all right."

"Don't see how we can lose," Lonnie said, eyeing the general ride down the line of march. He was so much like his father that Clay thought of Buford. He had the same lanky strength and green eyes and the same determination. Lonnie had joined the army before Bull Run and had fought in every engagement. Clay had tried to get him to stay home and take care of his father's farm, but Lonnie had said stubbornly, "No, sir, I'm gonna fight for mah rights!"

Now Clay looked at this tall man and thought how typical he was of the army that now wound around between two hills like a butternut-colored serpent.

His rights? Why, Lonnie doesn't even know what they are! he thought almost wearily. *He never owned a slave and never will, but he's going to war to fight for the right to own one.*

But the Army of Northern Virginia was composed of men like Lonnie Yancy. It was an army of hunters, riders, walkers—men who lived close to the ground. They were rebels against the new age of the machine birthed in the North, loving the dirt of the South fanatically.

Clay's eyes ran down the ranks of his own company, noting how *different* they were. His eye fell on Sam Griffin, who had come to war with nothing but his pants and shirts—and a rifle one of his ancestors had used at King's Mountain in the American Revolution. His eyes moved to James Huger, who'd first come to the Grays with a haircloth trunk full of fine shirts and a body servant to mend them. Clay smiled at how Huger had been tormented until he'd shared the shirts and sent the slave home. Now he wore the same rough clothing and floppy hat as Sam Griffin.

"Think we'll whip the Yankees, Clay?"

Turning quickly, Clay looked up at his brother-in-law, Maj. Brad Franklin, who was mounted on a fine bay stallion. He was dressed in a new uniform and looked every inch a soldier, his intense face smiling with anticipation.

Clay liked this man and nodded. Knowing that his men

needed to hear him speak positively, he answered, "We'll wear them out, Major. My boys are ready for a scrap!"

Franklin looked at the lean, tanned faces of the men of C Company and nodded. "I think we'll do them in this time, Captain. Never saw the army so fired up." His face grew serious. "Keep your head down, Clay." He grinned, then spurred his horse and rode down the line, pausing to speak to the men from time to time.

"We got some good officers, Captain." Waco Smith, the ex-Texas Ranger had moved up to walk beside Clay. He was a tall man who still wore a .44 in a holster on his thigh. He had the most direct gaze of any man Clay had ever seen— and was a tiger in battle.

"Got the best noncoms, too," Clay said fondly. "You mind what the major said, Waco. Don't get yourself shot." He added lightly to cover his concern, "Too hard for me to break in a new sergeant."

Waco Smith shot a quick glance at Clay, then grinned. "I was fixin' to say that about officers," he remarked dryly. The two marched along, speaking quietly of the affairs of the company. For both of them it was, for now, the center of their worlds. The men who marched with them were their concern, and each knew that when the battle was over, some of the men who walked with them would not be there.

Thinking, perhaps, of this, Waco finally shook his head. "Bad about Lowell. But at least he won't get killed." Both of them knew of men who had shot their hands off to get out of going into battle, and Waco added, "Lowell's going to make it, ain't he, Clay?"

"Yes." Clay's voice was slow, and he added, "But he's taking it bad, Waco."

"Figured he would. Young fella like that, he wants to be best at things. But he'll be all right." Waco looked back over the line, studied it, then shrugged. There was a streak of fatalism in the Texan, and he remarked, "Guess we'll lose some, Captain." The thought stayed with him, and his eyes were half hooded as he finally asked, "Why do some of us get killed and some don't?"

"No man knows the answer to that, Waco," Clay responded. He had wondered himself about this, but had come to believe that such questions had no answer. "A man can only do his best, and the rest is up to God."

The answer didn't satisfy Waco Smith, and as they moved along toward the north, he said, "Don't seem to fit, Captain, but it's shore the way things are." He had the old soldier's habit of putting such philosophical quandaries into some deep recess of his mind, and he became more cheerful. "How strong you think we are? And how many Bluebellies aim to stop us?"

"We've got about sixty thousand men, I think," Clay answered. "Don't know how many we'll be facing."

Smith looked through the clouds of dust raised by the feet of thousands of marching men. "Wal, there'll be more of them than they is of us." He spoke almost lightly, without concern. The veterans of the Army of Northern Virginia were accustomed to long odds. But they felt as Waco did as he dismissed the superior numbers, saying, "As long as we got Bobby Lee and Stonewall, I don't keer how many of them we got to fight. . . ."

Neither Waco, Clay, nor even Gen. Robert E. Lee could see into the future—no more than could Gen. Joe Hooker, who was leading the Army of the Potomac to meet them. Hooker had replaced Burnside after the Union failure at Fredericksburg.

The new general, forty-nine years old, was a graduate of West Point and a veteran of the Seminole and Mexican wars who had served in the Regular Army until 1853. At the outbreak of the Civil War he had been commissioned a brigadier general and had fought with distinction in several battles, earning the nickname "Fighting Joe." He had a reputation for loose living, loose talk, and insubordination, but his bravery and aggressive spirit were beyond question. In Lincoln's opinion these qualities outweighed his defects.

Hooker waited until April of 1863 was almost over, and the men knew that as soon as the roads were dry the new campaign would begin. After months of inactivity, they looked forward to it.

Lee's army still occupied its defensive position overlooking Fredericksburg. Hooker knew from Burnside's disastrous experience that a frontal attack would be fatal. Instead he planned a wide sweep around Lee's left flank, leaving a third of his army to cross the Rappahannock and hold Lee in his entrenchments. The Confederate commander, with 60,000 men—compared with Hooker's 134,000—would be in danger of annihilation if the Union movements succeeded.

The battle began on May 1. Lee, with characteristic audacity, divided his army and attacked Hooker's advancing force. The Union commander, having heard that Lee had been heavily reinforced, faltered, and the day's fighting ended inconclusively.

That night Lee and Stonewall Jackson decided upon a bold movement. Having found a guide who knew the way through the tangled wilderness, Lee sent Jackson with twenty-six thousand men across the front only two or three miles away to strike at Hooker's exposed right flank. It was a terrible risk for the Confederate army, for if Hooker struck Lee's remaining force, he would destroy it.

★ ★ ★

The men of the Richmond Grays saw little of the overall strategy of the battle of Chancellorsville. When Clay awakened them just before dawn, it was still too dark to see, but they could hear firing, skirmishers in heated dispute with the Federals.

They ate a hurried breakfast, and at six o'clock they heard the first artillery fire. Soon rolling clouds of powder smoke rose slowly, and the furious, ripping sound of small arms in volley ascended. Through the tangled wilderness, they saw balloons of smoke and points of muzzle blast from Federal gun positions.

Lonnie Yancy, standing beside Clay, stared at the blue forces that were gathering for the charge. "I didn't know there was so many of 'em!" he whispered.

They could hear their shouts of command, see the froth coming from the hardworking artillery horses as battery after battery was wheeled up, unlimbered, and run out, muzzles toward the Confederates. The Union flags snapped in the breeze, and mounted staff officers in clusters watched the army prepare.

"You wanted Yankees," Waco Smith said, grinning at the men. "Well, there they are—and hyar they come!"

The bugles sounded, and the blue carpet began to move, unrolling to the hoarse coughing of the cannons. They splashed across the small creek, some falling to turn the water crimson, but their places were filled by others.

Clay called out, "Fire by volley!" and he waited until the approaching wave of soldiers was fifty yards away before yelling, "Fire!"

The blue line suddenly was scattered and tossed by the hot lead. Clay yelled, "Come on, C Company!" He leaped forward, holding his pistol, and glanced down the line to see that Dent was leading his own men in the charge.

Lonnie Yancy had knocked down a soldier with his first shot, then reloaded and scrambled into the line. He knew no fear. That came before the battle—or afterward. He heard the high-pitched wailing, sustained and carried through the other noise like the screaming of animals, and realized that he was yelling along with the rest.

A blue-clad soldier appeared—undulating, weaving in the smoke—and he felt the shock of the rifle butt against his shoulder without even being aware that he had raised it. He bit off the end of the next cartridge, rammed it home, hammer back and cap pressed onto the nipple, then fired again. The blue haze ahead took shape, showing faces and arms and bright brass belt buckles.

Beside him he was aware of Sgt. Smith, and ahead was Lt. Dent Rocklin, taking aim and firing as calmly as if he were taking target practice at home. Maj. Franklin rode by on his fine horse, screaming and waving them forward, and other officers joined him.

Clay sent his last shot at the blue horde, then turned and picked up a musket dropped by Zeno Tafton, whose face was shot away. He loaded, fired, then reloaded.

At that moment he saw Brad Franklin ride forward and then reel in the saddle. "Brad!" he shouted and saw him fall to the ground, the horse running away in terror. Clay wanted to go to him, but there was no time.

Wrenching himself away from the scene, he saw that the Yankee line had begun retreating and yelled, "Keep firing!" He kept them at it until the Federals were back across the creek, but even as he ran to Franklin, he heard a slight cry to his right. Wheeling, he turned to see Lonnie Yancy drop his rifle and fall to the ground.

Clay called out, "Lonnie!" but when he bent over the man, he saw that a musket ball had struck him in the temple, killing him instantly.

How will I tell Melora? He was her favorite!

"Captain, Maj. Franklin's pretty bad!"

Clay looked up to see Waco standing over him, his face bloody and his eyes quick with anger. "We gotta get him to the hospital."

"Is he alive?" Clay demanded, as he ran back to where the officer lay.

"Yeah, but gut shot."

Clay saw that Brad Franklin was conscious, but he saw also the pool of blood that poured through his fingers. "They . . . got me this time, Clay!" Brad gasped.

"You'll be all right," Clay answered. Both men knew the chances of surviving a belly wound were almost nil, but Clay said, "We'll get you to the surgeon."

"Clay . . . tell Amy . . . I've always loved her . . . just in case, you know."

Clay nodded, but was filled with a sudden birth of faith. "Brad, I'm no prophet, but I think God's giving me a promise. I believe he's telling me you'll make it."

"Is that right, Clay?" Franklin stared through pain-filled eyes at his brother-in-law, whom he trusted greatly. He gasped, "Then I'll just go on your faith. . . ."

Clay directed the men as they picked Franklin up and carried him off to the hospital. Then he turned and walked down the line to where Bob Yancy was helping a wounded comrade. "Bob?"

Young Yancy glanced at him, and his face grew pale. Rising, he came to stand before Clay. "Is it Lonnie?"

"Yes, Bob." Clay put his hand on the young man's shoulder, adding gently, "He's gone, Bob. Gone to be with Jesus."

Tears sprang to Bob Yancy's eyes. They were always close, and the war brought them even closer together. Memories of childhood and hunting trips flashed through his mind. But he dashed them away and cleared his throat. "I don't know if I can go on without him here in the company."

"We'll all miss him, Bob," Clay said. "And we've got each other to lean on. Remember that."

Bob Yancy gave Clay a grateful look, then said, "I'll take care of him."

At that moment Gen. Jackson came riding up, his eyes pale. The soldiers called him Old Blue Light because of this. "Maj. Franklin is wounded?"

"Yes, sir. I've had him removed from the field," Clay answered.

Jackson wore an old forage cap pulled down over his eyes. He paused for one moment, then said, "I will pray for his recovery. You will take his place. I appoint you brevet major. Take the field, sir!"

The Grays saw little action the rest of that day. And the second day of battle was spent mostly marching through the wilderness to get into position. At twilight Jackson struck Gen. O. O. Howard's Eleventh Corps on the extreme left of the Federal line. Howard's men broke in confusion. Except for the falling night and an agonizing misfortune, a complete rout would have followed.

The misfortune came as Stonewall Jackson rode forward on the turnpike toward Chancellorsville followed by several of his staff. He surveyed the enemy's position, then headed back toward his own lines.

As he rode near to the Confederate troops just placed in position and ignorant that he was in front, the nervous soldiers opened fire on Jackson's party. Two of the number fell from their saddles dead. Jackson spurred his horse forward where he was met by a second volley. The general received three balls at the same instant. One penetrated the palm of his right hand, a second passed around the wrist of his left arm, and a third ball passed through the left arm halfway from shoulder to elbow. The large bone of the upper arm was splintered to the elbow joint, and the wound bled freely.

Jackson reeled in the saddle and was caught by his aide, who laid him on the ground. Dr. Hunter McGuire came at once and saw to the general's removal. As he was carried away, Jackson called out, "Gen. Pember, you must hold your ground, sir!"

At midnight Jackson's left arm was amputated near the shoulder. He made a good recovery at first, but pneumonia struck him and he weakened. On May 10 he died, a smile on his face. He said quietly and with an expression of relief, "Let us cross over the river and rest under the shade of the trees."

The day after Jackson was wounded, the battle resumed. Hooker lost control of himself and never was able to strike a hard blow at his enemy. By the end of the fighting he concluded there was no chance of success. Once again a much stronger Army of the Potomac had been vanquished by a smaller force under a superior general.

After the battle Clay walked beside the wagons loaded with wounded, some of them begging to be killed as they were jolted on the rough roads.

We've lost so many men, he thought, and the faces of the men in his company who had fallen rose in his mind. *This army will never be the same. I just don't see how we can win.*

The promotion to major meant nothing to him. He thought of Lonnie Yancy, buried in a shallow grave, far from the Southern fields he loved so well, and bitterness at the waste of it all rose in his throat. He thought of Brad Franklin, alive but just barely, and could only pray as he trudged along.

He saw in his mind more clearly than he had with his eyes the shattered forms on the field, the gaping wounds, the scattered arms, feet, and legs outside the surgeons' tent, the blood-soaked ground, the staring wide-eyed faces turning black and bloated almost before they could be buried.

He had always hated the war, but now he despised it with an intensity that shook him. But he could not turn back and so swept it from his mind, going from man to man to give what encouragement he could.

CHAPTER EIGHTEEN
To Be a Rocklin

★

The Army of Northern Virginia came home, and Richmond once again was filled with wounded men, for the wagons daily unloaded their bloody bodies at the doors of the hospitals. Chimborazo overflowed, and Mrs. Pember worked night and day caring for the shattered remains that were often dumped unceremoniously at the front of the ward. She longed for the help of people such as Rooney Smith, but knew that the young woman had her hands full at Gracefield.

Clay had come to Chimborazo to visit the members of his squad and, after spending time with each of them, went to Brad Franklin and his sister, Amy. Brad had amazed the entire staff by not dying from the worst type of body wound, and he had shown such improvement that he clamored to be sent to his home. Amy patted his hand as she pleaded with the doctor for this. She won her case, and Clay had volunteered to drive them to the Franklin plantation. He borrowed a wagon and took Brad and Amy home.

Before he could return to Gracefield, Clay had to stop at the Yancy place, for he knew he had to tell the family about the death of Lonnie. When he drove up, he was greeted with enthusiasm by the children, but with restraint by Buford and Melora. Clay said nothing about the death for a time, but finally when the three of them were alone in the cabin, he broached the unpleasant topic. He left nothing out, and the two listened intently. Finally he said huskily, "He was the best soldier in the regiment, Buford. Always up front, never shirked a duty. We'll all miss him greatly."

Buford Yancy sat loosely in a cane-bottomed chair, his sharp face grew tense. He had watched Clay's face during the recital, and now he said softly, "Lonnie was always a dutiful boy. Never was a better son." He said no more, and it was Melora who came to stand behind him and put her hands on his shoulders. The two of them were so still, Clay thought they looked like a portrait.

Then Melora looked at Clay, pride and sorrow mingled in her eyes. "Thank you for telling us, Clay."

That was all. He left soon afterward, promising that he'd give Bob a furlough as soon as he got back. "He's taking this hard, and I think you all need each other right now."

Melora had walked to the wagon with him, and when he got in, she looked up and asked, "Will you be leaving soon for another battle, Clay?"

"Not right away," Clay said. "The army's not ready. I'll be at Gracefield for at least two days. Will you come and visit while I'm there?"

"Yes. I'll come."

Just the promise was enough to lift his spirits, and he smiled, saying what had become a familiar refrain to them: "Soon I won't have to go away, Melora!"

"Soon, Clay," Melora echoed and stood there long after the wagon had jolted away down the rutted road and disappeared behind the line of trees.

When she went back inside, she found her father still seated in the worn chair. He gave her a peculiar look, then when she poured two cups of sassafras tea and brought them over, he asked unexpectedly, "Are you happy to marry him, Melora?"

Melora looked up quickly, aware that the pain of his loss

was sharp. *He's worried about me,* she thought, and then she nodded. "Yes, I am, Pa."

Buford took in the clean sweep of Melora's cheek, the erect figure, and the air of sweetness. He'd lost a son, and now there was an emptiness in him. Nobody could ever take Lonnie's place. Vaguely he was stirred with a desire to see more of the Yancy line, not to take Lonnie's place, but . . . He couldn't explain his feeling but finally made an attempt of sorts. "I hate to see things wasted," he murmured. "God put everything on this earth to be used. . . ."

He broke off, unable to find words to frame the emptiness inside him. But Melora understood. She was a woman of great discernment, and now she put the teacup down and put her hands over his.

"I know, Pa." She waited until his eyes came to meet hers, then nodded. "Don't fret about me. I've had a good life, and I know I'll be happy as the wife of Clay Rocklin."

"I should of made you marry a long time ago."

Melora smiled, and a dimple appeared on her cheek. "Cut a switch to me?" she asked.

Buford smiled at her. Melora could always make him smile. "I guess that wouldn't have worked. But you've give up your girlhood to raise these young 'uns."

"It's what God wanted me to do, Pa," she said simply. Then she squeezed his hands hard, saying, "But they're about raised now, and Clay is free." Her eyes suddenly grew warm, and she whispered, "One day, Pa, you'll have another boy child to hold—mine and Clay's."

She had never spoken like this, but somehow the thing had come to her—not in fragments and bits, but whole and entire. She was as sure of this as she was sure that the sun was in the sky, and the knowledge burned in her with a holy fire.

★ ★ ★

Lowell tried to force himself to be pleasant to his father. Clay had come home as soon as he could and for two days had moved about the plantation, mostly outside with Josh and the hands going over the work. But several times he'd come to sit with Lowell, and it had not been easy, for Lowell's reticence was like a stone wall.

Finally on the second day, Clay said to Rooney, "I can't break through to him, Rooney. It's like he's crawled into a deep cave and won't come out."

"I know," Rooney replied. She and Josh and Rena had tried everything to get Lowell to open up, but nothing had worked. Rooney had accepted Lowell's harsh remarks meekly, never answering in kind, but even that response seemed to anger him. Looking up at Clay, she said suddenly, "Maybe if we could get him to go to just *one* thing, it might get him out of that cave."

Clay stared at her, the idea taking root. "You have an idea, Rooney? About someplace to take him?"

"Well, he got a letter yesterday. It was from a soldier named Jimmy Peck."

Clay's eyebrows went up. "Why, Jimmy's the drummer boy of our company! I saw him at the hospital before I came here."

"Is he hurt bad?"

Clay nodded, pain in his dark eyes. "I'm afraid so Rooney. He's only fifteen years old, an orphan lad. He took some bad wounds, and Mrs. Pember told me he wasn't going to make it."

A cloud crossed Rooney's face. "Poor boy!" she whispered. "Only fifteen. That's younger than Josh and Rena!"

"What did the letter say?"

"He didn't write it himself. One of the women did. He asked Lowell to come and say good-bye to him."

Clay stiffened, and he shook his head, asking at once, "What did Lowell say?"

"He didn't say anything—not to me, anyway," Rooney admitted. Then she looked at him hopefully, adding, "But he didn't say he *wouldn't go*, Mr. Clay. Up until now nobody could even *mention* his leaving the house without making him mad."

"He and Lowell were great friends," Clay said slowly, thinking back. "The two of them were always into something together. Jimmy was such a fun-loving boy. Lowell looked on him as a younger brother, I think."

"Why don't you offer to take him, Mr. Clay?"

"I will!" Clay's jaw grew tight, and he nodded emphatically. "I'll put it to him that he owes it to Jimmy, which he does." Hope came to him and he said, "You come along, Rooney. You'll have to drive him back home."

Clay went at once to Lowell's room, and as soon as he was inside he said, "I just heard about Jimmy wanting you to come and see him."

Lowell gave him a startled look. He was sitting up in bed, reading a book, and for one moment couldn't answer. "I can't go to the hospital."

"Why can't you?" Clay demanded. He put his black eyes on Lowell, adding, "You're able to travel."

Lowell turned pale, and Clay saw that the fear of going outside of the room was torture to the young man. He ached for this son of his, but knew that the greatest kindness he could show was to force him out of the self-imposed prison Lowell had designed. "You're going, Lowell," Clay said evenly. "Make up your mind to it."

A flash of anger leaped to Lowell's eyes. "I'm not a child! You can't make me go!"

Clay said softly, but with a trace of iron in his tone—a tone that Lowell had encountered in the past—"I can't make you behave decently toward Jimmy, but you're going to face him, Son."

"I can't do it!" Lowell's face contorted with fear, and he grabbed at the first excuse that came to him. "My wound! It could start bleeding! I could die!"

This sort of thing had worked with Susanna, but Lowell saw at once that it meant nothing to his father, especially since the wound was mostly healed now. Clay Rocklin's eyes drew half shut, and he said, "Son, I'd rather see you die than go on being the sort of man you've become! You're a Rocklin! I know you lost a leg. Well, I'm sorry for that. But it doesn't give you the right to curl up like a whipped dog and whimper about how pitiful you are!"

"I don't—"

"Lowell, you're going to that hospital and say good-bye to Jimmy. Now, do you want me to help you get ready?"

Lowell glared at his father with hatred, but he saw that the tanned face was set. *I've got to go,* he thought with a sickness in his stomach. *If I don't, he'll pick me up and throw me into the wagon like I was a sack of meal!*

Lowell knew his father, knew the iron will that had carried him through half a lifetime of difficulties that would have killed most men. He'd seen him set his jaw in just the manner he saw now, coming back to face shame and disgrace and never once turning back. He'd seen his father maintain a marriage with his mother when almost any other man would have broken free from her. And he'd seen that expression in battle when Clay Rocklin had stepped into the hail of fire as though bullets were soft drops of summer rain!

"I-I'll get ready," Lowell whispered.

"Fine. I'll go get the wagon hitched. We'll put the wheelchair right in the wagon bed so you'll be comfortable."

Clay turned and left the room, aware that his fingers were trembling, and there was a nausea in his stomach. He had hated the scene! He hated to speak like that to Lowell, yet at the same time he felt a surge of hope. When Rooney came to face him, he nodded. "Get ready, Rooney, Lowell's going to say good-bye to his friend."

★ ★ ★

"All right, Lowell, hold steady now."

Lowell grasped at the arms of his wheelchair, and his father and a thick-bodied hospital attendant rolled it over the back edge of the wagon. He had made the ride in comfort physically, but the dread of being thrust into the busy world had so possessed him that he could not think. Now as the wheels touched the ground, he wanted to flee, but he was helpless.

"Thanks," Clay said to the attendant. "We can handle it from here." Clay stepped behind the chair, saying, "It's getting dark. I'll put you two inside, then go find us a room someplace."

"We can stay at the hospital," Rooney volunteered. She was acutely aware of Lowell's silence, and a feeling of dread had come over her as she thought, *Won't he ever say anything?*

Lowell's throat was constricted, and he found it difficult to breathe. As his father tilted the chair back and placed the front wheels on the sidewalk that led into the ward, he gripped the chair arms so tightly that his fingers cramped. Rooney stepped ahead and opened the door, and as soon as they were inside the long building, Lowell heard his name called!

"Hey! It's Lowell!"

"Well, look at you. Got an officer to shove you around! What an operator!"

"And got Miss Rooney waitin' on him! Lowell, you ort to be proud!"

Lowell felt the chair slow down, and as his father pushed him down the aisle, he saw familiar faces—men he'd fought beside in many battles. "H-hello, Ralph," he managed to say to a small soldier who had no hands. He thought of how many times Ralph Prentiss had entertained them all by playing on his banjo at a hundred campfires. Ralph saw that Lowell was struggling to find something to say and grinned. Waving his stumps, he winked. "Got to learn to play with my feet, Lowell!"

Lowell couldn't answer but managed a small smile. He spoke to other members of his company, and finally the chair halted next to a bed where a man with his eyes bandaged sat, his head cocked alertly to one side. "That you, Lowell?" he asked.

201

"Yes, it's me, Bailey."

"Well, I'm glad you come by, Lowell," the soldier said. "How you doin'?"

Lowell shifted uncomfortably in his chair, but said quickly, "All right, Bailey."

"Heard you lost a leg," Bailey remarked. "Now, thet's too bad, a dancin' man like you." Then he nodded confidently, adding, "But they make good legs fer fellers now, so they say." He paused and then shook his head. "Wisht they could make a pair of eyes fer me, but thet's past wishing fer!"

Clay said quickly, "I'll bring Lowell back later so you can visit, Bailey."

"Shore, Captain!"

When they moved out of that section of the ward, Lowell asked faintly, "Both eyes gone? No hope at all?"

"Minié ball tore them both out, Son," Clay answered. His answer seemed to cause Lowell to settle into his chair, and he said no more.

At the end of the building, the matron came out and put her eyes on Lowell. "How's the stump, Lowell?" she asked briskly.

Lowell licked his lips and nodded. "It's healing, Mrs. Pember."

"Fine! You'll be up soon." She noted that Lowell didn't respond and said briefly, "You came to see Jimmy. He's been asking for you for a week, ever since he was brought in."

"How . . . how is he, ma'am?"

Mrs. Pember stared at him. "Why, he's dying. I thought you knew that, Lowell."

"No hope at all?"

"No." There was a stark quality in Mrs. Pember's voice, and Lowell looked up to see that her lips were drawn tightly together. "The wound was too high to amputate—in the hip really. Dr. McCaw did the best he could, but there was really nothing he could do."

Lowell asked faintly, "Does he know he can't live?"

"Yes, it was only just to tell him."

Lowell was aware that the three of them were watching him closely. His head felt thick, and the pain from his stump had suddenly struck as it did at times, though not as often now. But he asked, "Can I see him?"

"Of course. He's back in the small ward. Come this way." She led them through a door that opened into a room with four beds, all of them occupied. "It's a little crowded for all of you," Mrs. Pember said. "Captain, would you put Lowell's chair close to Jimmy, then we can let them have some time."

"Yes, Mrs. Pember." Clay maneuvered the wheelchair into position beside the cot holding the small form of Jimmy Peck, then stepped back. "Rooney and I will visit the others, Son."

Lowell was not even conscious of their leaving. He was staring at the skull-like features of the young man on the cot. *He's nothing but a skeleton!* His eyes went to the blanket that covered the shattered hip, and he saw that it was black with blood.

Then the eyes opened, and a thin, reedy voice piped up, "Why, hello, Lowell!"

Lowell reached out and took the thin hand that the boy extended, saying, "Hello, Jimmy." He could say nothing for a moment, for his throat was constricted. "I'm . . . glad to see you."

Jimmy stared at him with fever-bright eyes. "I . . . been holdin' on, Lowell." He gasped for breath and then whispered, "Wasn't sure . . . I could do 'er!"

Lowell's eyes suddenly burned with tears. For the first time since he'd awakened to find himself missing a limb, he forgot about his own injury. The thin hand held to his, and he thought of the many fine times the two of them had—and some bad ones, as well. Jimmy had been so healthy, so full of life! He had been as agile as a squirrel, and his bright eyes filled with fun and laughter no matter how bad things had gotten. Now he was poised at the door of death, and Lowell felt he could not bear it!

"Tell me . . . what you been . . . doin'," Jimmy gasped. Lowell had no desire to speak of himself. The thought of how he'd been sulking in a room, refusing all help, came to him bitterly, and he choked and lied about how well he was doing. Finally he gave up his feeble attempts and whispered, "Jimmy, I never thought it would come to this!"

The dying boy moved his head and fixed his eyes on his friend. "Why, shoot, Lowell, . . . don't you worry none . . . about me!" He coughed a great tearing cough and then, after he got control, whispered, "Ain't got too long, Lowell. Got to tell you . . . something!"

The life was running out of the boy, and suddenly Lowell looked down and saw that the blood on the blanket was turning scarlet. He ripped the blanket back and saw that crimson blood was escaping in a small jet.

"Mrs. Pember!" he called out terrified, and at the same time he reached out and put his finger on the little orifice.

Soon Mrs. Pember appeared, followed by Clay and Rooney. "Don't move your finger, Lowell," she said quietly. "He'll bleed to death if you do."

"Do something!" Lowell pleaded. "Get the surgeon!"

"I'll send someone," Mrs. Pember said, then turned and left the room. "You stay with them, Rooney!"

Then they were alone, and Lowell's blood seem to beat in his ears. He kept his finger on the boy's artery, trying to pray and failing.

Jimmy whispered, "I got to tell you . . . that I wanna meet you in heaven, Lowell."

The simple statement struck Lowell Rocklin as hard as a minié ball. He stared at the dying boy, then nodded. "I'll do my best, Jimmy."

"Do you know Jesus?"

Lowell clamped his jaws together and then shook his head. "No, Jimmy. I don't."

"Well . . . kin I tell you how to git saved?"

Rooney stood there transfixed as the pale lips of the boy moved. He spoke of how he'd repented and called on Jesus.

Then in a fast-failing voice he begged Lowell, "You . . . do it, too, Lowell . . . please!"

Rooney saw the tears on Lowell's face and prayed, *Oh God, save him!* Then she saw Lowell's lips moving and heard his words faintly, ". . . just a sinner—but save me, like you saved Jimmy and Rooney, for Jesus' sake."

Rooney could not see, but she heard Jimmy gasp, "Did . . . you do 'er, Lowell?"

"Yes, Jimmy!"

Then the surgeon, Dr. McCaw, was there, and Jimmy looked up at him. "How long . . . can I live?" he gasped.

Dr. McCaw's face was lined with fatigue, but there was a deep compassion in his voice as he answered, "As long as Lowell keeps his finger on that artery, my boy."

Jimmy stared at the doctor for a long moment, then turned his wan face toward Lowell. He whispered, "Are you . . . saved, Lowell?"

"Yes, I'm saved, Jimmy!"

And then Jimmy Peck gave a deep sigh. He reached over and put his hand over Lowell's, the one keeping his life in. A peaceful smile touched his thin, pale lips. "You can let go, Lowell."

But Lowell didn't let go. For two hours he sat there, holding back the flow of blood. When his arm grew dead with the strain, the others tried to help, but Lowell refused, saying, "No, he's my friend!"

And then it ended. Jimmy opened his eyes and looked at Lowell. His pulse had grown so erratic that the doctor could not even find it. "He's lost too much blood. He's going!" the doctor had said.

Then Jimmy Peck stroked Lowell's hand, smiled, and whispered, "I'll see you . . . again, Lowell." Then his eyes closed.

Dr. McCaw said huskily, "He's gone, Lowell."

Lowell straightened up and sat upright in the wheelchair, staring at the small, pale face. "Good-bye, Jimmy," he murmured. Only Rooney heard him add, ". . . for now."

Rooney leaned down and said, "It was fine, Lowell! Just fine!"

And then Clay bent down and embraced Lowell, whispering, "I'm proud of you, my boy!"

Slowly Lowell looked up at them. His face was drawn with the struggle, but there was something in his eyes that had not been there before. And when he spoke, the hopelessness that had marked his tone was gone.

"I want to stay until Jimmy's buried," he said quietly.

"Of course," Clay answered. "I think that's what you should do."

Rooney was staring at Lowell's face, marveling at his expression—so different! She asked quietly, "And what then, Lowell?"

Lowell looked at her, then at his father. His face was pale, but there was a determination in his eyes. "Then I'll go home. And start living again!" He caught the hand that Clay held out, and Rooney took the other. Looking up at them, he felt so tired but so rested. Finally he said, "I'll meet Jimmy someday. I know that! But until that time, I've got to learn how to be a Rocklin!"

Clay stared down at his son, and pride laced his voice as he smiled and exclaimed, "You *are* a Rocklin, Lowell!"

And it was Rooney who bent over and kissed his cheek, whispering, "And now we can begin, Lowell! Begin all over again!"

PART FOUR
Josh

CHAPTER NINETEEN
Two Women

★

"I never saw such a change in a man!" Susanna's eyes were bright with pride as she spoke of Lowell to David. "Ever since he went to the hospital to visit his friend, he's been a different person."

"It's wonderful, isn't it, Grandmother?" Shaking his head, he added, "It's like he's risen from the dead!"

Susanna laughed softly. "You always did have a knack for overstating things!"

She left him then and entered the dining room. "Hello, Grandmother," Rena said. She asked without warning, "Grandmother, you told me once that Grandfather came when he was courting and serenaded you, didn't you?"

A smile touched the older woman's lips. "Yes, he did. Couldn't carry a tune in both hands, but he did it!"

Rena leaned back, staring at her grandmother almost enviously. "I think that's wonderful!" she sighed. Then she picked up her fork, nibbled thoughtfully on the fragment of pancake, and asked, "Grandmother, do you think any man will ever serenade *me?*"

Rena's expression was so woebegone that Susanna's heart went out to her. "I'm sure they will, lots of them," she said. Then she proved her wisdom by saying, "Oh, when I was your age, I thought I was plain and that no boy would ever like me. I had myself all primed to be an old maiden aunt living with my nephews—something dreadful like that!"

"Really?"

"All girls think that at a certain time, Rena." Susanna smiled and saw that her words had touched a fear that the girl had struggled with. "Of course! Didn't you know that?"

"No. I-I thought I was the only one."

Susanna sipped the last of her tea, rose, and went around to squeeze the girl's firm shoulders. "No, all of us feel like that, but you'll feel different soon. Why, I expect your father will have to run off some of your suitors with his pistol soon enough!"

Rena giggled and took an enormous wad of pancakes into her mouth. She felt a rush of relief and got up to embrace her grandmother, saying around the mouthful of pancake, "Oh, I *love* you, Grandmother!"

Susanna thought, *She needs so much encouragement—this war's robbed her of so much that I had!*

As Rena ran from the room, Dorrie came from where she'd been washing dishes. She'd heard the exchange and was not in the least ashamed of listening. Everything that happened to the Rocklin family was her business, and now she said, "Dat chile is growin' up, ain' she?" Her wise old eyes were sober, and she added thoughtfully, "Things ain't the same, is dey? Not lak when you was her age."

"No, Dorrie." Susanna thought of the days of her youth—carefree, happy times—times that would never come again. But she was too strong to grieve over what could not be changed. "She's a good girl, Dorrie, but she's had a hard life. And now she worries about losing her father."

Dorrie nodded but said strongly, "She's a Rocklin, ain't she? She gonna do *fine,* so doan you be worrin' yo' head. Gawd, he's knowin' 'bout all this! You heah me now?"

Susanna laughed and gave Dorrie a hug. "All right. Now, let's go to work!" She looked out the window, saying,

"There goes Josh. If Rena sees him, she'll make him take her fishing or something."

But Josh didn't see Rena that morning. He made straight for the backyard, where he found Rooney cooking lye soap. She was stirring the mixture in a big black pot, and when Josh rounded the corner and came to her, she greeted him eagerly. "Hi, Josh! Are we ready?"

"I g-guess so, R-Rooney." He lifted a small black bag, saying, "I got what we n-need."

Rooney looked across the yard to where two of the young slaves were talking. "Lucy, come and finish this soap, will you?" She waited until the two girls came and got their instructions, then said, "Come on, Josh."

As Josh followed her, a worried expression came to his face. The wind blew his hair over his eyes, and he brushed it back with his free hand, saying, "I'm a little n-nervous, Rooney."

Rooney glanced at him quickly, then said with a reassurance she didn't quite feel, "It'll be all right, Josh." As they approached the door, she slowed down and then turned to face him. Her mop of auburn curls had been blown so that they formed a soft crown, and her wide eyes were thoughtful. "Lowell's changed. You've seen how *different* he is, haven't you?"

Josh nodded, but there was a reluctance in his tone as he answered her. "Yeah, but I ain't sure h-he's changed *this* much!"

"Come on, Josh. I'm sure it'll be fine."

The two entered the house and moved toward Lowell's room. Rooney knocked on the door, and when Lowell called out "Come in," the two of them entered. Lowell looked at the pair with surprise, for both of them wore rather strained expressions. "Well, you two look like you've come to cut my other leg off!" He saw Rooney blink with shock, and Josh looked as if he wanted to turn and run back out of the door!

Lowell watched them but was thinking, *Guess I've made*

some progress—got to where I can make a joke about it, anyway. He noted that his mild remark had shaken them and said, "Well, come on in, both of you."

Rooney moved closer, and Josh followed, both of them as nervous as they'd ever been. Lowell noted this, then his eye fell on the bag in Josh's hands. "What's that you've got, Josh? You bring your lunch?"

Josh swallowed but could only shake his head. He gave Rooney an agonized glance, and she said, "Lowell, we've . . . been meaning to talk to you . . . Josh and me." Her face was pale, and she had trouble with her words.

Lowell stared at the pair, then said quietly, "Look, whatever it is, you don't have to be scared out of your wits. I'm not going to shoot you." He smiled, adding, "I've yelled at you enough since you got here so that at least you know my bad behavior won't kill you. Just tell me what the trouble is."

His manner was so mild that Rooney was encouraged, so she took a deep breath and began. "Lowell, Josh and me have been thinking, ever since you got hurt, that we might be able to . . . to help."

Lowell nodded and a smile touched his lips. "You have helped, Rooney, and you, too, Josh. Anybody else would have left me to wallow in my own pity a long time ago." He saw that his words made them both feel more comfortable, so he said, "Now, I guess your visit has something to do with what Josh has in his suitcase?"

"Well, yes, it has," Rooney replied. "You see, we got to thinking a while back, about those legs that soldiers get when they . . . lose a leg."

Josh spoke up, "I c-can make one, Mr. Lowell!"

Lowell stared at Josh, his face filled with surprise. "Make an artificial leg?"

"S-sure! I c-can do it!"

Lowell stared at the two, affection coming to his hazel eyes. "Why, I never doubted you could make anything you set your hand to, Josh, but—"

"We thought of it right after you got back, Lowell!" Rooney's eyes were alive with excitement. Now that she was certain that Lowell was not going to be angry, she threw herself into convincing him. "First we went to Richmond to see about having you one made. And there's only two places where you can get a leg."

"Guess they must be pretty busy," Lowell commented.

"That's the way it was," Rooney said with a nod. "They both said they'd have to put us on a list, but it'd be a long time before they can get to us."

"B-but I looked around while I was th-there," Josh said, his thin face stubborn. "And I s-seen how they made them l-legs!"

Lowell gave Josh a fond look but said doubtfully, "I guess that's a pretty specialized kind of work, making artificial legs. Not like making a plow or a table."

But Josh was adamant. "I asked th-the man about making one m-myself." Josh was the mildest of young men, but Lowell had noted from the first that when he got a notion in his head, he became stubborn. Now the boy's chin was stuck out, and he said, "He t-told me I couldn't do it—but I can!"

Rooney said quickly, "I asked him to let Josh come and watch him, just to learn how."

"What did he say to that?"

"He said no, but I kept after him until he agreed!"

"Sh-she shore did, Mr. Lowell!" Josh grinned broadly at Rooney. "She d-did it for sure!" Then he laughed as Rooney tried to make him stop. "She t-turned them b-big blue eyes of hers on that f-feller and let her l-lips go tremblin', and then she said, 'B-but my sweetheart n-needs this so b-bad!'"

Lowell shot an astonished look at Rooney, who blushed furiously. "You didn't!" he exclaimed.

"Well, he made me do it!"

"You should have s-seen her, Mr. Lowell!" Josh crowed. "She had h-him almost crying!"

Rooney's fair cheeks were red as roses, and when Lowell burst into laughter, she pouted, "Well, it worked, didn't it?"

"I guess so," Lowell finally answered, then added with a wink toward Josh, "But I'll be on my guard with you from now on, Rooney. A woman like you can get about anything she wants from a man!"

"Oh, don't be foolish!" Rooney snapped. She had begged Josh not to tell Lowell of the incident, and it had embarrassed her. But now that she saw that it had amused Lowell, she felt better. "Now, let's get down to business," she said. "Josh spent almost a week there, and he learned just about everything. Tell him, Josh!"

Josh began to speak, and both Lowell and Rooney noted that his stutter grew less noticeable as he became immersed in the explanation. Lowell glanced at Rooney, and she caught his eyes, nodding slightly. *How does she know what I'm thinking?* Lowell wondered. *Have to be careful around this girl!*

" . . . and so I *know* I c-can do it," Josh ended.

"Well, let's get started," Lowell said at once, and his willingness pleased the young man—and Rooney as well. "What's first?"

"First, Mr. Lowell," Josh said quickly, "we g-got to make a wax model."

"A model? Of what?" Lowell asked.

"Of your . . . s-stump." Josh faltered over the use of the word *stump,* but he and Rooney had already decided that they'd have to use the term. He saw a flicker of embarrassment in Lowell's eyes, so he hurried with his explanation. "Your whole weight w-will rest on it, see? So the s-socket of the new l-leg's got to fit just right."

"I guess I see that," Lowell said slowly. "Did you see them do this—at the shop, I mean."

"Oh, sure," Josh said, nodding. "Ain't nothin' to it. Just take wax and h-heat it. Then put the stump in so's it l-leaves an impression."

"Well, I guess we'd better do it, Josh."

"I'll heat the wax," Rooney said instantly and, taking the small case from Josh, left the room.

"That g girl's a caution, M-Mr. Lowell!" Josh said, shaking his head with obvious admiration. "Ain't n-nothing stops her when her m-mind's made up!"

"Tell me again about how she wheedled that leg maker into letting you stay," Lowell begged. He sat there, letting Josh retell the story, then urged him to give more details about the leg. They were interrupted when Rooney entered, bearing a basin with a cloth over the top.

"It's too hot, Josh," she said, placing the basin on the washstand. "We'll have to let it cool a little."

As the pair worked on making the cast, Lowell was so absorbed in the process that he realized with a shock that he was not embarrassed by the presence of Rooney. This was partly, he realized, because she had cared for him and was accustomed to his handicap. *With any other woman this would be hard,* he thought. *She makes it so easy!*

Finally the cast was made to Josh's satisfaction. "I'll g-get started on this," he announced and left the room.

"That's an amazing young man," Lowell said thoughtfully. He had settled back in his chair after dressing, and his eyes were thoughtful. He turned them on her, saying, "And you're an amazing young woman."

Rooney was making his bed but looked at him with a startled expression. She was not accustomed to compliments and said only, "Why, it's good to be able to help."

Lowell considered her, then asked, "Do you think you could manage this chair? I'd like to go out for a while."

"Oh, that would be nice!" She gave the coverlet a final tug, then came over. "You can see the new colt."

Lowell caught her wrist as she moved to step behind him. Rooney broke off her remarks and gave him a startled look. He held her firmly, looked up, and said, "Rooney . . ."

And then he could not find the words to express what was inside him. He struggled for a long moment, then taken by an impulse, lifted her hand to his lips and kissed it.

215

"Oh—Lowell!" Rooney gasped, and her lips trembled. No man had ever kissed her hand, and something about the gesture brought a sudden rush of happiness to her. Finally she took a deep breath, then smiled tremulously, saying, "Let's go outside, Lowell."

She took him outdoors, and the warm May breeze blew against her face—but she knew the weather was not the cause of the flush her cheeks felt as they moved along the walk.

CHAPTER TWENTY
Man in the Saddle

The Confederate army had won the battle of Chancellorsville, but at a ruinous cost. The Army of Northern Virginia lost veterans, and there were no replacements. Supplies were exhausted, and the leaders of the Confederacy were aware that the Army of the Potomac would be back—larger and more powerful than ever.

One hope burned brightly for the South—the hope of recognition from Europe. England made a pretense of neutrality, but the aristocracy and ruling classes sided with the South. Agents of the Confederate government reported that if Gen. Lee could establish his army firmly on Northern soil, England would at once acknowledge the independence of the South. This meant that ample loans could be obtained from that country to shore up the failing resources of the Confederacy.

At this same time an antiwar movement called the Copperhead movement was gaining strength in the North. President Davis hoped that it would cause the North to falter, perhaps even to declare the war over.

Lee had informed the president that an offensive against the North was the only hope for the South. "If we wait for them to come to us," he'd said, "we'll be surrounded, and we cannot win a long siege."

217

So as spring gave way to summer, men were looking north, and the Army of Northern Virginia felt the stirrings of far-off battles. . . .

★ ★ ★

"Well, h-here it is!" Josh stood before Lowell holding the new leg in his hands. "Sure h-hope it works."

Lowell had waited anxiously for Josh to finish the work on the leg, but now that the moment had come, he felt an unexpected rush of fear shoot through him.

What if it doesn't work?

He tried to banish the thought, but there was such uneasiness in his expression that Josh said quickly, "We m-might have to work on it a l-little, but I *know* it'll work!"

Josh's assurance seemed to brace Lowell somewhat, for some of the tension left his face. "All right, Josh, let's see how she goes."

Lowell stripped off the robe, and Josh came to help him fit the device. He'd been to the hospital with Rooney, and the two of them had studied the way the limbs had been strapped into place. Josh had also taken his workmanship back to the shop in Richmond, where the owner had been highly impressed. "Excellent job! You can come to work for me anytime!" he had said. He'd given Josh a few suggestions but had indicated that there were few improvements to be made.

Now Josh knelt and fastened the limb into place. He had worked with Lowell, taking measurements and making sure that the straps were exactly right. Finally he looked up and asked, "That too tight?"

Lowell was staring down at the leg. It was made of cork and was very light, but he was filled with doubt. "Let me put my pants on, Josh," he said.

"Sure!"

Lowell had not worn trousers since arriving at the hospital. Such a garment would have made it difficult to dress his stump and would have been uncomfortable in any case.

218

Now, however, the urge came to him, and he struggled into the trousers with Josh's help.

"There you are." Josh nodded and stood up. "Ready to t-try it?" He was nervous, for he'd thought of little but getting Lowell on his feet ever since he'd started the project. Now that the time had come, he wondered what he'd do if his work didn't measure up.

Lowell sat still, looking down at himself. There was no difference in the legs, he saw at once. Josh had used his remaining leg as a model, carving the artificial limb to exactly the same measurements.

His voice was hoarse as he said, "Feel like I'm about to get on a wild horse, Josh." But he shook his head, mustered up a grin, then said, "All right. Here we go!"

Josh put his hands out. Lowell took them, then heaved himself to his feet. For one moment he looked surprised, then gripped the young man's hands hard. "Room is going around like a top!"

"J-just hold what you g-got, Mr. Lowell," Josh urged. "You been down f-for a long time."

Lowell nodded and stood there until the room settled down. Cautiously he swayed back and forth, then side to side. It was a strange sensation, completely unlike anything he had ever experienced. He seemed to be balanced on his remaining leg, and there was no feeling of having the other foot on the floor. Looking down, he assured himself that both feet were planted, then gave Josh a crooked grin. "Seems to be working . . . so far," he muttered.

"Does it h-hurt?"

"Well, a little bit," Lowell agreed. "Not too bad, though."

"The man in the shop said you'd toughen up. No w-way to do that except to u-use it a lot."

"Like forming a callous on your hands, I guess," Lowell said. Then taking a deep breath, he nodded. "Hang on, Josh. I'm pretty shaky." Gripping the hands of the boy, he placed his weight on his sound leg, then twisted his body as

Josh had tried to instruct him. He leaned forward, and the artificial limb swung into place. Then he tried to put his weight on it while swinging his other leg. But he had no confidence, so he staggered and loosed his grip on Josh's hand. He waved his arms wildly, then fell into Josh, who caught him about the waist and kept him from falling.

Josh held him, saying, "Hey—don't w-worry! I've g-got you!"

"Put me back in the chair!" Lowell gasped.

"Mr. Lowell!"

"Put me back, blast you, Josh!"

Josh helped his friend to move backward, and when Lowell was seated, he saw that his face was pale and perspiration covered his brow. He waited, knowing that this was a critical time. The limb maker in Richmond and the nurses at the hospital had warned him that many men simply gave up and refused to use the limbs, choosing a wheelchair instead.

"I can't do it!" Lowell whispered. "I can't do it, Josh!"

Josh was in a strange position. All his life he'd looked on men like Clay Rocklin and his family with awe. They were rich and influential, far above his station. Josh still felt that way, but he had thrown himself into helping Lowell walk, and despite his shyness, there was a stubborn streak in him. He came from hill people who took the back of no man's hand, and now as he looked down at Lowell, courage rose in him. He knew that gentleness would not do here—that Lowell Rocklin had to be pushed!

"Mr. Lowell, you g-got to do it," Josh said. And when the man shook his head stubbornly, the boy said, "You ain't a coward, are you?"

Lowell looked up at Josh abruptly, as startled as if the boy had slapped him across the face. He reddened and cried, "Get out! Leave me alone!"

"No, sir, I c-can't do that!" Josh's face was pale, but his jaw was set, and he stared right into Lowell's face. "I guess if any of the Rocklins are cowards, n-nobody ever found out about it. Are you aimin' to b-be the first?"

Lowell stared at the boy, anger rising to choke him. He wanted to throw himself at the boy, to strike him down with his fists! How did he dare!

And then Lowell thought of the sacrifices the boy had made—all to help him. And now he saw Josh was almost trembling, though he held himself upright and taut. *It took a lot for him to speak up to me that way,* he thought. *He's got plenty of nerve—more than I have!*

Josh watched as the anger seemed to drain from Lowell's face, and Josh said in a pleading voice, "I don't l-like to talk to you bad, but you just g-gotta make it!"

Lowell let his eyes drop to his hands, then to his legs. He understood clearly at that moment that he had come to a fork in the road, and his choice would follow him the rest of his days. *I'll either get up and try again—even if I fall a thousand times—or I'll crawl into bed and be helpless for the rest of my life!*

Seldom had any choice been so clear to Lowell. And he thought of Jack Bailey, who had said, *They make good legs fer fellers now, so they say. Wisht they could make a pair of eyes fer me, but thet's past wishing fer!*

That thought put a desperate courage into Lowell Rocklin, and he prayed silently, *Oh God, don't let me give up!*

Josh saw Lowell look up, and he was filled with encouragement, for there was a defiant look in Lowell's hazel eyes. And then he grinned faintly, saying, "Well, you're a pretty good preacher, Josh. Now, let's try it again!"

"I knowed you w-wouldn't give up!" Josh took the hand of Lowell Rocklin, heaved him up, then said, "N-now, we'll take it r-real easy. . . ."

★ ★ ★

While Lincoln fumbled in his attempts to find a commander who would fight, the Confederate army repaired itself, knowing that the onslaught would soon come.

Col. Taylor Dewitt called Clay to his headquarters one sunny morning, giving him an order. "Maj. Rocklin, I've got a hard duty for you." Taylor's eyes gleamed with humor, and he laughed aloud. "Doggone it, Clay, I wish you were the colonel and I was the major!"

"Don't think I'd like that, Colonel," Clay said, smiling. "What's the duty?"

"Recruiting," Taylor said. "Our ranks are stretched too thin. Get out there and get some men for us. You'll be close to your people, so tell them all hello from your colonel!"

Clay had drawn a horse, and after listening to the moans from Dent—with broad hints about favoritism from his "old buddy Taylor Dewitt"—he rode out of the camp and made his way back to Richmond. He made several stops on the way and was surprised at winning several young fellows over to signing up. He was not a high-pressure salesman, but something in his quiet manner made the young men want to be in his company. Several of them were afraid the war would be over before they could get in it, and Clay didn't argue, though he knew better.

When he got to his own county, the recruiting went even better. He was known by most of the planters, and the Yancy boys had spread the word about the Richmond Grays. It had been filled with young aristocrats at first, but now Clay was looking for hard fighters, not dancers!

Finally he drew up in front of Gracefield just after noon on Tuesday. He'd worked hard and had a good catch, enough to please the colonel, so he had no guilt over taking a couple of days at home. Highboy met him, white teeth gleaming, and when Clay threw him a piece of hard money, his head bobbed up and down violently. "Sho' is good to see you, Marse Clay!"

"Grain him good, Highboy. I've ridden him hard." He pulled a large sack from behind his saddle, dismounted, and made his way up the steps.

He was met on the porch by Rena, who threw herself into his arms, nearly knocking him off balance. "Whoa! Be careful with an old man!" he protested, but grasped her around the waist and swung her around so that her feet flew out.

She protested, but it was a game he'd played with her for years, and she loved it!

"Now, I'm out of breath," he said, putting her down, but keeping his hands on her waist. "You're getting fat," he announced.

"I am not!"

"Are too!" Then he kissed her and whispered, "You're the best looking woman I've seen in these parts!"

Clay picked up his sack, and the two went into the house, Rena chattering and hanging onto his free hand. Clay was relieved to see her so happy. He'd been concerned over leaving her, but she'd finally cast off the heavy burden he'd seen on her after Ellen died.

Moving inside, the family all came to greet him, and Dorrie said, "Come on and set down. Dinnuh's ready."

Clay went to her, put his arm around her ample waist, and said, "I've got a present for you in my bag here."

Dorrie gave him a look that was at the same time avaricious and suspicious. "Whut you done got me?"

"I'll show you." He opened the sack, rummaged through it, then pulled out a thin package. "Here you are."

Dorrie took it, saying her thanks, but when she started to leave, Clay shook his head. "None of that! Open it and see if it fits."

Dorrie looked around, protested, then opened the package. She took one look inside, her eyes flew open, and then she hurriedly closed the package before the rest of them could see what was inside.

"What is it, Dorrie? I couldn't see," Rena protested.

But Dorrie merely shut her lips tightly and shook her head. Then she looked at Clay who was grinning broadly and who prompted her, "Don't you like it, Dorrie?"

The tall black woman drew herself up and clutched the package firmly. Then she stared at the tall man whose eyes were laughing at her, and she said, "Mr. Clay—you is *bad!*" Whirling, she left the room.

Clay said, "Never saw such ingratitude!"

223

Susanna was laughing, for she had caught a glimpse of the present. "That would have made a good piece for your balloon, Rooney."

Then they all went in and sat down at the table, and Clay began passing out gifts for everyone. "Just my way of saying how important you all are to me," Clay said in explanation for his generosity.

Dorrie and Lucy began bringing in the food, and Clay looked around for Rooney, for he didn't notice her leave the room. Then she entered, smiling at him in a rather mysterious fashion. Clay said, "Come and get your gift, Rooney."

But she didn't come to him as Clay expected. He glanced at his mother and saw that she too had a look of excitement on her face. Everyone, in fact, had that same expression.

"What's going on?" Clay asked, looking around. "You all look like the cat who swallowed the canary."

"We've got a gift for you, too, Mister Clay," Rooney said.

"A gift for me? Well, let's have it," Clay insisted.

Rooney moved back toward the double door she had passed through and whispered something that Clay couldn't hear. He couldn't imagine what was going to happen but knew that for some reason everyone was grinning broadly.

And then he heard steps—a strange tread that somehow didn't seem exactly right. Something about the rhythm of it. . . .

And then Lowell appeared!

Clay had never been struck so hard in his life. He'd spent sleepless nights praying for—for exactly what he was seeing now! Lowell was wearing a fine gray suit with a white shirt. He held a cane in his right hand, and there was a proud smile on his lips. "Hello, Father," he said and then began to walk across the floor.

Clay had wisdom enough to stand and wait. He wanted to run and grab Lowell but knew instinctively that this would be wrong. Lowell moved across the floor, swinging his right limb and planting it firmly. It was awkward and ungainly, but Clay didn't care! As Lowell came to stand before him, Clay's eyes filled with tears. He made no move to hide them, and if he had looked around, he would have seen that he was not the only one so moved.

"Lowell," he whispered. "I . . . I can't tell you . . . what this means to me!"

"You'll have to thank Josh and Rooney, Father," Lowell said unsteadily. He cleared his throat and thrust his hand out. "Welcome home, sir!"

Clay grasped the hand, then could not restrain himself. He put his arms around Lowell and held him fiercely. Then he released him, turned, and pulled out a handkerchief. Blowing his nose, he waited for a moment, and when he turned around, he said evenly, "Well, let's eat!"

It broke the tension, and all during the meal, Lowell spoke of how it had come about, always giving the credit to Josh and Rooney. He had a different spirit, and Clay did not miss the expression in Rooney's eyes. She never took her eyes from Lowell for more than a few moments, and when she saw Clay observing this, she flushed and dropped her eyes.

Finally the meal was over, and Lowell said, "Father, I want some of your time."

"Of course."

Clay rose and followed the young man outside. Lowell led him out the side door, for it was only one step—much easier to navigate than the front porch. Clay walked along, adjusting his pace to Lowell's, and found himself at the pasture where the horses were kept. Lowell leaned against the fence, put his fingers in his mouth, and whistled shrilly.

"I could never do that," Clay stated. Then he saw Midnight, Lowell's favorite mount, appear from around the barn. The beautiful horse came up to the two men, and Lowell gave him a bit of biscuit he pulled from his pocket. "Beautiful animal! Never saw a finer one."

Lowell patted the smooth muzzle, then turned to face his father. His face was as earnest as Clay had ever seen it, and he began to tell Clay how he'd struggled to learn to walk.

Once again, he gave Josh and Rooney all the credit. "I must have fallen a thousand times, but they always picked me up," he said quietly.

"We'll always owe them for that. They're quality." He was aware that Lowell was framing something, trying to find a way to ask him something. "What is it, Son?" he asked. "I'll do anything I can for you—you must know that."

"All right, I'll tell you." Lowell put his hazel eyes directly on Clay and took a deep breath. "I want to stay in the army." He saw the surprise on Clay's face and quickly went on, "I know it'll be hard, but I can do it, sir."

Clay was troubled and showed it. His brow furrowed, and he said, "Why, Lowell, you know what the army's like. It'd be too hard for you. You'll learn to walk much better, but I don't think you'd be able to keep up over some of the terrain we'll be marching through."

"I know, but I want to be a courier." Lowell saw the idea make a change in his father's face. "I can't march, but I'll be able to ride as well as any man."

Clay nodded slowly, then said, "Well, now that's so, I guess." He stood there, letting the idea sink in, and finally said, "Nobody will look down on you if you don't go, Son. You've done your share."

Lowell shook his head stubbornly. "I've got to do it, sir!"

"And you want me to find you a place?"

"Yes, sir!"

"Well, I'll do it." A thought came to him, and he exclaimed, "Why, Gen. Stuart—he'd be glad to have you, Lowell!"

"I never thought of that!"

"He was very impressed with you," Clay replied. "I'll be glad to speak to the colonel about you transferring and not being mustered out."

"Do you really think he'll have me?"

Clay looked on Lowell's eager face, and pride swelled in him. He gripped Lowell's arm tightly, then said, "Son, *any* general would be glad to have you on his staff!" Then he laughed and shook his head. "Well, I'm a little prejudiced, I guess." He looked at the black horse and then at Lowell. "When do you want to go, Son?"

Lowell thought, then said, "Josh and Rooney will help me. And it won't be as hard as learning to walk." He did some fast figuring, then said, "I'll be ready in two weeks, sir."

"Two weeks," Clay said thoughtfully. He did some addition of his own, then smiled briefly. "That'll be plenty of time, I think."

"Where will the next battle be?" Lowell asked.

"I think it'll be in the North. We've got to hit the Yankees on their own ground."

"I'll hope to be with you, sir!"

Clay suddenly asked, "What about Rooney?" He smiled at the startled expression on Lowell's face. "You can't take her with you, as you did last time."

"I-I guess not," Lowell stammered. Then his face brightened. "But she'll be here when I get back."

Clay didn't respond, but even as he turned the conversation toward the probable tactics of Gen. Hooker, he was thinking, *He's in love with that girl—and I don't blame him!*

CHAPTER TWENTY-ONE
Rena Loses a Friend

"Easy, Midnight!"

Lowell held the reins firmly as the black horse snorted and tossed his head. He had always been a difficult animal to mount, requiring strength and great agility, though he was quickly obedient once a rider was on his back. He was not in the least a vicious horse, but for some reason he refused to stand quietly as a rider stepped into the stirrup.

Lowell had saddled Midnight in the barn, then led him outside into the brilliant sunlight, stopping in the center of the small corral built of split rails. Although he did not take his eyes off the prancing stallion, he was aware that he had an audience. Behind him Highboy and two other hands were standing at the door to the barn, and to his left he knew that Rooney, Buck, Josh, and Rena were standing outside the tall fence.

They had all seen him ride Midnight. For two weeks he'd left early in the morning every day for a ride, but he'd always been helped into the saddle by Josh or one of the hands. What they didn't know was that Lowell had gone several times to practice getting into the saddle with only Highboy present.

And those sessions had been disasters! Even now as Lowell held the horse fast, he thought of the many falls he'd taken, and he heard Highboy whisper, "Oh, Marse Lowell . . . be keerful!" The tall slave had begged the young man not to attempt mounting on his own, saying, "I'll go to the army wif you, Marse Lowell! Lots of soldiers takes dey body servants, and I can hep you git on dat hoss every time!"

After Lowell had been tossed to the ground several times, he'd been sorely tempted to accept Highboy's offer. But he'd shaken his head grimly, saying, "No thanks, Highboy. I'll get on my own horse or I won't go!"

Finally he'd managed to pull the trick off once—and was elated. It wasn't the end of the thing, of course, for Midnight had no intention of reforming! However, he'd stayed at it until he could manage getting astride the horse at least nine times out of ten, so he'd announced at breakfast that everyone was invited to watch.

Now as he hauled in on the reins, he was aware that if he got thrown, he'd look like a fool and a failure, but he was ready to risk it. There were rumors about the army moving into the North soon, and Lowell was determined to be a part of it.

"Easy, boy," he said, gently but firmly. As he pulled the horse's head down, he moved to the side, his movement somewhat jerky. Keeping Midnight's head down, he leaned under the glossy neck, tossed the reins over, and caught them, then held them tightly. Midnight tried to toss his head and prance away, but Lowell jerked him into place almost roughly.

The trick was to mount quickly, he had discovered. One false move and Midnight would be sidling off to one side or giving that little half-buck that made it impossible for him to throw his artificial leg over the saddle. *Good thing it was the right leg instead of the left,* he thought. *I'd never be able to balance in the stirrup on the cork one.*

Giving the reins a steady pull, he stepped to the side and balanced on his artificial leg—and this was the critical moment! He had learned that if he could hold that balance, lift his left leg, and jam it into the stirrup, it was possible to lift himself with one surge of power and throw the other leg over the saddle even if Midnight tried one of his tricks. But if he missed the stirrup with his left foot, he was helpless and usually was dragged to the ground in an ignominious fall.

Now he jerked down on the reins to hold the horse steady for one moment, lifted his left foot, and stabbed at the stirrup—and was elated when his boot entered! He'd had Josh enlarge the stirrup so that it was easier to insert the toe of his boot, and now as it hit home, he instantly grabbed the saddle horn with his right hand, gave a sharp heave, and threw his right leg up and over the broad back of Midnight. Just as he did, Midnight gave a forward lurch, but the momentum of his effort carried him into the saddle, and he knew he was safe! He heard Highboy yelp shrilly and identified Rooney's voice as she cried out, "That's the way, Lowell!"

As he pulled Midnight up sharply, he glanced down to his right and lifted his body, shoving the toe of his boot into the stirrup, which had been specially designed by Josh so that it hung low enough to allow his leg to lock. Josh had also taken the forward sway out of that stirrup by means of carefully designed strips of white oak. This device prevented the stirrup from swaying forward when his boot hit and also held the leg firmly in place.

Flushed with his success, Lowell turned Midnight's head toward his small audience and swept off his hat. "Guess I'll be able to get a job with a circus!"

They all laughed, and he wheeled the horse around and called for Josh to open the gate. Then he gave a shrill cry and sent the sleek animal out at full speed. Leaning forward, he exulted in the speed of the animal, and a joy he thought he'd never know again came to him. *I'm as good as any man when I get in the saddle!* He drove the horse at a breakneck speed, then turned him sharply and was pleased that he'd mastered that trick. There was some loss of response, perhaps, but so little that he knew he could still do the job.

He put the horse through every difficulty he could devise,

then slapped him on the neck fondly. "If I do as well as you, boy, I'll get a medal!"

When he returned to step down from the tired horse, he saw that Rooney was waiting. "Take good care of him, Highboy," he said fondly. "We've got a long way to go, him and me!"

Rooney came to meet him as he moved through the gate. She took his arm, and Lowell knew that it was partly to help him, for she had learned to serve as a brace for him since he'd almost given up his cane. He still used it, but now he put his arm around her waist and smiled. "Maybe I could take you along when I go back. You could cook for me and wash my clothes, just like in our ballooning days."

Rooney gave him a swift glance, longing in her face. "Oh, Lowell, I wish I could!"

She had such a woebegone expression that Lowell almost laughed. "Well, I doubt if the general would favor that."

"I don't see why not." They were walking along the open space that separated the barns and outbuildings from the main house, and Lowell gazed at the place, realizing how fond he was of Gracefield. He knew that he might never see it again, for no one was safe in battle. He'd grown up here and knew nearly every stone and blade of grass, and it gave him a wrench to think this might be his last glimpse of it.

"When will you be going?"

Startled, he looked down at her. "Why, day after tomorrow, I guess."

They had come to the scuppernong arbor, and the white lath work was covered with vines, most of them returning to the green of summer. Rooney stopped abruptly and turned to him, and he saw that she was very serious. Her blue eyes contained some sort of sadness that was rare, for she was a happy girl as a rule. Something was in her mind, he saw, for her lips were pursed as they were when she was making a decision, and there was a hesitancy in her manner.

"What is it, Rooney?"

"Oh, I don't know. . . ." She was not tall and had to tilt

her head upward to look into his face. Lowell admired the freshness of her skin, the clearness of her eyes, and her long, thick lashes. "I wish you weren't going!" she said abruptly. Then she took the lapels of his suit coat and suddenly leaned against him.

Lowell was taken by surprise, for he had not seen this side of Rooney for a long time. She had been the strong one, always giving him confidence and never showing fear. He put his arms around her, thoroughly aware of the intense femininity that he held in his arms. Finally without drawing back, she lifted her face and said simply, "I love you, Lowell!"

And then Rooney Smith did something that she would not have dreamed of doing only a few months before: She released her grip on his coat, reached up, and pulled his head down, kissing him firmly on the mouth.

For Lowell, there was a wild sweetness in her gesture, and the softness of her lips stirred him, so that he gripped her and pulled her closer. He half expected her to draw back, but instead she pressed herself against him with an impassioned gesture as if she were afraid she would lose him. He could smell the sweetness of the scent she wore, and her hair brushed against his cheeks, stirred by the wind.

There was no reserve in Rooney, and it was as if all the fears she'd had about men had never been. As Lowell held her, it was a natural thing, and she had no other thought but *I love this man!*

Finally she drew back and shyly dropped her eyes—and then raised them. She waited for him to speak, and though she had almost no experience with real love, she knew that Lowell felt some of what was in her so powerfully. Finally he whispered, "And I love you, Rooney!"

She laughed then, and when he kissed her again, it was as if she'd come home to safety after a long and difficult voyage. She pulled back, drew him to the bench and, when they were seated, began to speak of how she'd fallen in love with him. He listened, charmed by her honesty and openness as much as by her fresh youthful beauty. Finally she stopped and reached out to stroke his cheek. She started to speak and halted, a troubled look in her eyes.

"What is it, Rooney?"

"I-I'm not the kind of girl men like you . . . care for," she said quietly.

He read her thoughts and caught her hand. Holding it firmly he said, "Yes, you are! You're honest and brave and beautiful. What else is there for a man?"

Rooney said with difficulty, "My family!" She could not say more and turned her face away. "When my mother gets out of . . . jail, I'll have to help her. You—you wouldn't want a woman like that in your—" She almost said, "in your family," but realized that Lowell had said nothing about marriage. She thought of the long line of Rocklins, men and women of distinction, and fell silent.

"Rooney, I can't say much right now," Lowell said quietly, then paused, thinking, *How much has changed in just a few weeks! When I had two legs, I'd never have thought of marrying a girl in her social class. Now, it's what I want more than anything in the world!* He had not himself realized this fully, and the suddenness of it shocked him. He'd been firmly fixed in his own little world, but the blast of a cannon had completely destroyed his dreams and ideals. Now, looking at Rooney, he understood that he'd let go of them along with the bitterness that had filled his spirit. *I want her more than I ever wanted all those things I set such store by! Why, I can't even think of the future without her in it!*

Carefully he said, "Rooney, it's you I love. I've got only one leg, and you've got a mother with terrible problems. We have to take each other with the difficult things as well as the good things." He stroked her hair, for he loved the wild soft curls that crowned her head, and he began to tell her how much she'd come to mean to him. He'd never done this, but the words came easily, without effort. She kept her eyes fixed on him, her lips half parted, and there was such trust and joy in her expression that finally Lowell said, "You're the one woman in the world for me, Rooney!"

"Oh, Lowell!"

"But I've got to go," Lowell added. "It's something I have to do. When I get back . . . well, we'll have lots of plans to make."

"Yes, Lowell." Fear came to Rooney, as it did, perhaps, to all women who sent their men off to face the cannons, but she kept a smile on her lips. "I'll be waiting for you."

He got to his feet and, when she rose, embraced her briefly, then said, "That makes all the difference, sweetheart!"

If the pair had known they were under careful observation, they might have behaved differently, but neither of them realized that a pair of sharp eyes was watching them from the door of the hayloft.

Rena had persuaded Josh to take her rabbit hunting, and she'd joined him in the loft, helping to throw down hay for the farm animals. Josh had been pleased that Rena was going, but he turned to see her staring out the window instead of helping throw down forkfuls of the fragrant hay. Curiously he stepped behind her and peered over her shoulder. One glance and he pulled her around, "You ain't g-got no business watching such!"

"Lowell is kissing Rooney!"

"W-well, is it any of your b-business?"

Rena saw that Josh was angry, but she wanted to see more. She tried to pull away, but he held her arm so tightly that she couldn't move. "Let me go!" she cried angrily.

"No! It's not right spying."

Rena flushed with anger—and guilt. She'd known it wasn't right to watch the pair, and now that Josh had caught her at it—and refused to join her—it made her very angry. Without thought, she swung her arm and slapped him on the face, the blow, making an ugly sound.

Josh stared at the girl, conscious of the stinging blow, but hurt worse by Rena's act than anything else. He was terribly sensitive, and it had been a new world when Rena Rocklin had shown him such kindness. Now as the sound of the blow seemed to echo in his ears, his eyes grew bleak. Dropping his grip on her arm, he turned and walked away. Without a word, he leaped from the loft into the pile of hay, caught his balance, then ran out of the barn.

Rena was transfixed, unable to move. She had not *meant* to strike Josh! It had been her pride that had made her do it, and she leaped forward to the ladder, crying, "Josh! Josh! I didn't mean it!"

But he was gone, and though she searched for him everywhere, she couldn't find him. Finally she went to her room, fell across her bed, and wept until she was weak.

When she went downstairs, Susanna saw at once the trouble that lurked in her granddaughter's eyes. "What's wrong, Rena?" she asked.

Rena stared at her with tragic eyes and began to tell Susanna what she'd done. By the time she'd finished, her voice was trembling and tears were brimming in her eyes. "I was so mean to him, Grandmother! He was right, and I was wrong!"

Susanna remembered how small things were enormous to the very young. She'd seen that the young man had been good for Rena, and now she saw that the girl's affection for Josh ran deeper than she'd thought. Putting her arms around the girl, she murmured, "It'll be all right."

"I've got to find him . . . tell him I was wrong." She looked up and saw that her grandmother had an odd look in her eyes. "What is it?" she whispered.

"Josh has gone home for a little while, Rena," Susanna said, pity in her tone. "He told David he had to help his father with the work there."

Rena's face turned pale, and she whispered, "He's mad at me! And he's right!"

Susanna stood there, trying to comfort the weeping girl, but knew that there was little she could do. *When you're sixteen, a thing like this is as big as a mountain,* she thought.

Aloud she said, "Rena, he's hurt, but he's a good young man. He'll get over it, and you two will be friends again."

"No, he won't come back," Rena said, shaking her head. "You don't know how shy he is—but *I* knew it! He's so ashamed of his stutter he doesn't make friends, Grandmother. And . . . and I was his friend!"

Rena tore loose from Susanna's hands and ran out the door, disappearing around the corner of the house, shaking with the sobs she tried to hold back.

Susanna stared after the girl, then picked up the tray of food and made her way to Mark's room. "I've fixed you one of those omelets you like, Mark," she said, setting the tray down.

Mark Rocklin knew this woman very well. One glance at her and he demanded, "What is it, Susanna? Bad news about the boys?"

"Oh no." Susanna hesitated, then sat down and related the problem to him. When she had finished, she sighed and looked at him, weariness in her eyes and in the lines of her face. "She thinks it's the end of the world, Mark."

"The young always think that." He toyed with the omelet, then looked at her with a tired smile. "You carry so many people on those small shoulders, Susanna." And then he added, "You've always been the finest woman I've ever known."

His praise shocked Susanna Rocklin, bringing a tinge of red to her cheeks. "Why, Mark—," she started to protest, but he cut her off.

"It's true. I should have told you years ago. And Rena's like you," he added. "She's had a pretty bad knock, but she'll make it."

"I think she will, but it's good to have someone else tell me." Susanna leaned over and stroked Mark's hand, noting with a sudden fear how frail it was. The two of them sat there, speaking quietly, and somehow they both felt a closeness that had been gone for years. Neither of them knew how to speak of it—and neither did. But when Susanna rose to take his tray back to the kitchen, she gave a sudden sigh of relief. "You've made me feel better, Mark."

"I'm glad. Good to be of some use." He caught himself, saying, "That sounds like self-pity, and there's nothing I hate worse than that in a man!" He hesitated and for one moment seemed on the brink of telling his sister-in-law something.

Susanna caught the look on Mark's face and asked, "What is it, Mark? I've thought for some time you've wanted to tell me something. I'd like to hear it."

Mark Rocklin had spent his life alone, for the most part. Only a few times had he been able to speak his mind and heart to another, and he longed to speak now. But the habits of a lifetime were strong, and he found no words to express what was in his heart.

"Sometime I'll tell you, Susanna," he said and then wearily lay down and turned his face to the wall.

Susanna stared at him, then shook her head and left the room without a word. Going to her sewing room, she closed the door and sat down in the worn rocking chair. She began to rock, and the motions of the old chair were as even as the tides or the spinning of the globe. She picked up the worn, black Bible, but did not open it. Holding it in her hands, she closed her eyes and her lips began to move. "Dear Lord, hear my prayer. . . ."

CHAPTER TWENTY-TWO
"Jine the Cavalry!"

Some officers were so colorless that they could pass through a crowd without being recognized. Gen. Ulysses S. Grant was one of these. He wore the uniform of a private at times, the only mark of his rank being the stars pinned to his coat. Grant was so plain in appearance that once when he was boarding a gunboat, smoking a cigar, the guard, a new private in the army, stopped him and addressed him roughly: "You—throw that cigar away!" Grant had smiled, tossed his cigar away, then passed by saying, "I like to see a soldier who does his duty."

Gen. James Ewell Brown Stuart was definitely *not* one of these drab officers! The general—better know as Jeb Stuart—would never be overlooked in any crowd. His uniform consisted of a pair of thigh-high black boots, tan breeches, a flowing cape with scarlet lining that rippled in the wind as he rode his horse at a full gallop, and a black ostrich plume crowning his rakish hat. Stuart surrounded himself with men only slightly less colorful than himself, and his entourage included one man called Sweeny, who had been a professional minstrel. Wherever Stuart camped, one could hear the lively plunking of the banjo and the laughter of his men.

As Lowell guided Midnight through the ranks of tents that practically surrounded Richmond, he was seized by a sudden tension. *I must be crazy doing this! Every young fellow in the South with a horse wants to ride with Jeb Stuart. He can get all the men he wants with two legs. No reason for him to take me.*

As he moved past the line of tents that marked the camp of the infantry, he heard the tinny, plinking sound of a banjo. Drawing closer he heard a fine tenor voice singing:

We're tenting tonight on the old camp ground,
Give us a song to cheer
Our weary hearts, a song of home,
And friends we love so dear.

Many are the hearts that are weary tonight,
Wishing for the war to cease;
Many are the hearts that are looking for the right,
To see the dawn of peace.
Tenting tonight, tenting tonight,
Tenting on the old camp ground.

Rows of small tents framed the background of the cavalry encampment, but Lowell made his way to a large Sibley tent set out in front. The conical canvas shelter could accommodate twenty soldiers, but by the ensign flying from the polished pole beside it, Lowell knew that it housed Gen. Jeb Stuart.

Pulling Midnight to a halt, he spotted the general at once. Stuart was in the midst of a circle of officers who were being served a meal by two black servants. Lowell noted at once that there was a holiday air about the group and decided that all he'd heard about Jeb Stuart's ability to draw men and hold them was true.

"I'm Lt. Collins. What can I do for you?"

Glancing around with a start, Lowell looked down at a tall, long-legged lieutenant who had advanced from his left and now positioned himself directly in front of Midnight. He was wearing a heavy Dance revolver, a Confederate copy of the Colt .44 Dragoon and the favorite weapon of Stuart's troopers. "Why, I'd like to speak with Gen. Stuart, Lieutenant." He fished an envelope out of his pocket and extended it to the officer. "I have a letter from Col. Benton of the Richmond Grays."

"Wait here," Collins replied, then eyed Midnight with a practiced eye. "Better keep your eye on that hoss. Some of our folks might decide to requisition him."

Lowell grinned and nodded, then watched as the long-legged officer approached Stuart. He saw the general glance at him, then tear the envelope open and scan the single sheet of paper inside. He nodded and waved Lowell forward. The officers surrounding the general watched the new arrival curiously, and Lowell felt a moment of awkwardness. *I can't ride Midnight through the middle of them, but if I get off, they'll know I've got a wooden leg.*

Setting his teeth, he slipped off Midnight and moved forward. No matter how much practice he'd put in, he was acutely aware of the halting gait he was forced to use. He was also aware that Stuart was watching his progress thoughtfully. But the general smiled, wide lips almost hidden behind his ferocious beard and moustache. "Well, Sgt. Rocklin, we meet again!"

"I'm surprised you remember, General."

"I might have forgotten you, but I never forget a good horse." He put his bright blue eyes on Midnight, then shot at Lowell directly, "I'll buy him from you, Sergeant—name your price."

Lowell shook his head. "Sorry, General, but I couldn't sell him."

Stuart nodded his approval. "I'd have been disappointed if you had." He put that thought aside, then studied Lowell carefully. "Too bad about that balloon getting destroyed." He glanced at his staff and gave them a brief history of the balloon. When he finished, a chunky young major eating from a tin plate said, "I wish we had some of those things. They'd come in handy."

Stuart nodded absently, still engaged in some sort of thought. "That's right, Maj. Malone." He studied Lowell, then said, "You took a pretty bad wound. Gen. Able told me about it."

"Yes, sir, I lost a leg," Lowell said instantly and was aware of the scrutiny the staff officers gave his legs. He knew that this would be the issue and wanted to get it into the open. He had hoped to see the general alone, but there was no chance of that now.

"Your colonel writes that you want to jine the cavalry."

"Yes, sir, more than anything!"

"Well, Sergeant, I admire your grit, but we're a pretty rough bunch." Stuart hesitated, seeking for the best way to put what was in his mind. Finally he shrugged and said bluntly, "Lots of men with two legs can't stay up and take the punishment we have to take. It would be difficult for a man with only one."

"If I fall behind, take my horse and leave me!"

A mutter of approval went around the circle, and Maj. Malone observed, "A man can't say fairer than that, General!"

Lt. Collins put in slyly, "Be a good way to get another good hoss, sir."

Stuart looked over Lowell's shoulder at the fine lines of Midnight and hesitated. Then he shook his head firmly. "I'm mighty tempted, but it wouldn't be fair. I'm sorry, Sergeant. I admire your spunk, but—"

Sensing rejection coming, Lowell said quickly, "General, I can give you two reasons why you should take me."

Stuart had already settled the matter in his mind, but Lowell's statement caught at him. "And those two are?"

"The first is that I can play a harmonica as well as Mr. Sweeny there can play a banjo."

Sweeny was a short man with a bushy head of black hair and a pair of bright black eyes. "Why, let's have a sample, Sergeant! If you can do what you say, I'll be on your side. Some of these so-called 'musicians' in this troop can't tell one note from another!"

Lowell had learned to play the harmonica from Box. He

had a great deal of natural ability and had spent long hours making up tunes and acquiring new skills. Knowing of Stuart's love of music, he'd stashed his harmonica in his pocket, hoping for just such a chance as this. Pulling it out, he put it to his lips and began playing a lively tune, employing the trills and half notes he'd learned. Sweeny listened critically for the first few notes, then nodded gleefully. "The man can do it!" he cheered, then his hand began to move across the strings of his banjo.

The two instruments formed a wonderful harmony on the stillness of the air, and Stuart, Lowell noted, enjoyed the duet. He beat his thigh with a hard hand and moved his head in time with the music. When the two reached the end, giving a run of staccato notes as a final flourish, he led the loud applause that went up and said loudly, "Never heard better mouth organ playin' in my whole life, Sergeant!" Then he added regretfully, "But a man's got to be more than a musician to ride with me. What's your second reason?"

Lowell knew his last chance had come. "Why, General, I don't see how you can turn down a man who can beat anybody in your whole cavalry in a horse race!"

"Ho! That's pretty big talk!" Stuart blinked. Memory came to him, and he said, "As I recollect, we settled that awhile back. Me and Skylark beat you and that black horse right smartly!"

Lowell suddenly grinned. "No, sir, all we settled was that any private should have enough sense *not* to beat a general in a horse race—or anything else!"

A shout of laughter filled the air, and Maj. Malone's voice rose over it. "He's got you there, General! Why, even a *major* knows better than to win against his commanding officer!"

Stuart's genial expression gave way to a sudden flare of anger that brightened his eyes. "That's the squeal of a loser!" he exclaimed, his pride touched. "Man that can't win has to blame it on something!"

Lowell said carefully, "Sir, I don't suppose you'd give me and Midnight another chance?"

Stuart understood at once what the sergeant was up to. He could not suppress a grin. "I can guess the stakes," he shot back. "If you beat me, I let you into the troop."

"Yes, sir!"

"What do I get if *I* win?"

"Why, you prove to your staff that you've got the best horse, General."

"Don't see how you can refuse the man, Gen. Stuart," Maj. Malone urged slyly, winking at his fellow officers.

"Well, by george, I'll have to show you clodhoppers *again* what a real horse is!" Turning his head, Stuart yelled, "Turner, saddle Skylark!"

The officers all ate hastily, and in the background Lowell could see the troopers had gotten word of the race. He stood talking with Maj. Malone, who asked about his background and then listened intently. "I've met your father," he said, nodding. "Fine officer!" Then he glanced at Stuart who was swinging into the saddle. Leaning forward he whispered, "Make the race half a mile or more. Skylark can beat anything on four legs for a quarter of a mile, but that black gelding of yours looks like he's got more bottom!"

"Thank you, sir!" Lowell nodded gratefully. He stepped into the saddle, aware that eyes were taking in his actions critically. When Stuart rode forward, the two of them moved together along the line of tents into the large open field where drill took place. It was occupied now by a lieutenant drilling his company, but when he saw Stuart and Lowell followed by the staff—and by many of the troopers who hurried to see the race—he called out loudly, "Let's take a break, men. We can watch them imitation soldiers play with their hosses!"

Lowell grinned, for he himself had made fun of the easy life of the cavalry. Then Stuart pulled up to say, "Now, I don't want any excuses after we get this thing done, so you can pick the distance and the route, Sergeant."

Lowell was prepared and lifted his arm. "How about to that big tree and back, sir?"

Stuart blinked at the choice and gave Maj. Malone a hard glance. The major returned his stare blandly, and the general nodded shortly. "That's half a mile to that tree."

"We can make it shorter, sir," Lowell said, "if that distance is too much for your horse."

A muffled laughter ran around the men who watched, and Stuart glared at them furiously. "That will be fine—to the tree and back. Maj. Malone, you can give the start. We go on the count of three!"

Lowell guided Midnight forward, and the big horse knew as well as his rider what was happening. He quivered with eagerness, the powerful muscles bunching as the two horsemen brought them side by side. Lowell held the eager animal in check as Malone's voice rang out, "One—two—*three!*"

Midnight shot forward, but Skylark was faster. As Lowell had expected, by the time they had reached the tree, the smaller bay was four lengths ahead of the big gelding. Stuart rounded the tree and shouted as the two passed, "Too bad, Sergeant!"

Lowell leaned into the turn, and when he faced the crowd of cheering men across the field, he leaned forward, shouting, "Midnight, get him!" He felt the surge of power that pulled him back as Midnight lunged forward, and he let out a wild cry as he saw the gap began to close.

Gen. Stuart cast a look over his shoulder, a startled expression crossing his face as he saw the big black coming up fast. Whirling, he began to lash his horse with the reins, but it did no good. As Lowell pulled up even, Stuart's face was swept with chagrin.

Lowell urged Midnight on, but as he approached the starting point he was tempted to pull the animal back. *No, I'll beat him as bad as I can!* When he shot into the gap left by the spectators and glanced back, he saw that he'd beaten Stuart by three lengths. Pulling Midnight to a stop, he slipped to the ground, where he was surrounded at once by a group of admiring troopers who beat his shoulders in congratulations.

Maj. Malone took Skylark's reins as Stuart came to the ground and tossed them to him. "A good race, General," he stated. "The boy has a fine animal."

Stuart stared at him accusingly. "Did you give him any advice, Malone?"

"Why, yes," the major confirmed. "I told him that he'd better choose a long distance because no horse alive could beat Skylark in a quarter of a mile."

"Why, you . . . you *scoundrel!*" Stuart almost stuttered, anger in his flashing blue eyes. For one moment Malone thought he was about to be transferred to the infantry, but then Stuart's good humor won out. He stared at the group of admiring troopers and officers who surrounded the big black horse and laughed aloud. "Well, he'll be your responsibility, Major. See that he keeps up—or I *will* have that black horse!"

"Yes, sir," Malone said grinning, knowing his man. "And I think we'd better have another race . . . this time for a shorter distance."

"Right! Can't have a mere private beating his commanding officer!"

"Why, Rocklin's a sergeant, General!"

"Not any more," Stuart slyly stated. "He'll have to earn his stripes all over again. Come along, Major."

Lowell turned from speaking with the men who pressed in to shake his hand and stroke the sides of Midnight. He waited for the general to speak, fearful that he'd lost his chance despite winning the race.

But Stuart smiled, and Lowell's heart seemed to leap as the bearded general said, "Well, looks like you jined the cavalry, Pvt. Rocklin. Now, let's see if you can keep up!"

Lowell didn't miss the fact that he'd been demoted, but that meant nothing to him. "Thank you, General!" he responded quickly. "I'll do my best to do that."

"You'll serve in Maj. Malone's troop, and we'll have a race tomorrow." Stuart's bright blue eyes twinkled as he added, "This time for just a *quarter!*"

"Yes, sir!"

As Malone walked away with Lowell to show him his quarters and acquaint him with his sergeant, he said, "Private, I don't think I'd win that race tomorrow if I were you."

The words were gently spoken, but Lowell understood at once that he was being given what amounted to a command. "No, *sir,*" he said vigorously. "Midnight never does well two days in a row, especially against generals!"

Malone laughed and then sobered. "I'm not sure I did the right thing, helping you get back into this war. We'll be leaving shortly to join Gen. Lee."

"We'll be going north?" Lowell asked, excitement in his voice.

"It's no secret." Maj. Malone's rugged face was suddenly tense, and he shrugged his thin shoulders. "Everybody seems to know what's coming. I just hope Hooker doesn't know what Lee is up to."

"Major, thank you for helping me!"

Malone had a sudden vision of this eager young man lying dead on a battlefield. *It'll be all my fault if that happens, but I can't think on that.* "Your home is just outside of Richmond?" he asked suddenly.

"Yes, sir."

"I wish mine were! Well, there's no time for training you. You can serve as a courier for the general. That means you'll be a messenger boy, but I don't have to tell you how important that is."

"I understand, sir. It's great just to be here!"

Again a picture of this keen-eyed young man lying bloodied in a distant field flashed through Malone's mind, and he said impulsively, "After the sergeant gives you your instruction, take what time there is and be with your people. We won't pull out for four days—be back by then."

"What about the race, Major?"

"Wait until the general beats you," Malone answered with a dry smile. "Then go see your people." They were almost to the spot where a sergeant stood watching them, and he added quietly, "Enjoy your time with your family. It may be the last you'll have for a time."

★　★　★

Mark and Rooney had grown very close, and Rooney often thought of what the tall man had said about loving a woman named Beth. She had said nothing about the matter and was certain that he had no memory of it. But she had grown fond of him and wished that he would confide in her. One afternoon she was sitting with him, reading from a novel called *Ivanhoe,* and when he seemed bored, she put it down. Idly she asked, "You never thought of marriage, Mr. Rocklin?"

Her question troubled him, she saw, and he hesitated before saying, "Yes, I did think of it once." He let the silence run on, then shook his head. "I wish now that I had married."

"Why didn't you?" Rooney asked quietly.

Mark stared into the fire, his dark eyes grown moody. When he spoke, it was in a low voice, almost a whisper. "Pride, I guess. She wasn't of our class—" Suddenly he realized what he was saying and gave Rooney a startled glance.

He's thinking I'm not of Lowell's class, Rooney knew instantly. She saw that he was embarrassed and said, "It's all right. I understand."

A look of relief washed across his face, and he said, "You're a discerning young woman, Rooney."

She was exactly that, and as she sat there listening to the fire crackle, the missing pieces of Mark Rocklin's life fell into place. His family all realized that he was a man who was incomplete. He'd been a driven man, traveling much and coming home to Gracefield as if it were a safe harbor, but restless and unhappy even when there.

He fell in love with a poor girl, but wouldn't marry her because of his family, Rooney thought. *I wish he'd married. He's been so unhappy!* Then she asked, "What became of her, Mr. Rocklin? Did she marry somebody else?"

"No, she died." The words were harsh and almost grim, and Rooney knew the door had slammed shut. She began to speak of other things, but she understood Mark Rocklin's unhappiness now, she felt, more than his own family did.

Buck suddenly burst into the room, crying, "It's Lowell! He's ridin' in!"

Rooney threw down the Sir Walter Scott book and ran through the door, closely followed by Buck. They found Rena, Susanna, and David on the front porch, and there was Lowell riding in on Midnight!

"Lowell!" David exclaimed as the young man dismounted. "We didn't expect you back."

"Well, I left a sergeant and came back a private, David, but I'm serving under Gen. Stuart!"

Susanna could not have cared less about his rank but simply put her arms out. He gave her a fierce hug, then did the same for Rena. "Dad'll be home soon. I met him in Richmond." Then he turned and clapped his hand fondly on Buck's shoulder, saying, "I've got a present for you in my saddlebags. It's a Yankee officer's pistol. Go get it, but don't shoot anybody!"

Buck leaped off the porch with a yelp and was soon brandishing the pistol wildly. "I hope it's not loaded," David said, grinning at Buck.

"No, it's not." Lowell turned to Rooney then, and there was a sudden silence. Susanna broke it, saying, "Rena, you come and help me fix this man something to eat."

Rena started to protest, but Susanna gave her arm a sudden pull toward the door. "David, take Midnight to the barn." She herded Rena inside, pausing at the door to give Rooney a sly smile. "Bring him in when you're through with him, Rooney," she said.

Lowell smiled suddenly and took Rooney's arm. "My

grandmother is a smart woman." They stood there, looking at each other, and then he demanded, "Come with me."

"Where are we going?"

"To the scuppernong arbor," Lowell said, a sly grin forming. "That's where us Rocklin men take pretty girls to kiss them!"

Rooney blushed, but then said, "All right, I'll do it." He laughed at her red face, then led her around the house to the arbor. When they were inside, he looked around. "I wasn't joking about this place, Rooney. My father said he got more kisses here when he was courtin' than anywhere else. He even proposed to Melanie Benton right on this very spot."

"She turned him down and married your uncle Gideon, didn't she?"

"That's right. You've really boned up on my family history." He reached out and took her by the arms, but when he tried to embrace her, she resisted. "What's the matter?" he asked. He'd looked forward to this moment, but now she was apprehensive. Thoughts had come to him, such as *No woman wants a man with only one leg!* And now he stood there waiting for her to tell him that she'd changed her mind.

But Rooney was thinking about what Mark had said. *She wasn't of our class.* Rooney slowly lifted her eyes and said, "You come from a proud family—"

At once Lowell expelled his breath. "Never mind the family!" he said almost roughly. "I'm not asking you to marry the family. I'm asking you to marry *me!* If they don't accept you, we'll go make our own place!"

Rooney's eyes filled with unbidden tears, for it was what Mark should have said to that girl years ago. Throwing her arms around him, she cried out, "Oh, Lowell, I love you so!"

He held her fast, kissed her, and then said huskily, "My father said he'd horsewhip me if I let you get away—and my grandmother is just about as bad!"

They stood there relishing each other's company for close

to an hour—until Buck's head poked around the corner. "You two gonna stay out here all day? Come on, Lowell. You gotta show me how to load the pistol, and Miz Rocklin wants to see you." He frowned at Rooney, adding, "You sure are selfish, Rooney, hoggin' Lowell so the rest of us can't have him."

Rooney laughed at Buck, then went to him and asked, "Do you know what a brother-in-law is. . . ?"

★ ★ ★

Mark awakened himself by uttering a short cry, the result of a ragged pain that tore across his stomach and brought him out of a fitful sleep. Cool hands touched his brow, and he heard Mclora's voice saying, "Drink this, Mr. Rocklin." He swallowed the bitter liquid she held to his lips, then lay back on the bed.

"Sorry to be such a baby," he muttered. "You don't have to sit up with me, Melora."

"I'm not sleepy." Melora pulled the oak rocker by the window up to the bed and began knitting. As she worked, she talked quietly of the small affairs that made up the lives of the Rocklins and the Yancys. Not the war—she didn't speak of that. She spoke of the new calf, the fox that Box had killed carrying off a chicken, the church supper that had been such a success.

Mark lay there rigidly until the pain subsided, then relaxed as the room grew fuzzy. Her voice was warm and soft and pleasant. As she spoke and he felt sleep dragging him down, something came to him. At first he thought, *It's none of my business,* but the thought persisted. So he said carefully, "Melora?"

"Yes, Mr. Rocklin?"

"When are you and Clay getting married?"

"Why, we haven't decided."

Mark felt a sharp disappointment at her answer. He fought off the drowsiness that fogged his mind, opened his

251

eyes, and struggled to sit up. Then Melora blinked and said, "What's wrong? Is it the pain?"

"No, it's not that." Mark had pulled himself into a sitting position, and Melora leaned forward, anxiety in her eyes. "Melora, don't put it off! Marry Clay as soon as you can—tomorrow!"

Melora was startled by the passion in Mark Rocklin's voice. She knew him to be a man who kept his emotions under strict control, but now his face was set in a grim expression. "Why do you say that?"

"Because I waited too long once. There was . . . a girl I loved. And I let her slip away." Haggard lines creased the sick man's face, and he reached out to Melora. When she took his hand, he said hoarsely, "Nobody has tomorrow, Melora. All you and Clay have is *now*. I know Clay thinks it would be unfair to marry you until he's back safely from the war. But if you love him, give him what time there is. If it's only a day, that's better than missing love altogether!"

The medicine hit Mark then, and he lay back. His eyes closed, and he muttered a few words before dropping off into a deep sleep. Melora remained to be sure that he was all right, then rose and left the room. It was after midnight, and she knew that he would sleep, so she went to her room. For a long time after she went to bed, she thought of Mark's words: *All you and Clay have is now.*

The next morning she rose early and said little to anyone. Mark seemed not to remember the incident, and she did not mention it. All morning she worked, then in the afternoon she changed and went for a long walk in the woods. As she moved across the soft earth through the path beside the creek, she thought of the times she and Clay had walked there in earlier days.

Finally she turned and walked back down the path, and when she came out of the timberline, she saw Clay riding down the road. He saw her at once and spurred his horse. Dismounting, he moved toward her, and she put her arms up. Clay said with surprise, "Melora, what is it?" She was not a woman to parade her emotions, but now she held him tightly, lifting her face. He kissed her and as always was totally aware of her femininity.

"Clay, I want to get married—now!"

Clay's face stiffened with surprise. "Why, Melora—," he began to protest, but she cut him off by placing her fingers over his lips.

"I know. You're afraid you won't come back. That I'll be a widow. Clay, I've waited for you too long. I want you, even if it's only for a day or a week!"

Clay was amazed at Melora's intensity. Her dark eyes pleaded with him, and her lips were soft yet firm with purpose. "But what if there's a child?"

"Then I'll have something of you, Clay. I love you, and we have little time. All we have is now. Let's not let it slip by!"

Clay pulled her close, kissed her again, then lifted his lips. "Day after tomorrow you'll be my wife, Melora!" Then he laughed, and there was a joy in him that Melora had never seen. "Come on. Let's go tell Mother to start baking the wedding cake!"

Hand in hand they ran like children down the road, and Clay's mount threw his head up, puzzled at this sudden freedom. Then with a whicker, he moved into the field and began cropping the tender blades of emerald grass.

CHAPTER TWENTY-THREE
Now Is Forever

Clay walked out of the house and headed for the barn. The sky was painted a hard, bright blue, and clouds white as cotton sailed majestically overhead. He'd never felt better and had given Rooney a tremendous hug, stating firmly, "I'd have horsewhipped this boy of mine if he hadn't proposed to you!"

As he moved toward the stable, he heard a voice and turned to find Rena running out the front door. "Daddy, are you going to the Yancys'?"

"Sure am. I'm taking your grandmother's wedding dress to my bride-to-be."

Rena looked pale and hesitated slightly. "Take me with you, Daddy."

"Why, sure! Come along. You're going to be the maid of honor, so you and Melora can make all the plans." He'd spoken with his mother, asking why Rena was so subdued. She'd said, "She and Josh had a spat," and Clay had thought little of it, saying, "They'll make it up."

Now as he climbed into the buggy, he noted the girl's pale face and asked, "Are you sure you want to go, Rena?"

"I have to go with you, Daddy," she said, lifting her chin defiantly.

Clay hesitated, for on this trip he wanted to be alone. But

there was a vulnerability in his daughter's wan face that made him say, "Why, sure, Rena. I'd have asked you if I'd known you wanted to go."

Rena climbed into the buggy, and soon Gracefield was left behind. "I've missed you," Clay said, turning to smile at her. "And Dent said to tell you that you and your grandmother will be staying with Raimey after the wedding." He put his arm around her, squeezed her, then added, "You've got to go see that my grandson gets raised the right way!"

Thomas Denton Rocklin was born to Dent and Raimey in early March, and no one at Gracefield had the opportunity to spend much time with the newest Rocklin.

Rena tried to pull away, but he held her fast. She really liked to be held and was glad that he kept his arm around her. "Daddy . . . ," she said tentatively, "I was horrible to Josh. . . ."

As the girl poured out the story, Clay understood how important this thing was to her. She was sensitive—too much so, he thought at the time—and the boy had been someone her own age to talk to. Susanna had told him how fond Rena was of Josh, and now he listened, then said carefully, "Too bad! Nothing much worse than hurting a friend, is there?"

"He hates me!"

"No, he doesn't," Clay said firmly. "Josh has too much sense for that. His feelings are hurt, but he'll get over it."

As they drove along, he talked to her easily, keeping his arm around her shoulder. He had a very special love for this daughter of his and knew that she was very dependent on him. He had never escaped the sadness over the loss of the years when he'd been away. He'd missed so much of her girlhood, and she'd missed having a father. Now he was determined to make it up to her. The war had come, and he had to do all he could during the fleeting times that they were together.

Finally they drove into the opening where the Yancy cabin sat and saw the smoke pouring out of the chimney. Clay said,

"Hope that smoke means Melora's cookin' up somethin' good!"

As he stopped the team, the door opened and Buford stepped outside, followed by Melora and the others. "Well, I never!" he exclaimed. "Comin' round at dinnertime again!"

Clay stepped down, then turned to help Rena. Melora came over to put her arm around Rena. "I'm so glad you came with your father, Rena. You've got to help me plan everything."

Clay reached into the buggy and brought out an oblong box. "I hope you're the same size as my mother was when she married. She says you are."

"I won't be as beautiful as she was, Clay."

"That's your opinion, not mine." Clay smiled warmly and winked at Buford. "How much dowry do I get for taking this old maid off your hands, Buford?"

"Daddy!" Rena exclaimed. "You ought to be ashamed!" But Clay only laughed at her and sat down with his host to drink some fresh buttermilk. He was exuberant in a fashion that none of them had seen before, and for the next ten minutes kept them all smiling as he spoke of how he was robbing them of their cook.

Rena watched Josh, who said not one word—and had not even looked at her. All of the younger Yancys crowded around her, and she smiled and talked with them, but she felt a sharp despair when Josh retired to a dark corner of the room and sat with his face turned down.

Clay had observed this, too, and thought quickly. "Melora, do you still have that case of books I sent—the old ones?"

"Why, yes, Clay." Melora had been watching the little drama, not missing the misery on the faces of both Josh and Rena. She understood at once what Clay was up to and said, "They're up in the bedroom in the loft."

"Josh," Clay said, "hop upstairs and find me a book called *The Last of the Mohicans*, will you?"

"Yes, s-sir."

Melora waited until Josh had disappeared up the steep ladder and exclaimed, "I forgot. I put that book in another box. Rena, go tell Josh to look in the small box, not the big one."

Rena blinked and cast a nervous look at Clay, who said, "Go on, Daughter, do what Melora tells you!"

When Rena reached the top of the ladder and stepped into the large room, she saw Josh turn toward her. She had dreaded this moment—yet longed for it for days. At once she walked across to him and whispered, "Josh, I'm . . . I'm sorry I hit you! You were right, and I was wrong!"

Josh was stunned, and as he looked down and saw how afraid she was and noted the tears beginning to gather in her eyes, he swallowed, saying hoarsely, "Aw, it w-wasn't nothing."

"Yes, it was!" Rena tentatively put her hand on his arm, and her voice was so low that he could hardly hear her as she said, "Will you be friends again, Josh?"

Josh had been miserable since leaving Gracefield. He'd gone about his work with a dullness and lack of interest, so that his family knew that something was very wrong with him, but he had not spoken of his problem.

Now as he looked down and saw Rena's dark eyes looking at him in a woeful manner and her soft lips trembling, he couldn't stand it. "I'd like that," he muttered, then added fervently, "I missed you something awful, Rena!"

"Did you, Josh? Really?" Rena suddenly threw her arms about the boy and held him closely. "I was so miserable I thought I'd die!"

Josh was shocked almost witless by Rena's embrace. He stood there awkwardly, not knowing what to do with his arms. The pressure of her form against him sent a shock through him, and he stood there stiff as a ramrod. Then he put his arms around her and patted her on the shoulder. "Let's never fuss again, Rena!" he said.

Rena drew back suddenly. "Josh! You're not stuttering!"

Josh blinked and realized that she was right. "I guess you scared it out of me!" he marveled.

"Oh, Josh!" Rena was so excited that without thinking, she leaned forward and kissed him on the lips—and then she froze, realizing what she'd done. Josh, she saw, was staring at her, and finally she said, "Well, it was only a little kiss! Didn't you ever get kissed before?"

Embarrassed by her boldness, she turned away and started for the door, but he leaped after her, caught her, and whirled her around. "Not by such a pretty girl," he said. And then he heard himself saying, "But I like it fine, Rena." And he leaned forward and kissed her cheek.

He drew back, and they stared at each other wordlessly. Finally Rena said, "Will you come back, Josh? And take me coon hunting and fishing?"

Josh nodded, answering at once, "Sure, I will." He stared at her, then said again, "I've missed you a heap, Rena!"

Clay and Melora noted the expressions on the faces of the two young people when they finally returned with the book. Clay couldn't resist saying, "Must have had to look hard for that book, Josh."

But Melora said, "Now stop that, Clay." She rose and headed for the door, saying, "You can come and help me feed the stock."

"I'll do that," Buford protested, but Melora gave him a warning look, and he mumbled, "Well, I guess not."

Clay walked with Melora, taking her hand. "I guess Rena and Josh made up," he remarked. "She was miserable."

"So was Josh."

They fed the stock, then she took his hand and led him down past the barn to the small pond. They stood there looking at their reflection in the still water. "Remember when the snapping turtle bit me and wouldn't let go?" she said with a smile.

"I remember."

Clay let his mind go back and thought of the twelve-year-old Melora, her eyes filled with tears as he'd worked to get the small turtle to release her. "It must have hurt like the dickens, but you didn't cry out loud."

"No, I didn't, did I?" Melora was caught up in the memory and said gently, "We have lots of memories, don't we, Clay?"

Clay Rocklin took her in his arms and saw her eyes widen. He bent his head and kissed her, savoring the softness of her lips. Then he lifted his head and said, "Melora, I love you."

"I love you, too, Clay." *I've loved him since I was a little girl,* she thought. *He may not come back from the next battle. I want to have all of him I can—and to give him all that a woman can give a man.*

"Melora!" Clay stroked her black hair, and he held her in his arms. The still green water of the small pond mirrored their image, and there was a holy quietness over the earth.

Finally he said huskily, "I can't promise you how long—"

Melora put her fingers over his lips and lifted her face, saying, "Now is forever, isn't it, Clay?"

CHAPTER TWENTY-FOUR
"With This Ring I Thee Wed"

✦

"Clay, for heaven's sake sit down!" Col. Taylor Dewitt had joined Clay in the pastor's study. The faint sound of the organ filtered through the door, and Clay had been pacing the floor like a caged lion. As Clay's best man, Taylor felt it his duty to keep the bridegroom from exploding, and he said in disgust, "It's only a wedding, man! Why, you didn't get this nervous at the Bloody Angle!"

Clay halted abruptly and glared at his friend. "This is worse than going into battle, Taylor," he muttered grimly. "I'd rather get shot than go out there!"

The two had been friends for years, and Taylor came to lay his hand on Clay's broad shoulder. "I guess I was the same when I got married. Goes with the territory, I suppose—" He broke off as a short man with fair hair and intense blue eyes entered. "Glad you came, Pastor. The bridegroom's about ready to make a run for it."

Rev. John Talbot, pastor of Faith Church, the largest in Richmond, was accustomed to nervous bridegrooms. "Quite natural," he said, smiling. "But let me tell you this, Maj. Rocklin, fifteen things may go wrong when we go out there. The maid of honor may fall flat, one of the guests might drop dead of a heart attack, the roof might fall in . . ." Rev. Talbot paused dramatically, his lips lifting in a smile as he added, "But when you walk out of that church, you'll be a married man!"

Clay laughed, amused by the short minister. "I trust you for that, Rev. Talbot. But all the same I'd just as soon we'd eloped."

"And rob the women of a chance at a good cry?" Dewitt jibed. "Not likely! Anyway, you couldn't cheat Melora out of a big wedding."

Clay knew that Taylor was right. He himself had wanted to have the ceremony at the small church near Gracefield, but the pastor was serving as a chaplain with Lee's army, and the church would never have held the crowd. Clay had stood outside watching the crowd arrive, and the sight of what seemed to be half the people in Richmond and the surrounding countryside shook his nerve.

"Let's go over the ceremony one more time, Reverend!" he pleaded.

"Now, Major, there's no reason for that. You just do what I tell you, and everything will go all right. Col. Dewitt, you have the ring?"

"Ring?" Taylor stared at the pastor blankly, then snapped his fingers. "I left it at camp."

"You did *what!*" Clay shouted. "Why, I should have known better than to—"

Taylor laughed loudly and pulled the ring from his pocket. "Of course I have the ring! Now calm down, Clay. It'll soon be over, and it won't hurt a bit."

"You make getting married sound like pulling a wisdom tooth!" Clay glared at him. His nerves were frayed, and he asked nervously, "What time is it?"

At that moment the organ music swelled, and Pastor Talbot said, "That's our signal. Now, you two just follow me."

Clay walked stiffly through the door behind the minister. As he took his place with Dewitt standing beside him, his jaws were tightly clenched, and he swallowed hard. The church was illuminated by bright waves of pale yellow sunlight that streamed in through the high windows. Clay forced himself to relax, and slowly he took in the crowd that had gathered in the large sanctuary.

His mother sat in the first row to his right. Susanna Rocklin was a serene woman, but her fine eyes were filled with satisfaction as she smiled at him.

David, dressed in a fine gray suit, sat next to Susanna, and next to him were Dent and Raimey. Dent's face was turned so that his scar was invisible to Clay, but when he turned, the jagged slash was obvious. Clay glanced at his daughter-in-law—blind but lovely as a young woman can be! And nestled in her arms was Clay's infant grandson, Thomas. Clay didn't think he was biased when he thought that this was the most beautiful baby in the whole world. And then his eyes fell on Lowell and Rooney, both of them beaming at him.

Clay noted briefly the other members of the Rocklin clan—the Bristols and the Franklins with all the younger ones. Then far back in the balcony, the black faces of Dorrie, Zander, Box, and the slaves he'd known for years.

On the other side, he saw the pews were filled with Yancys and their kin. Most of the men were gone to the war, but the women and children were there, dressed in their cotton dresses and Sunday shows. And throughout the church he saw faces of friends. He also was shocked when he recognized some of the leaders of the Confederacy—including Alex Stephens and Jefferson Davis!

Then the great organ swelled, and everyone in the building rose and turned to see Miss Rena Rocklin, the maid of honor, as she came down the aisle. She wore a light blue gown that Clay had never seen, and there was such joy on her face and such grace in her figure that he could hardly believe what he saw. *She's become a woman, and I'll never have that little girl again!* Glancing to his left, he saw Josh standing with his family, and there was an expression on his youthful face that was close to worship. *He loves Rena, and I wouldn't be surprised—*

But he never finished his thought, for once Rena was in

place the great organ filled the sanctuary with the beginning chords of Mendelssohn's Wedding March. Clay's head turned to the entrance, and there she was—Melora!

She wore a dress of pure, shimmering white silk with a high lacy bodice and a long train. The dark sheen of her hair was set off by a filmy veil, and her beautiful green eyes glowed as they met Clay's.

Buford Yancy, wearing a worn black suit and a string tie, was at her side. Melora took his arm, and the two of them made their way down the aisle. A calmness enveloped Melora, a serene air that was a reflection of her spirit. She was smiling slightly as she came to stand before Rev. Talbot, but Clay saw that her eyes glistened. She looked at Clay, handsome and tall in his ash-gray uniform, and thought, *He's the only man I've ever loved!*

"Who gives this woman in marriage?"

Buford Yancy swallowed hard, then nodded. "Reckon I do." He did his part by placing Melora's hand in Clay's, then went to the front pew and seated himself.

As the minister began to speak, Clay could feel the pressure of Melora's hand. He returned it and found it strong and warm. The moment he took her hand, all nervousness left him, and he listened carefully as Rev. Talbot spoke of marriage and the sanctity of it.

When it came time for the two of them to say their vows, Melora's voice was not loud but so firm that those in the balcony heard her clearly. *"I, Melora, take thee, Clay, to be my wedded husband . . . to have and to hold . . . to love and to cherish . . . in sickness and in health. . . ."* She turned to look at Clay, and diamonds were in her beautifully shaped eyes. Then as he spoke the old words to her, her lips quivered but still were soft with a smile.

"With this ring I thee wed."

Clay slipped the gold band on Melora's finger and then lifted her hand and kissed it. The unexpected gesture brought a sigh from the women in the audience, and the pastor smiled. "Very well done, Major. I hope you will be doing the same on your golden anniversary!"

Clay looked at him, then put his eyes on Melora. "You may be sure of that, Reverend!"

"By the authority vested in me by the sovereign state of Virginia, I pronounce you man and wife! Major, you may kiss your bride!"

Melora turned her face upward, and her lips were tender and yielding as Clay bent to kiss her. For one instant she clung to him, then stepped back. "Now, Mister Clay," she whispered, using her familiar old name for him, "you finally belong to me!"

Then the music swelled, and the couple made their way to the back of the church. They could not leave, of course, for a reception had been planned. "We have to be patient," Melora whispered, seeing the anguish on Clay's face. "Everyone wants to wish us well."

For over two hours the newlyweds were subjected to well-wishing. Clay's back was slapped and his hand was shaken until it was sore, and Melora was the recipient of many kisses.

The first to come brought a shock, for it was none other than Jefferson Davis and his wife, Varina. The president shook hands with Clay, saying, "Congratulations, Major! My prayers will be with you!" Then as Mrs. Davis bowed to Clay, murmuring her congratulations, Davis moved to Melora. He was an austere man, not given to gestures. But perhaps it was the face of Melora, so peaceful and full of joy, that moved him to lean forward and kiss her on the cheek.

"Why, Mr. President!" Varina Davis exclaimed. "You're becoming quite a courtier!" And then she, too, stepped forward and kissed Melora, whispering, "I hope you will love your husband as well as I love mine!"

Finally the line ended, and Melora and Clay had one brief moment with Susanna. She kissed them both, then stepped back, saying, "I wish your father were here to see this. Now, be on your way!"

Clay and Melora were struck by a hail of rice as they stepped outside. Both of them were startled when a command rang out: "Draw sabers!"

Clay got a glimpse of his old comrade Bushrod Aimes standing at the end of a double line of gray-clad troopers. A grin adorned his round face as the men drew sabers. The gleaming sabers flashed in the sunlight, and the sound of clashing metal broke the stillness of the morning. Clay and Melora moved under the canopy of bright steel, and Clay noted the grinning faces of his comrades-in-arms as they held the sabers rigid.

When they reached the end of the line, Bushrod stuck his hand out. "Get out of here quick, Major! There's talk of one of those fool shivaree things!"

"Thanks for the warning, Bushrod," Clay said, grinning. He helped Melora into the buggy, took the lines, and when he spoke sharply, the team leaped instantly into a fast gallop.

Watching the dust, Bushrod said to Taylor Dewitt, who'd come to stand beside him, "Looks like they're in a hurry, don't it?"

Taylor watched the dust rising from the wheels of the buggy and shook his head. "I don't blame them," he murmured. "They've only got a few days. I don't reckon they want to waste a second of them!"

★ ★ ★

"Oh, Clay! It's perfect!"

Clay had helped Melora out of the buggy, and the two had entered the small cabin nestled on the bank of a small lake. "It's not the Majestic Hotel in Charleston," Clay said quickly. "Actually it's a hunting lodge, but it's private."

Melora was delighted as they entered the cabin. "Look, Clay, everything is so neat—and someone filled the cupboard with all kinds of groceries!" Clay smiled as she dashed around the room, making new discoveries. Finally she turned to ask, "How did you do all this?"

"Well, actually I hired Mort Jenkins and his wife to get it

ready. They live about five miles from here." A humorous light touched Clay's eyes, and he said, "Let me show you the rest of the place." He moved across the room and opened the door, and when Melora came to stand beside him, she looked inside to see a large double bed. A brightly colored bedspread was turned back to reveal freshly starched sheets. Melora felt her cheeks grow warm, and she refused to turn and look at Clay. He said nothing, and finally she turned and met his eyes. "It looks . . . very comfortable," she managed.

"I'm sure it is."

Melora suddenly giggled and, giving Clay a gentle shove out of the room, said, "Get my bag. I need to change out of this wedding dress." When Clay's face brightened, she rolled her eyes. "Mind yourself, Mister Clay. I'm going to put on another dress so you can show me the lake. . . ."

They roamed the trails of the dense woods holding hands, and the sound of their laughter frightened a small herd of deer. As they fled away, Melora cried, "Oh, look, Clay—a fawn!"

Later they moved around the path that bordered the edge of the lake. "We can dig worms and come fishing," Melora said. When Clay remarked blandly that he might find better things to do, she pushed him suddenly so that he couldn't catch his balance and fell into the water. He came out and ran after her, catching her in his arms and threatening to toss her in. But she clung to his neck and begged, so he shook his head and put her down. "You treated me much better when you were nine years old!"

Melora gave him a slanting glance—infinitely feminine—and murmured, "Oh, I don't know. I may treat you better than you can imagine, Mister Clay!"

Clay's eyes grew wide in anticipation—and surprise at Melora's forwardness. "Why, Mrs. Rocklin!" he said in mock innocence. He reached for her, but she ran away and he pursued.

Later she cooked supper, and they ate by candlelight. When they had finished, he helped her with the dishes, and then they went outside to walk beside the lake. The moon glowed brightly in the sky, then came down to repeat itself in the glassy surface of the pond. Crickets sang their monotonous song, and a frog they startled cried, "Yikes!" and plunged, *kerplunk,* into the water. They watched the circles spread over the pond, and when the lake was finally still, Clay said quietly, "I wish we could stay here forever, Melora!"

She reached up and touched his face, then announced, "We'll come here often. It'll be our place." She hesitated for one brief moment, then said quietly, "Give me a few minutes, Clay."

He watched her as she moved back toward the cabin, then turned and breathed the air laden with the scent of earth and water and evergreens. Old memories flooded him, but he shut them out. *This is a night to think of the future!*

Finally he turned and walked slowly back and entered the cabin. Melora stood in the kitchen wearing a white silk gown. Her eyes seemed enormous as she gave him a look that he could not understand.

He took her in his arms, marveling at the incredible smoothness of her skin, savoring the scent of violets—but stronger than that was the fragrance that was simply Melora—feminine and mysterious.

She was trembling in his arms, and Clay whispered, "Are you afraid, sweet?"

"Just a little." But then she put her arms around his head and whispered fiercely, "But I'm your wife now, Clay. All that I am is yours!"

Clay said huskily, "Melora, I'll never stop loving you—never!" When he found her lips, they were soft and vulnerable, but at the same time firm and willing. He then led her to their bridal bedroom.

★ ★ ★

"Are you going to sleep all day?"

Clay woke up with a start to find Melora standing over him pulling his hair. He caught her arm and pulled her down. She struggled, but he ignored her efforts. "No, I'm not going to sleep *all* day."

Melora's cheeks were bright with color, and she couldn't meet his eyes for a moment, then she gave his hair a jerk so hard that he yelped. "Do you want breakfast or not?" she demanded.

Clay rubbed his head, then smiled. "Come here, Wife!" he commanded.

Melora colored even more brightly, but she came to sit beside him. "I must be an obedient wife," she whispered against his chest as he held her.

Clay stroked her back, then said, "You know, I've often thought that you had a tiger in you—but now I know there's a whole menagerie!"

"You're *awful!*"

"You didn't think—!"

Melora leaped up and ran out of the room, crying, "I'm going to throw your breakfast out the door!"

"Hey—don't do that!" Clay yelped in alarm. "Give a man a chance to get his pants on!" He struggled into his clothes, then went into the other room to find his breakfast on the table. "Pancakes and bacon!" he said with satisfaction. "You always did make the best pancakes in the world!"

They ate, then Clay rose and said, "Come on. Let's go fishing."

"Now?" Melora asked in surprise. "Let me do the dishes first."

Clay said, "Fishing is more important than washing dishes." He paused then and came to her. Taking her hand, he studied the ring on her finger, then kissed the hand as he had during the wedding ceremony. Then he pulled her close, and when she was enfolded, he whispered, "Melora, I love you more than life. I . . . I feel like a man who's wandered in some kind of . . . of deep dark woods, who finally finds his way home. Wherever you are, sweetheart, that's home to me!"

Melora rested against him, feeling the steady strong beating of his heart.

"Clay, let's always be that—a home for each other!"

"We don't have long."

Fiercely she clung to him, and as her arms tightened about him, he heard her whisper, "We have *now*, Clay—and now is forever!"

GILBERT MORRIS is the author of
many best-selling books, including
the popular House of Winslow series
and the Reno Western Saga.

He spent ten years as a pastor
before becoming professor of
English at Ouachita Baptist University in Arkansas and earning a Ph.D.
at the University of Arkansas. Morris
has had more than twenty-five
scholarly articles and two hundred
poems published. Currently, he is
writing full-time.

His family includes three grown
children, and he and his wife live in
Orange Beach, Alabama.